BEFORE
WE
DIED

BEFORE WE DIED

JOAN SCHWEIGHARDT

RIVERS ❖ BOOK 1

A FIVE DIRECTIONS PRESS BOOK

ISBN-13 9781947044166
ISBN-10 1947044168
LCCN 2018902975

Published in the United States of America.

Publisher's Cataloging-in-Publication Data

Names: Schweighardt, Joan.
Title: Before we died / Joan Schweighardt.
Description: Wallingford, PA : Five Directions Press, 2018.| Series: Rivers ; book 1. | Summary: Two Irish American brothers from New Jersey set out in 1908 to make their fortune as rubber tappers in the rainforests of the Amazon.
Identifiers: LCCN 2018902975 | ISBN 9781947044166 (pbk.) | ISBN 9781947044173 (ebook)
Subjects: LCSH: Brothers--Fiction. | Irish Americans—Fiction. | Rubber industry and trade--Brazil--Fiction.| Amazon River Valley--Fiction. | Brazil--Fiction. | Hoboken (N.J.)--Fiction. | BISAC: FICTION / General.
Classification: LCC PS3619.C49 B44 2018| DDC 823 S39--dc22
LC record available at https://lccn.loc.gov/2018902975

FIVE DIRECTIONS PRESS

Contents

MORE BY JOAN SCHWEIGHARDT

The Last Wife of Attila the Hun
The Accidental Art Thief
Virtual Silence
Homebodies
Island

Dedicated to Arútam,
identified by the people of the South American rainforest
as a spiritual force that enhances the life force,

And to Adam and Alex,
foremost byproducts of my own life force,

And to John, my father,
who liked to say, "All goes well when you ring the bell."

PRAISE FOR *Before We Died*

"An exciting fictional account that explores the very real issues around the consequences of greed and misunderstanding between cultures. Schweighardt's story happened with rubber tappers a century ago; it continues today around oil, lumber, cattle, soy, and the mining of crystals and other resources. This book, besides being a good read, is a wake-up call!"

—John Perkins, *New York Times* Bestselling Author

"With great skill, Schweighardt brings to magnificent life the colors, smells and sounds of Amazonia in this compelling tale of love, loss and honest men butting heads with privilege and greed."

—Damian McNicholl, author of *A Son Called Gabriel* and *The Moment of Truth*

"The story conveys an epic scope, taking the reader across countries and the vast inner landscape of human desire, where the hunger for meaning and love intersects with the suffering of loss and redemption. Beautiful and enthralling, impossible to forget."

—Rocco Lo Bosco, author of *Staying Sane in Crazy Town* and other titles

"Narrator Jack Hopper is the perfect guide—bawdy, brutally honest, brave, and sometimes overwhelmed... An adventure story that takes you into the steamy heart of the Amazon jungle as confidently as it explores the passions and confusions of the human heart... Will leave you breathless and wanting more."

—Julie Mars, author of *A Month of Sundays: Searching for the Spirit and My Sister* and other titles

PREFACE

In 1876 British explorer Henry Wickham smuggled 70,000 rubber seeds out of Brazil and into London. Some of these seeds became plants, and some of the plants were shipped to Ceylon, Singapore, and the Malay states. Eventually the offspring of these first plants became components in successful rubber plantations throughout Southeast Asia. But it took years for this to happen, and in the meantime, the rainforests of South America continued to meet virtually all of the world's rubber demands.

At first this was an easy task, as rubber was used mainly to manufacture hoses, shoe soles, and some industrial parts. But over time innovators realized that rubber bicycle tires were better than wooden ones, and when the automobile came along, the rubber boom in South America began in earnest.

Tapping for rubber in the rainforest was extremely challenging. Wild rubber trees don't grow in groves; they are spread throughout forests thick with vegetation and fraught with danger. Nor can trees be tapped throughout the year. Still, people rushed to the jungle to make their fortune in rubber.

The greed of some of the barons at the top of the industry hierarchy knew no bounds, and many of the people at the bottom wound up as little more than indentured slaves. Often the rubber tappers died—from malaria, yellow fever, snake bites, starvation—before they could pay off their debt to their sponsors. Some crafty barons began to see the advantage of using the indigenous people of the forests to do the work. They did not let the fact that most indigenous people did not want to become rubber tappers stand in their way.

At the height of the boom, the Asian plantations began to produce, causing the South American rubber market to fall off suddenly and sharply. For those who had profited so prodigiously, this was an all-out disaster. For others, it was a blessing.

1908–1910

1

It was Clementine, the old Italian hag who passed herself off as a fortuneteller, who started it all. Mum began seeing her regular after Da died, as she purported to know exactly what Da was thinking over there on the other side. How many times me and Bax gave over all our energy trying to make Mum see the hag was only after her dough, what little she had of it. But she would hear none of it. Then one day, after one of their "sessions," Mum tells us Da told the hag—and the hag told her—that we, meaning Bax and me, needed to get away from the docks and have ourselves an adventure, because we were for fair spending too much time being miserable since Da's passing. We knew Da didn't say no such thing, but we also knew he would have said *just that* if he could look down from above and see the sorry state we were in. We *were* miserable. Me more so than Bax because he at least had the lovely Nora to console him. Mum was all for it back then, this adventure idea, when it was fresh from the hag's lips to her ears. Fuck, she was all for it as recently as the day before.

But now here was our ship—all twenty thousand tons of her, double-masted with one great funnel, booming her kisser like the wild sea lass she was—preparing to cast off, and here was Mum, clinging to our shirt sleeves, bawling and keening like it was Da's funeral all over again.

Nora was there too, of course, with her arm wrapped around Mum's shoulders, trying to persuade her to let us go before it was too late. "Just pull away," she snapped at Bax, her ire on the rise. We looked at each other, me and Bax, but we only continued to try to reason our way out of Mum's grip. She was our mammy after all.

Finally her shrieking became a whimper and she let go of us and we kissed her quick and ran like hell. And sure enough, we were the last two to board. By the time we got up on deck and pushed our way to the rail, we were already pulling away from the dock. "There," Bax hollered. He'd found her in the crowd—her yellow dress, her hat that looked like a rose garden planted on a steep slope—hunched over and sobbing into her handkerchief like an old woman as Nora led her away. I thought my heart might break, it was such a sorry sight. But just then Nora—ever the rip—who'd been bent over Mum, consoling her, straightened and looked back over her shoulder, right at us, and flashed her most winning smile, all gums and bright white teeth. I laughed, because at first it seemed she was beaming at me. Then I felt my cheeks go hot. She was beaming at Bax, of course. He was wearing the new black derby she'd bought him to remember her by. He took it off and bowed and she blew him a kiss. Then she turned back to Mum and resumed her caretaking.

Our sea journey took fourteen days. I brought along a satchel of books, and while Baxter was off becoming intimate with the captain, the crew and all of our fellow travelers, I finished off Jack London's *The Call of the Wild*, which I deemed appropriate given our destination. In the evenings, when Bax had knackered himself sick making new friends and it was too dark for me to read (we'd been told not to light lanterns unless it was an emergency), Bax would ask me how my book was going, which was his way of saying he wanted the story in as much detail as I could remember.

We'd established the pattern back when we were kids, because Da didn't give much credence to a boy who spent too much time behind a book, and while I had nothing to lose going against Da's whims—as I was never going to be the favorite anyway—Bax had the nut hand there and he could not afford to lose it. So Bax got the benefit of my hard work; I read and then I summed things up and related them to my brother, enabling him to learn almost as much as me about books without having to actually crack one. It could have been our little secret too, but Bax was too spirited to try to get away with something like that. "My brother's the bookworm," he'd tell anyone who cared to listen. "I get all my learning secondhand from him." Sometimes he'd add, because it made people laugh and also because it was mostly true, "And he gets all his living secondhand from me." The only book Baxter had brought along was an English-Portuguese dictionary, because he was determined to be able to speak to our fellow *seringueiros* (rubber tappers) in their native tongue.

Nora had been in the same room with Jack London just the month before, when she'd gone across the river to Manhattan with her auntie to attend a lecture given by Mary Ovington, one of the leaders in the women's rights movement and a member of the Socialist Party. Nora had come back jazzed, saying she planned to work with the socialists while Bax and me were away, to advocate for affordable housing for the Negroes. My first thought at the time was, *Now, ain't that ironic? Here she don't really even have decent housing herself, her and her auntie.*

Nora's parents, native-born in New York but from Irish Catholic stock like our own, died of consumption when she was a toddler. All she remembered of them was their coughing, their spitting up of blood. She'd been raised by her Aunt Becky, her father's sister, a short round woman who never married, a socialist and anti-imperialist who gave speeches and rallied workers to fight for their rights, and who often dragged her niece along with her to secret meetings— *so as to indoctrinate her,* Mum and Da always said with a good ounce of scorn. They lived in two tiny rooms in a dilapidated boarding house for women on Jefferson Street. Aunt Becky worked in a garment factory when she was younger—which was where she first took note of workers' rights, or lack thereof—but now she had enough dough (Mum and Da had always speculated the socialists were paying her a stipend to keep her gob running) so that she didn't need to work at all and could spend all her time rousing others to higher states of social awareness. It couldn't have been all that much though, that stipend, judging by their living conditions.

We'd been sitting in the parlor that day, listening to Nora go on and on about how handsome he was, London, how smart, and how she planned to read all his books, which she could do easily enough as she worked in a bookstore now that she was out of school, and she got her books for cost. He was my man too, London was. Here was a fellow could clean a clock when he had to but could also write what was in his head and even what was not. I hoped to do as much myself one day, maybe writing stories for the papers or for a magazine, so long as I was never chained to a desk in an airless office where the risks and thrills of a life well-lived could be denied me. I wanted to ask Nora if he'd talked about his adventures in the Klondike, but just as I was about to open me useless gob, in jumps Bax, saying, "This London fellow… Would you say he's handsomer than me?" Nora stared at him a moment, her mouth open and her eyes wide, feigning to be aghast he would ask so impertinent a question. But then all at once she'd squealed with delight and leaped off her chair and planted a loud smacker on Bax's cheek and told him no, never; no one was as handsome as he was, except maybe me (and her gaze came sliding my way, leaving me, as always, with my cheeks ablaze) as I had the same genetic coding, if Gregor Mendel with his pea plants could be believed.

While he didn't care for reading, it was Bax who put our plan together, him and Nora. They combed the newspapers and made a list of New York agents and exporters working rubber in South America and wrote letters to a few of them. Or, to be more accurate, Bax dictated and Nora did the writing; neither of us had good penmanship. One agent-exporter, a Portuguese by the name of Manuel Abalo, wrote back, and when he was in New York on business, Bax took the ferry across the river to meet with him. Abalo wanted to meet me too of course, but our boss on the docks, German fellow who Da had had great respect for, said he'd fire both our skinny arses if one didn't stay behind and get the work done.

Nora and Bax were standing at the door when I got in from the docks that night. I had to plow my way through to get inside and out of my jacket. Even Mum was standing nearby, wringing her hands and looking jazzed. Bax had been back from his meeting for a while by then, but he'd made the ladies wait till I got home, not because he didn't like to repeat himself—old Bax never had a problem there—but because he wanted to feed the drama, as was also his way.

"So he says to me," Bax said to us soon as I sat down, referring to this Abalo chap. "How do I know you can do the work? Why would I want to be pouring money into men I have no proof can keep up? I heard longshoremen were a shiftless lot."

Bax took a step back, so that he was dead center in the room, to demonstrate how he answered. With his chin raised, his legs apart, and his arms folded over his chest, he could have been Hercules himself standing there. "Shiftless, you say? Listen here, I says to the old kinker, I could well name some shiftless bods out there on the docks, but me and Jack would not be among them. I says to him, Me and Jack, we've carried sugar, flour, beef and coal, and much more, in crates weighing twice as much as our own woebegone selves on our young backs, and no one ever saw us as much as flinch. Me and Jack have labored in the piercing cold of winter morns, before there was even a glim in the sky, and under the hottest midsummer sun, working sometimes twenty hours straight, doing what must be done to get our ships loaded and out to sea. We have worked with sponges tied over our ugly gobs to keep the fumes from some of them hauls from choking us down. We have worked bruised and cut and oozing pus from the bottoms of our feet. We have worked sick as dogs. We have worked bleeding like goats, me and Jack have. We have forced our big bodies into wee narrow spaces to take on cargo, and we have lifted above our heads barrels that would kill us fast if one of the other macs was to lose his footing. So say what you will about longshoremen, my good man, but don't dare say it about Jack and me, and never say it again in my presence."

Baxter nodded once, to let us know the drama was over for now—though he maintained his heroic stance in the middle of the room. Nora turned to Mum at once, her jaw dropped open with delight. Mum stretched her lips out flat in response, closest she could get to a smile these days. "And what did he say to that?" I asked. My brother could be a doozer when he wanted. I was the serious one, the thinker. Sometimes I found me miserable self with thoughts behind my thoughts. But I could never have come back at Abalo the way old Bax did. And I will not deny it grieved me some to be lacking Baxter's fire.

Bax waited to be sure he had our full attention. "He said, You and your brother, you've got yourself a job."

We all laughed then, even Mum. I got up to shake my brother's hand, and Mum and Nora stood up behind me, just to be nearer.

Abalo would become our *patrão*, Bax explained, meaning he would arrange our passage to Amazonas and provide us with the tools we'd need to get started as *seringueiros*. We would have to pay him back at the end of the first tapping season, but if we did a good job and brought in enough rubber, we'd have more than needed to cover our expenses. Abalo said we might even want to become agent-exporters ourselves after a few seasons of hard work. There was *that* much money to be made in the industry.

We whooped and hollered when Bax was done with his blather, and the three of us—Mum was watching from the entrance to the kitchen by then—began to dance in a circle, our hands on one another's shoulders just as we did when we was wee wild brats. "We're going to be rich!" Bax cried, and he leaned over to plant a smacker on Nora's bobbing cheek. "We'll have ourselves our own business," he went on. "We'll take turns going to South America to oversee, but eventually we'll hire an overseer, and then we'll conduct our business from here. I'll take you to Paris..." (this to Nora, naturally) "...and we'll have tea with your precious Picasso. We'll live here, of course—because if you can't live safe and full on the Emerald Isle, where better is there than here in Hoboken in the grand state of New Jersey—but we'll have ourselves a swank office on the top floor of a grand building across the river just like Manuel Abalo. Just like him, we'll look out the window and see the Flatiron reaching for the sun each day, making us feel like anything is possible. It'll be a fine life after all."

His "after all" hit me like a bolt of lightning. "I only wish Da was here to share it," I said. I dropped my hands from Baxter's and Nora's shoulders and our little jig fizzled to an end.

Mum sighed loudly and excused herself, and we watched as she disappeared into the depths of the kitchen. Then Baxter laughed. "If the hag is right," he whispered, "Da knows all about it already!"

"The hag's nothing but a hocus, and you know it as well as I do," I snapped at him. "She wants us to have an adventure for fair, but not because Da's spirit said so. More likely it's a plot to get us out of the way so she can glom even more of Mum's money."

"Whatever your mum pays her," Nora broke in in a rapid-fire whisper, "it's a small sum for the hope and happiness she receives in return. Besides, your mum told me Clementine refers to things she can't possibly know, things that were intimate between them two. So there may be some truth to it after all. Consider that. Or at least respect it."

Her eyes flashed from me to Bax and back again. They went a deeper blue when she got beefed. We took the argument no further.

2

FINALLY WE TURNED INTO a channel from the Marajó Bay and arrived in Belém, a seaport maybe sixty miles inland from the Atlantic, with fishing boats and ships of all sorts bobbing in the harbor like corks, not unlike the scene at the docks back in Hoboken. The only difference was it was hotter than hell and more humid than it had ever been in Hoboken—all because we were sitting just about right on the equator. Abalo had said that he would be in Belém to meet our steamer soon as it docked and would travel with us to Manáos, where he had his shack and where we would get our supplies, but we waited on board for over two hours—until the captain told us to scram—and he never did show up.

Since we were carrying little money (Abalo had said we wouldn't need any, so we'd left most of our savings with Mum), we figured we'd have to find a grassy clearing to spend the night if Abalo didn't show by dark. In the meantime, we set out to learn what we could about Belém.

Walking along on the crowded docks we saw plenty of black people, who, I had read, had for centuries been brought over from Africa—until slavery was abolished some twenty years earlier—to work on sugarcane plantations. Others we saw were African-Caribbean workers—you could tell by their accents—pouring in from Barbados and other islands to work in the rubber industry like our own eager selves, or to help build the new railroad line that would one day transport rubber from the Mamore River in Bolivia to the Madeira River in Brazil. There were lots of Portuguese people of course, and there were lots of *caboclos,* "copper-colored people," which is to say those who were Portuguese and Indian combined. There were plenty of *brancos,* white people, like us too.

There were footbridges all about, to go with all the waterways, and we crossed over one to have ourselves a nice long look at an imposing orange brick fort. When we saw that the palisade surrounding it was stocked with grand cannons that looked like they hadn't been ignited in centuries, and that there seemed to be no one watching guard over them, we turned to each other to establish agreement and then ran quick to the furthest piece and took our stations behind it. Bax, who'd assumed position of Commander along the way, hollered, "Now!" and I, being the lowly Loader, quickly shoved an imaginary bag of black gunpowder into the muzzle and stuffed it in with an imaginary rammer and followed it through with an imaginary projectile. Then Bax, having now become the Ventsman, came with his pick to pierce the bag through the vent hole… And it was all going along so bloody well when two overweight uniformed men came running out of the fort, weaponless but red in the face and screaming in Portuguese. I ran right and Bax ran left, and like two shafts from the same bolt of lightning, we were past them before they knew what struck them, and next thing we knew we were back on the footbridge, bent over and holding our guts together, laughing like the fuckin loogins we were.

Later we headed for the city center, where we were gobstruck to see that Belém had electric street lights. It had only been four or five years since the oil lamps on the streets in Hoboken had been replaced, and Hoboken was as modern a city as anyone could want. Transportation in Belém was provided by horse-drawn trams that ran on tracks from one side of town to the other, but posters nailed to the sides of buildings bespoke construction beginning on trolleys that would run on electric, for which workers were needed. There were trees and flowers galore, and church steeples, and plenty of fancy blue tiles included in architecture. "Fuckin charming," Bax said. *Charming* was Mum's favorite word, and she said it not when she meant it but when she meant just the opposite. We laughed, and having had our fill of our self-guided tour, we returned to the docks.

We watched the fishermen clean the day's catch and admired the produce that sat in sale piles everywhere. We ate a meal of *pato no tucupi* (duck served in a yellow-colored broth, the lady said) on the wooden deck of a café overlooking the water, and when it got dark we went back into the heart of the city and found a place to sleep in the courtyard of one of the churches. We slept fitfully, because of the bugs. In the morning we were covered over with bites and sores from where we'd scratched ourselves raw in our sleep.

We returned to where the steamer was docked. It was already being loaded for its return trip to New York. An old mucker sitting against the side of a nearby warehouse, using a fish bone to clean between the gaps in his teeth, saw us watching the loading process and yelled out that it was *borracha*, rubber, in the wooden crates. That made us feel a wee bit less vexed. We were tired and hungry and hot and itchy as blazes, but we had for fair entered the gateway to the industry now, and when we returned to Hoboken, it would be with stories aplenty—and dough to start our futures.

Abalo still did not show up. There was nothing for it but to wait, so we sat in the shade of the warehouse and told the old man, who spoke some English, of our plans. The fellow wanted to know where we'd be going to tap. Somewhere outside of a place called Acre, Bax informed him. The old man laughed. The word Acre, he said, came from the Indian word *aquiri*, which translated as "river of caimans."

"What's a caiman?" Bax asked.

"Alligator," the old man said. He brought his elbows together and made his arms and hands into a giant snapping gob which went for Baxter's noggin.

Bax jerked back so fast his derby fell off his head. He brushed it off and put it back on. "Our *patrão* is giving us rifles," he said. "We'll have nothing to fear."

"Don't shoot them *selvagens*, the savages," the old man warned. "You think you can kill 'em because you have guns, but they come back at night, and you can't hear 'em or see 'em any more than you could hear or see a *duende*, a goblin. They come with poison arrows, and if they decide not to kill you then and there, they drag you off and cut you into pieces and boil your head and eat your feet…"

Baxter and I laughed, but when we looked back at the old man, we found he was serious, staring back at us with his bottom lip hanging loose and swinging side to side like he was considering if we were even worth the warning.

He'd been a sketch at first, but time passed, and then neither of us wanted to talk to him anymore. We shared a look, to agree we both knew what the other was thinking, and saying we were hungry, which in fact we were, we got up and wandered about the docks and found another place to sit where we could still see the steamer we'd come in on. "What if he doesn't show up?" I said after a bit.

"He'll show."

"What if he doesn't?"

"Ever the optimist, ain't you?"

I was getting under my brother's skin, I knew, but I was feeling narky by then and I didn't much care. "We splurged on supper last night. Now we don't have enough dough for another meal let alone passage home," I added for good measure.

"Then we'll have to get work, won't we, you miserable loogin." Baxter jutted his chin towards one of the call-for-work posters tacked to a nearby warehouse wall. "We'll lay trolley lines until we have our passage."

A rat ran by, not far from our feet. Its hair was coarse and shaggy, and it put me in mind of Nora's porcupine, even though that was five or six years ago by then. When Mum learned we were keeping a porcupine in the basement, she raised the roof. "A porcupine is a rodent same as a rat," she'd cried. "Only with quills, which makes it worse." She softened a bit when we told her it was nothing but a shaggy-haired baby, quill-less still, and that Nora had found it. Some older kid had shot its mammy out of the low branches of a red oak down near the river with a slingshot, and when he'd gone, the mammy porcupine in a thick burlap sack thrown over his shoulder, Nora found the little one under some leaves at the foot of the tree and brought it to the field where Bax and me were horse-playing with some other buckos and begged us to shelter it until it was old enough to manage on its own. We'd been down to check on it every hour all that afternoon, and the last time we'd had to search for the wee thing, because it had managed to curl itself into a fist and cover itself over with the leaves and twigs and small stones that Nora had brought in earlier in the day to duplicate its proper environment. If we hadn't been up and down the stairs so many times—the three of us until Nora went home for supper—Mum might never have got wise to us and demanded an explanation. Once the secret was out, Bax and me insisted she come down and see the creature for herself. But the first thing we saw as we descended the stairs was Nora—who should have been home in bed by then, who had sneaked out of her auntie's flat and come back in through the cellar door—sitting in the circle of light cast from her oil lamp with the thing up on her chest like a wee dote. She'd flashed that smile then too, she did.

I looked to Bax, to see if he was reading my thoughts. He was chewing on the end of a stick, staring ahead, focused on the steamer and the dock where it was tied.

"Imagine, going back home and telling everyone we never got started in rubber because your man Abalo never showed up," I said. Something had come over me and I couldn't stop myself.

"I already have," Baxter muttered. One of the dark-skinned men who'd been helping to load crates onto the steamer turned and looked our way. I thought I'd seen him look at us before too. But then he turned in the other direction and walked off. "You'll want to shut your ugly gob before you vex me much further," Bax added for good measure.

"Hmmm," I said, because I was back thinking about Nora.

She was a scamp, Mum always said so. A scamp and a cooch. She did exactly what she wanted to do. Mum knew darn well she'd snuck over to the house a time or two in the middle of the night, when, as she liked to say, any decent girl would be in bed, and that at least on a few occasions (that she found out about; there were many more), we'd gone back outdoors with her. "Girl needs a mother," Mum groused when Nora was ten and twelve and fourteen. "For fair, Becky can teach her to be uppity," she declared any number of times, "reading all them books and dragging around to events where her little arse don't belong, but did Becky ever tuck her in at night? Sing her a lullaby? Rock her when she cried? Hell, that woman don't even smile." If Da was in the room, he'd say, "That young lass cries? I doubt that, Maggie me love."

It was no secret that Becky planned to skedaddle the minute Nora turned eighteen—less than a year now—to live with a friend who had settled in Boston. She'd been telling Nora all along, since she was a wee dote, to get herself prepared. She was doing this good deed, this caretaking, straight from the center of her heart because Nora was her only brother's daughter. But once her surrogate years were behind her, she needed to be moving on, while there was still time for her to "get to know" herself. "Cold as a dead fish," Mum said whenever the subject of Aunt Becky's looming departure came up. Nora would stay behind, in the two dingy boarding-house rooms, with their ugly peeling wallpaper and their undersized windows looking out not on the sun and the sky or the river but on the brick wall of the building beside, all alone—at least until she found a suitable roommate, which she'd have to do quickly if she didn't want half the neighborhood looking down their noses at her and questioning her respectability—to figure out her path in life. I never mentioned to Mum but Nora once told us she'd come home one evening to find her aunt wrapped in the arms of another woman, both of them naked and horned up.

Fifteen minutes later I saw the same dark-skinned man coming back again, passing the steamer, and moving in our direction, walking with purpose, if I wasn't mistaken. "That Abalo?" I asked.

"You shite-faced beggar. Does that look like the kinker I described?"

It didn't; the man Bax had described was a tall light-colored Portuguese in a finely cut three-piece suit and calf-button boots. This man was a *caboclo,* and he was barefoot. And while he wore breeches and a white shirt not unlike what we were wearing, his outfit was characterized by multiple strands of white stones dangling from his neck. As he got closer, I said, "Bugger me sideways. They ain't stones; they're teeth!"

Bax jumped to his feet. The dark man said, "Hopper, *sim?*" and Bax quickly replied, "Yes, that's us," and extended his hand. The other man didn't look at it, let alone take it. "*Vocês vêm,*" he said brusquely. *You come.* And he turned and headed off in the opposite direction.

He walked quickly, never looking back to see if we were even behind him. We had to scramble to gather our packs and catch up. We followed him down to the far end of the docks, to a double-decked steamer that was a smaller version of the one we'd come in on, a *gaiola,* the locals called it, a bird cage. Its engine was running and there were men along both sides untying lines and getting ready to cast off. We stood uncertainly, watching as the dark man called out "*Capitão!*" and the captain turned to look down on him from the deck. The dark man indicated us with a jut of his chin and jumped on board and almost immediately was swallowed whole by the crowd of men at the front of the boat. It was *o capitão* who finally signaled that we'd better hurry on board too. The craft was already pulling away from the dock by then and we had to make a jump for it. "You Hopper?" the captain asked in English as we regained balance. Bax nodded. "That's C brought you on board. He'll get you to your destination."

"C? Like the letter?" Bax asked, but the captain didn't answer.

"He'll be your outfitter and your guide, your *mateiro*. He'll get you to Manáos, and from there to your camp. He don't talk much and you'll only rub him wrong if you bother him with questions."

"But then how will we know—?" I began.

"You'll know," the captain answered curtly, and he turned and headed towards the stairs to the wheel room on the upper deck.

The *gaiola* was not nearly as accommodating as the one we'd made our ocean passage on. Not only was it half the size but it carried twice the number of people—all of them men. We'd been told once we reached the region we would be expected to sleep in hammocks, but there was cargo everywhere, wooden crates carrying who knew what. It wasn't clear where a hammock could even be strung.

It took several hours to cross open water and put the seaport behind us, and then we found ourselves navigating through channels that twisted amid islands large and small at the mouth of the jungle. I saw a herd of wild pigs peering at us from behind some trees along the bank. "Fuckin look at that!" I shouted. A moment later Bax pointed out an alligator, a caiman, sunning itself on the beach, and we both hooted.

Still no word of Abalo, but we were en route at least. We were headed into the jungle. Before long we were seeing parrots done up in fancy colors, like church-going ladies on a Sunday, and squirrel monkeys squawking and flinging themselves tree to tree. Rose-colored dolphins swam at the side of the boat, one of which seemed to take a liking to me, or so I thought. I was half over the rail trying for a better view of him when Bax called me a shite-faced beggar and grabbed me by the back of my cacks and pulled me arse back down. "I saved your fuckin life," he said. "Don't ask me to do it ever again." I laughed. I hadn't felt so chuff since before Da died.

Just as it was getting dark, C appeared with two manky burlap hammocks that smelled of damp and the previous users' body odors. We accepted them with gratitude but then stood like the loogins we were waiting for instruction on where to hang them. C stared at us for a moment—pulling on his chin, disgust and wonderment fighting for space on his flat moon face—and then snatched the hammocks back and turned portside. We grabbed our packs and followed. Within a minute C had found hooks to secure the hammocks from the outer wall of the central cabin to the beam at the edge of the upper deck, in a narrow chasm between two huge crates. He hung them crisscrossed, one over the other. The lower one nearly touched the deck floor. "I'll take that one," I said. "At least I won't have to worry about falling too far if we hit something in the night."

"It'll be hot down there," Bax warned.

I shrugged. "As long as you don't fart, I'll take me chances."

The days that followed were more or less the same. The steamer kept close to the shoreline, because the current was less strong there, leaving us to observe the scenery at close range. We saw jungle, nothing but jungle, but every patch of vegetation was different than the one before it, and my eyes did not surrender their appetite for it. And there were dramatic variations too, depending on time of day. The mornings often brought dense fog that lifted gradually—like a whore lifting her skirt by degrees, Bax said—to reveal trees and plants glittering with dew; the flora along the edge of the river stood out in sharp relief in the afternoons, and twice so because its reflection spread out over the surface of the water as well; the evening sunsets were snazzy for fair, with pink and purple and orange clouds overhead and, once again, reflected in the water, sometimes muted and sometimes so forceful it nearly took me manky breath away. We were in a different world. I'd never seen nothing like it.

Every now and then we passed a small settlement, generally consisting of no more than three or four houses up on stilts and a string of small boats tied to trees near the bank, but these became fewer and fewer as we traveled further along the great Rio Amazonas. We kept our eyes out for animals, and we saw our share, especially the playful river dolphins. We watched for Indians too, but if there were any, they were too clever to make themselves known. Occasionally we saw fishing boats out in the river. Sometimes we saw great ships heading east.

We worked on our language skills by listening to the stories shared among our fellow travelers and checking the words we could make out in Baxter's dictionary. With so much time on our hands, it wasn't long before we were able to determine the subject matter, if not the content, of the conversations on which we eavesdropped, and more often than not it was the Indians. The men spoke of the *selvagems* with fear and disdain.

As far as we could tell, these men were all Portuguese who had been working rubber for some time and had risen to the position of overseer. They were all well dressed and none of them looked as if they'd done a hard day's work in a good long time. For fair, the sight of them—Bax said their muscles were scarce as hens' teeth—made us wonder if we really aspired to become overseers ourselves, and in the end we concluded that we would engage in both tapping *and* oversight, just to keep ourselves hardchaw and ready.

They were not friendly, these other fellows on the boat; they made no attempt to speak to either of us directly, but that was all right, even for Baxter. I had finished *Call of the Wild* by then and started on a collection of stories by Herman Melville. I began with *Bartleby the Scrivener*, which I could see was about the oppression of workers, and I couldn't help but think how swell it would be if Nora was there to discuss it with me. She would have had all sorts of theories about the significance of Bartleby's "I would prefer not to." Bax was more interested in the fact that poor Bartleby had to work in a stuffy office without any windows, while here we were traveling along on a river in the heart of the natural world, sleeping outdoors in hammocks, learning a new language, and about to build a lucrative career around a simple substance that was more likely to change the world than any other material since the beginning of time.

Eventually we traveled into the region where the Rio Amazonas and the Rio Negro flow side by side. This was the most remarkable sight I had ever seen because the Rio Amazonas was yellow and the Rio Negro was black as me mum's best tea. The line that divided them was irregular but resolute, with the yellow and black waters refusing to merge. The "meeting of the waters," as it was called, meant we were nearly to Manáos.

We had seen nothing but jungle for days and days by then, and it was hard to believe that a grand city would suddenly rise up out of the forest. Bax bet me my last clean handkerchief that the stories about Manáos' riches would turn out to be exaggerated; that it would be nothing more than a slightly more civilized version of Santarém, one of the larger settlements we'd passed on the Amazonas. Our senses had already adjusted to the world of thick, tangled vegetation, and it was unthinkable that civilization of any sort could survive in such a setting. But the stories of Manáos had not been overstated, and its sudden appearance on the afternoon of the same day, on the heels of such dense greenery, was jolting.

Manáos' harbor was large, and filled with fishing boats and river launches and ships of all sizes bearing flags we didn't recognize. The docks we could see as we approached were the very ones I'd read about, free-floating, built on concrete platforms held up by pontoons, and thus able to rise and fall with the fluctuations of the river levels, which, I'd heard, could vary as much as sixty feet from wet season to dry. These docks led to warehouses on the hilly shore. A series of cables overhung the platforms, ready to help move goods—rubber, that would be, the very substance that had brought us all this way!—back and forth from ship to shore. Being longshoremen ourselves, we couldn't help but admire the apparatus.

The Customs House, with all its intricate carvings and fancy archways around its windows and doors, looked out over the docks, as did its tall tower and turret adjoining it. I'd heard some of the men saying the concrete blocks and bricks for the Customs House had been shipped all the way from Britain. The talk was nothing in Manáos had come from South America.

Our steamer docked alongside a smaller boat from which squawking caged birds and monkeys were being unloaded. From another small boat, docked just behind it, lads were handing fruit and what seemed to be dead turtles up into the waiting hands of their workmates. Bax pointed out fish being cleaned, not on wooden benches like back at home but on slabs of marble fit for the floor of a palace.

We turned in circles, trying to swallow it all. And then all at once there was C, whom we'd seen hardly hide nor hair of for the entire trip, appearing out of nowhere like the kinker he was and signaling we should follow him. We hurried behind him, passing a gathering of twenty or more coffee-colored women in gay frocks clacking away as they beat their laundry against the rocks on the banks, and more women, carrying large baskets of produce and who knew what else on their heads. Between the birds and the women, the air was full of music and color, and I will be the first to admit I was fuckin elated.

Soon we were away from the docks, making our way up the hill along a wide street—lined with stucco and tile houses and filled with swanky hacks and trolley cars—moving towards an area of grand hotels and mansions. The architecture here was even more ornate than what we'd seen in Belém. We saw church steeples, and banks and restaurants, and of course, in the distance, the great copper dome of the opera house that was so famous even our mum, who knew little of the larger world—if you didn't count what she knew of the sweet great isle where her heart still dwelled—had heard of it. Exotic trees and flower gardens were everywhere, and the parks we passed featured large stone fountains in which water flowed from vases held by bronze cherubs. We were moving too fast to take in everything, but I saw enough marble, crystal and gold shining through the windows of the various buildings to assure myself it was true the people here were making enormous amounts of dough in the rubber industry. Manáos had been little more than a squalid riverside village before the boom began. And now here it was, an international city—in the middle of the jungle!—that imported its street cobbles from Portugal, its ironwork from Poland, its marble and gold leaf from Florence, its crystal from Venice. Even some of its trees had been imported, I'd heard.

C led us to a grand structure that was the size of any two buildings together back in Hoboken. Situated on a wide cobblestone street, it was only three stories high but half a city block wide, with decorative balusters and columns supporting balconies on the second and third floors. An observatory towered above us from the third floor. The windows were arched and multi-paned, trimmed in white against dark gold stucco. All around it were lush gardens and marble pathways for strolling through them.

I thought it must be a grand hotel, though there was no sign identifying it as such. It was not the kind of place I had expected to find myself at any time during our journey. C told us to wait and left us out in front and disappeared around the back of the building. We waited out there, in the screaming hot white sun, watching the well-dressed passersby—one of whom, a lady carrying a squawking parrot in a cage in one hand and a fancy white parasol in the other, stopped to have herself a good long look at us, for which we would have had choice words but for the fact she *was* a she, and that we were only jazzed to be where we were—for over an hour. Then C returned, and before we had the opportunity to ask where we were and why in fuck we had been detained so long, the front door opened and a lovely dark-skinned girl wearing a stark white apron over a high-collared grey dress motioned us to step in. We looked at each other, Bax and me, then we turned to look at C, but his face and stance told us only that he would not be accompanying us inside. When the girl saw our uncertainty, she laughed and grabbed my sleeve and tugged on it to get me moving. We followed her into the foyer, and there, finally, was a feller who could only be the great Manuel Abalo.

Abalo approached with his large hand extended. "Baxter, my boy. How have you been? How was the trip?"

"Quite fine, sir, but I'm Jack," I said.

Abalo laughed and turned toward Bax and shook his hand next. "You didn't tell me he was your twin!"

"He's no twin of mine, the ugly bugger. He followed me fifteen months after me own grand entrance into the world, and he's been following me since. If I stopped short I'd likely find him up me arse."

Abalo didn't catch Baxter's little joke. He was too busy looking us over, his gaze sliding back and forth like a clock pendulum. He was a big man, well over six feet, with a waxed mustache and a robust gut, maybe in his early fifties. "I see," he said. "Now that you say so, I see the difference. Jack, is it? You've got the rounder face. Baby face, eh?"

"Our da got himself jarred one night and stepped on his gob when Jack was still a wee dote. That's why he looks that way," Bax cried cheerfully, but Abalo didn't snag that one either.

"But aren't I the lucky one!" Abalo exclaimed. "Two strapping young men. Black hair and blazing blue eyes. Skin as white as a ghost moth's." He turned to Bax. "Ireland, you say. I never think of Irish as raven-haired. I think of yellow and red like the birds here." He threw his arm out, as if the birds were there in the hall with us. He laughed. "Well. And the trip was good, you say?"

While Baxter began answering—politely choosing to blabber on about the good weather and all the creatures we'd seen on the river (rather than the fact that Abalo hadn't showed up in Belém and that C's curtness had almost caused us to miss our passage to Manáos)—Abalo led us into a small parlor off the foyer. It contained only a table and chairs and a China cabinet. "Louisa," Abalo snapped, speaking over the tail end of Baxter's story. The girl with the white apron appeared at once with a tray of beverages and an assortment of cakes. Abalo invited us to sit. We pulled ornate red velvet-cushioned chairs away from the highly polished mahogany table and sat our happy arses down. While we were choosing from among the cakes, Abalo withdrew a piece of paper and a pencil from his inside jacket pocket. "Now," he said, "let's get right down to business. We'll make a list of all the things you'll need, and by the time your launch leaves for Acre in the morning, your provisions will have been delivered to you by some of my men."

As our mouths were already full of cake—we'd eaten nothing yet that day—we could only look at each other. But I had no doubt our thoughts were the very same: Here we were with our benefactor, our *patrão*, eating delicious cakes in his beautiful mansion, and about to make a list of *our* needs. We'd dealt ourselves a nut hand if ever there was one, all right.

It took no more than an hour. By the time we were done we had ordered everything from extra shirts and trousers to canned foods (including meats and sardines and condensed milk), to strips of *carne seca* (salted dried meat), to a barrel of *farinha* (a flour made from manioc, which Abalo promised was delicious mixed with meat or beans or even water and would become a staple in our diet), to medicines, including quinine for malaria, to whiskey, to rifles and ammunition, to tapping tools—enough provisions to keep us going for a full year. Abalo said there would be two other men going to our camp. They would be joining us there in Manáos that night and we would all travel to the camp together, along with a second group of men arriving in the morning and bound for yet another camp. Once we arrived at our destination, C would help us build ourselves a proper dwelling and show us the rubber-tapping process. We would have to learn fast, because by then it would be the beginning of wet season. We wouldn't be able to tap much once the rains started; first, the trees didn't bleed as well then, and second, the rain was so fierce it would rip down the cups meant to catch the bleed from the bark, and even if it didn't, water would mix with what rubber milk there was and ruin it. But we would have the chance to become familiar with our surroundings, and as soon as the rains stopped we would be ready to work. At the end of the tapping season, C would escort us to a nearby base camp, where we would turn in our rubber for money, less the cost of our travel expenses and provisions. "Sometimes," Abalo mumbled as he showed us to the door, one huge paw on each of our backs, "it can take more than one season to get your expenses behind you and realize a profit. Not likely to happen with fellows like you, but worth considering."

C was standing outside, just where we'd left him. As soon as the door closed behind us, he began moving back toward the harbor and we were right behind him. "What did he mean by that?" I asked Bax. "That it could take more than one season…?"

"You heard what he's giving us? We'll have everything we need—"

"I understand that, but I expected to make plenty of dough during season one. You led me to believe that was what he told you when you met—"

"You calling me a liar, Jack? That's what he fuckin said all right. And if you think I'd tell you otherwise, you can *pogue ma hone*, and bugger me sideways."

"Bugger your own fuckin self sideways, arsewipe. You heard him with your own ears. He said it could take more than one—"

"You flunky shite-faced beggar boob. And so what if it does take more than one season? You going to be hankering so bad for your mammy you won't be able to hang in? You're a lag, you're—"

"And you're a manky blowhard who don't know what he's talking about half the time and is lying the other half."

"Jack, you creeping snag. I'm trying to educate your fuckin arse here, so listen good. You got to think of this as an investment in our future. That was his house we were at. And he started out just like us, an ordinary tapper—"

"And did he say that?"

"He implied. Otherwise where'd I get it?"

"Woolgathering, perhaps?"

Baxter shoved me, and I shoved him back. But then we both thought to look and see where C was, and sure enough he was turning a corner well ahead of us. Much as I was ready to have a go at my loogin arsewipe of a brother, there was no time for it. C would only keep going and we'd be lost on the docks and have to go back to Abalo's house, if that was even what it was, and ask for directions. But I was fuming. Everything had been all laid out for us, all the supplies, all the plans, everything…except for the payment part. It sounded a wee bit to me like that was being left to the fickle freaks of fortune, and I did not like it any more than I would have liked having me plums pinned in a vice.

C led us to a small river launch and indicated, with a combination of words and gestures, that we would sleep on board that night and the launch would leave first thing in the morning. Then he left us on our own and headed back towards town. We climbed on board and entered the one small cabin. It was empty except for an oil lamp on one wall. Bax lit it, and after lifting the shutters on the windows— three on each side—to let in some air and the diminishing light, we sat on the floor and waited for our fellow tappers to arrive, but no one came. Finally Baxter broke the silence, saying, "We might as well go find something to eat."

I was about to remind him that we had very little money when a wee voice from outside the cabin door called out, "Hopper?" We jumped to our feet and I opened the door at once. Standing there was the dark-skinned girl who had led us into Abalo's home and served us cakes and beverages in the small room off the foyer: Louisa. She was carrying a large basket, which I took from her straight away as I could see it was heavy. She'd been hunched with the weight of it, but soon as I had it from her she straightened, winked, and turned to go. "Wait," I called.

She turned back, but now I wasn't sure what to say. "You speak any English?" I managed in Portuguese.

She shrugged, but she smiled too.

"Mucker, she don't know what you're talking about," Bax said flatly from behind me.

I turned to look at him. "Shut your stinkin' pud-breathing gob," I said, and I turned quickly back to Louisa. "Amigo," I said, thumping my thumb on my chest. "Me, amigo Jack."

Bax sighed behind me. "Leave her be, arsewipe. What do you want from her?"

I looked at him again. "Someone to talk to besides you, beggar." I turned back to her and pointed. "Amiga?" I asked.

She laughed. "*Eu trabalho para o Senhor Abalo*," she said, and she hurried across the deck and climbed back down onto the dock.

Baxter slapped my shoulder. "Good job, Jacko. You've got a way with the ladies. Now if only you could scare off the insects just the same…"

The basket contained an assortment of breads, dried fish, vegetables and fruits, along with two bottles of Port. I was so hungry and everything looked and smelled so good that

I nearly forgot how raging mad I was at my brother and answered civilized when he asked me if I thought we should eat our share now—we had to assume we were meant to share the food with our fellow *seringueiros*—or hold off a wee bit longer. Except for the cakes at Abalo's we hadn't eaten all day. It took us only one glance at each other to make our decision. We divided everything quickly, taking exactly half for ourselves, along with one of the bottles of Port. By the time Ted and Leon came on board, darkness had fallen and we were sprawled out in opposite corners of the cabin, full to bursting and with buns to match.

"I hope you saved us some," Leon, the taller one, said.

Bax jumped to his feet. "You speak English!"

"Of course we do. What did you expect? We're second generation. Both of us. German."

"This is grand!" Bax flicked his thumb toward me. "We've had only each other to talk to for weeks now, and lately he's getting my goat." He looked at me. "See, beggar, what do I always tell you? If you wait long enough—"

"From Pittsburgh," the smaller one, Ted, interrupted. "In Pennsylvania. You know it?"

"Do we *know* it? Why, sure we do. You fellows invented the Nickelodeon, God bless your natty-arsed souls!"

"I don't know we was the ones to invent it. Could be though," said Leon. "But it was our very own Andrew Carnegie was the inspiration that brought us here."

"We know about that too!" Bax cried. "A fellow we used to work with, he brought in an article his brother sent from the *Pittsburgh Gazette*. It was all about how someone'd approached Carnegie on a train and asked him if he had to do it all over again, would he still go into steel. And your fellow Carnegie says, *Best opportunity today is rubber, that's where I'd put my time and energy if I was just starting out.*"

"That's it, the very same!"

"We're brothers, from the grand state of New Jersey, by the way. American born, parents from Ireland." Bax shook Leon's hand, then Ted's. "A town called Hoboken. Ever hear of it? I hate to one-up you first thing like this, but we invented baseball. The four of us, Americans. How 'bout that? Let the good times roll, huh?"

It went quiet, and when I looked up again, I saw they were all staring down at me. Since the newcomers had come in I'd been working on getting to my feet, but the booze had rendered me rat-arsed, and all this time I'd only made it to my hands and knees. One limb at a time I came to a kneeling position and then slowly stood. Then, so as not to be outdone by my brother, I smiled my biggest Irish smile and shot out my hand. But I had me more of a bun than I realized, apparently, because I didn't know until my hand got slapped down hard that I'd offered it to Bax. Anyway, we all had a hell of a good laugh.

An hour later Leon and Ted, who said they'd been friends since childhood, had finished eating and were halfway through their own bottle of booze and we four were engaged in a game of poker. Since no one had much money, we kept the antes low, and Bax, who was winning, said it stood to reason he would finally get jammy when there was no kitty to speak of. I didn't need a nut hand myself to feel jammy, and I don't think Bax or the other two did either. Many of the men who were coming to the jungle to tap were Brazilians from the northern part of the country, men who had abandoned their small farms and left behind their loved ones for the chance to get out of debt. Or they were coming from the Caribbean in dire need of income. Either way, they were down on their luck, surely sullen, and they wouldn't know much, if any, English. Four Americans working together increased the chances we would have us a wee bit of *craic*, as me Mum would have put it, and make some dough to boot. It was a gift we hadn't expected.

As the evening wore on, we toasted to brotherhood. We agreed we would work our skinny arses to the bone, that we would help one another and cover for anyone who took sick. We would share our food. We would help to keep one another's spirits high, no matter how tough things got.

On and on we went, dealing new hands, making new toasts, slugging down more booze, and thinking up new and ever more creative names for our *mateiro*, C, who Leon and Ted had only met that day but already disliked. When the cabin door opened and a little dark head popped in, we were all startled into wide-eyed silence. At first I thought it must be Louisa come to collect the empty basket, but then she spoke, saying, "Amigo Jack?" and I realized it was not the same girl.

"What does she want?" Leon scowled.

"Me, apparently," I said, getting to my feet.

The others burst out laughing, but once I'd made it to the door, the girl motioned me to follow her. I looked back, as gobstruck as any of them. "I'll see what she wants and be back swiftly. Don't nobody touch my dough."

The girl wrapped her shawl tightly around her narrow shoulders and started off fast, walking down the docks. I could hardly manage a straight line let alone keep up with her. For the next five minutes I snaked and stumbled as I followed her small figure past the long line of boats in the moonlight. I had to laugh at myself, thinking how I'd look to anyone watching, weaving and bucking like a cock-eyed doodle out on a spree. The docks were mostly quiet now. Crews were preparing for the early morning bustle. A few lanterns were lit on a few fishing boats, and the voices of men clacking and laughing floated over the edge of the dock along with the smell of dead fish.

She stopped and turned to see where I was. When I caught up, she indicated that we would be turning down the slip at hand and boarding a river launch not unlike the one I'd just come from. She started towards it, and pulling her skirts about her, she hustled up the plank. As I climbed on board behind her, I wondered if I should be afraid, if I had been lured there for a purpose, if someone with a knife would grab me from behind and threaten to slit my throat if I didn't give over all my dough. I had to chuckle. All the money I had was back at the launch, being watched over, or so I hoped, by me very own brother.

The cabin was dark. She struck a match and lit a candle that had been in a corner and the room illuminated somewhat. There was no one there waiting to slit my throat. So what did she want, I wondered?

She stared at me and I back at her. She was a *cabocla*, like Louisa. Her dark eyes were large and shiny and her chin came to a delicate point. I remembered that she had called me Amigo Jack, and using my best Portuguese language skills, I asked her if she was a friend of Louisa's. "*Louisa trabalha para o Senhor Abalo,*" she answered. "*Bruna...*" (she pointed to herself; she was Bruna) "*...trabalho para Senhor Fabiano.*"

I tried asking if this Fabiano and Abalo were business partners, fellow *patrãos*, or maybe just cronies. She shrugged. She didn't understand the question. I didn't know what else to say. Truth be told, I wanted to return to the game. Ted, the wee one, had shown himself to be a piker, making wee bets to match his stature. But Leon was betting like the rat-arsed kinker he was, and me and Bax were beating him handily. If any hoodoo came slinking in, it would be because of me, for breaking the circle.

A shadow washed over me, and just like that, I was off me trolley. I slid down against the wall thinking I might be needing a bit of a kip before I returned to the game. I let my legs sprawl out in front of me. Maybe she's only lonely, I thought, a young lonely girl looking for a friend, an amigo. And then I thought about how this was the first time I had *not* felt lonely since Da died the year before. If nothing else, the hokum psychic Clementine's manipulation of me mum—or at least its result, this venture—had cured me of my loneliness.

My mind drifted, and pickled as I was, I found myself there all over again, standing in Murphy's backyard back in Hoboken, Bax right beside me, not knowing in that moment we were about to lose our da. Mrs. Murphy had gotten herself plugged, finally. The shindy was for her, to celebrate.

Lots of moolah, the Murphys had. They had a piano, and someone inside was playing "Nellie Dean" on it. Roses and hostas and hydrangea galore there in the garden. People clacking, laughing loudly, some dancing. Mac Todd, friend of Da's, saying we were living in the age of magic, why with electric street lights up and down Main and a handful of places where you could use a telephone.

I remember thinking he was right; it was a swell time to be alive. I wanted to hear more, but I got distracted by some of the ladies standing nearby. They were gossiping, getting louder by the minute, and their ringleader was none other than me own dear mammy. "It's a good thing she finally got herself pregnant," she was saying to the others, "because she was crazy as a bedbug there for a time, I tell you, telling anyone who'd listen she was being punished for something she done back before she married." She hesitated to look each of her listeners in the eye. "Something dark," she added, her brows rising, her voice an octave lower. She shuddered. "Never did say what it was."

Bax and me exchanged a look. Our mum could be a gossip when there were other women around. If Da had been there, he would have said, "Now, Maggie...," and then he'd have winked at me and Bax, as if to agree that the men in the family at least knew darn well what Annie Murphy had done that was so terrible. But he wasn't there. He was working that night, down at the docks—or so we thought at the time. When he'd left the house, he'd said he'd try to make the shindy, maybe towards the end of the night, if he wasn't too tired.

I returned my attention to the cabin and was startled to see that Bruna had removed her belt and was slowly unbuttoning the tiny buttons that ran all along the front of her dress. There were tears in her eyes and she looked terrified, but one by one the buttons came undone. While I sat there, sensible as a rock in a rainstorm, she slowly stepped out of her frock and began to unbutton her undergarment. When her bottom lip began to quiver, it hit me hard: Louisa had thought I'd wanted to buy a whore! She'd sent me Bruna!

"No, no, no, no, no," I cried, forcing myself to my feet.

"*Não?*" she asked softly, her fingers resting on a button.

"It's not that I wouldn't want to, believe me, but I have no money. Louisa got it wrong. No dough! You see?" I pulled my pockets inside out and showed her.

Her eyes flooded with more tears. I couldn't tell if she was crying for relief or because she'd wasted her time and was not to be paid after all. As she began the task of re-buttoning her garment I saw that she was bruised on her right shoulder. I lifted the candle from the floor and brought it closer. She covered the bruise immediately, but I put my hand over hers, and when I felt her relax I gently moved her hand aside. The bruise was purple and blue. It looked recent. "Who did this to you?" I whispered.

She shrugged and glanced at her dress on the floor. I picked it up and handed it to her and took a step back. While she slid it over her head and began to button it, I wondered what would happen if she went back without any money, if someone would beat her for returning empty-handed.

"Fabiano, does he know you're here?"

She nodded. I couldn't tell if she'd understood. Her dress was back together again.

"Come on," I said, and I reached for her hand.

"*Não*," she cried, jumping back like I was hoodoo.

But I kept my hand extended in the space between us and finally she took it and I blew out the candle and returned it to the floor and she let me lead her off the boat and down the docks and eventually back to the slip where my launch was tied.

We climbed on board and I threw open the cabin door, startling the card players. My money was still sitting there in a pile just where I'd left it. I scooped it up and turned to Bruna and handed it to her. She put it into a small leather poke that hung from her belt.

"Are you a fuckin booby?" Baxter cried.

I took Bruna's arm and gently pulled her in. "Someone named Fabiano all but owns her. If she goes back without any money, he'll beat her."

"How do you know all that?" Leon asked.

"That's the way it works, man! And she's got bruises."

Leon and Ted laughed. "How'd you come to see her bruises?" Baxter asked.

"We had a misunderstanding. By the time I figured out why she'd called me out and led me away, she'd half undressed."

Baxter was staring at me, waiting for me to go on. "So, now you got to pay her for her whoring?"

"We didn't do nothing, Bax. Look at her. She's terrified."

Baxter looked at her. Then he looked back at me. He pondered a moment, then he sighed and bent forward and scooped up all his money, which was considerable even with the small antes, and handed it to me. "You sure?" I asked. Baxter nodded. I turned and gave the additional money to Bruna.

"What the hell is going on?" Leon shouted, getting to his feet. "Does this mean the game is over without me or Teddy having a say? Or a chance to win our dough back? You take us for suckers? Or is she a shill of some sort?"

Baxter, on his feet too now, leaned in toward him until their noses were almost touching. "We been toasting all night to brotherhood," Bax said slowly. "Now you get to see what it looks like. Be thankful for that and keep your ugly gob shut."

They stared at each other for a long time—the small veins popping on both their foreheads, their lips clamped, their fists clenched and their knuckles white—while me and Ted watched closely to see what would happen. If a fight broke out, I'd be forced to step aside. I couldn't sock someone like Ted, who was only half me size and looked more frightened than Bruna had when she'd thought I was there for a mow. But no one made a move, and when the spell broke and everyone looked away, Bruna had disappeared into the night.

3

THE CRATES AND BARRELS containing our provisions arrived in the morning, and so did another six men, all of them *caboclos* in their late thirties or early forties, four of them going into the jungle to tap at the second camp and the other two being C, of course, and Sam, who was the boat's captain.

The new *seringueiros* were Paulo, Gomez, Bonito and Cabeça de Galinha. Sam, who spoke some English, explained that Bonito's real name was Nuno, because he was the ninth son in his family, but he liked everyone to call him Bonito, which means handsome, because he was so ugly.

The four of us stared in gobstruck silence, for it was true: Nuno Bonito was as ugly as a mortal sin in the Catholic church, with drooping eyes that were so far apart they were almost at the sides of his head, a mouth that was pushed up too close to his nose, and no more than one or two or three teeth to fill it, and all of them black at that. But then Sam began to laugh loudly, and so did Bonito, who seemed to be looking at us with only one eye, like a bird or a fish. Bax was the first in our contingent to join in. He stepped up and shook Bonito's hand and slapped his back and called him by name (his name of choice, that is) and said he was pleased as Punch to know him. Then me and Leon and Ted did the same. We all turned to Cabeça de Galinha next. Teddy, who had taken the trouble to learn quite a lot of Portuguese before arriving in Amazonas, whispered, "I think his name means chicken head." We chuckled in anticipation. We thought Sam would laugh too and explain why he was called such an arseways name. But Sam left it at that. "This is Cabeça de Galinha," was all he said. And while Cabeça de Galinha, who was as handsome as Bonito was homely, shook hands all around, he didn't as much as crack a smile.

The new men were a friendlier bunch than those on the steamer from Belém to Manáos, and while everyone stayed mostly to himself during the day, looking out at the shoreline and perhaps, like me own pensive self, reflecting on the events that had brought him to the middle of the jungle, at night when we docked, we played cards in the cabin or on the deck and drank from the whiskey bottles that had been included in our provisions. The only exceptions were Sam, who played cards but didn't care for drink, and C, who kept watch until he decided not to and then retired to his hammock on the bow of the boat.

Since me and Bax were without money, we played for provisions at first. In two nights' time, Baxter lost a bottle of whiskey and a pair of cacks, and he would have lost his black derby too if I hadn't given him one of my own whiskey bottles to keep him in the game. I'd been winning modestly, and I feared my brother's streak was over and we'd lose half our possessions before we even got to camp.

The problem was Baxter didn't know how to keep a poker face. If he had a good hand, his face lit up like the city of Manáos in the middle of the black jungle night, and everyone knew about it. "You might as well lay down your cards and let everyone gawk for themselves," I said to him many a time in disgust. But Baxter's luck returned, and soon we both had dosh enough to stay in the games without sacrificing our precious belongings.

As the days went by, our knowledge of Portuguese improved ninety to the dozen. The other men made it easy by refusing to try to learn any more English than they already happened to know. The only new words they seemed interested in were "Pittsburgh" and "Hoboken." For reasons unknown, saying either was enough to send them into peals of laughter, even Cabeça de Galinha, especially when they were drinking. "Hoboken" was especially funny to them. Nuno Bonito, who loved to get everyone started, took to yelling "Hoboken!" whenever he laid down a nut hand. One evening when I finally felt I had me the skills for it, I told them how Hoboken had once belonged to an Indian tribe and *brancos* had bought it from them for some beads and a barrel of beer. The men laughed hard when they heard that. Nuno Bonito said he wished they could buy the forest from the *selvagems*, the savages, here that easily; it would solve a lot of problems. I didn't say anything, but I wondered why Nuno Bonito would say such a thing being as it was clear he had some Indian blood himself. They all seemed to hate the native tribes.

The other thing the *caboclos* liked to joke about was Ted's size. While all the rest of us stood six feet or were at least edging on it, Teddy was short, maybe five foot and five inches, and thin as a boy, with a boy's narrow shoulders and scraggly neck. Cabeça de Galinha called him *peixe pequeno*, which meant small fish. Each time he said it Ted would drop his head and Leon would mumble, "Don't you worry about Teddy boy. He'll pull his weight all right. He's tougher than he looks." In spite of the occasional teasing, a bond began to form among us. Only C remained outside of it.

Days and days of traveling—ten, twelve, I lost count—on the water called for diversion, and the further we got along our way, the more we drank and shared stories. Paulo was a doodle if ever I saw one. After enough whiskey, he would often interrupt a card game to say he had a story to tell and laughter would follow even before he began—because Paulo always laughed so hard at his own stories. Paulo always stood to tell a tale, and Captain Sam always jumped up to stand beside him to translate to English, so we *brancos* wouldn't miss anything. Paulo giggled like a lass. He could never get through a single line without squeaking and squealing and falling forward from his waist in fits of laughter, his eyes red with drink and foolishness.

"*Havia um caçador que tinha dez cães,*" Paulo, the top banana, said one night.

"There was a hunter who had ten dogs," Sam, second banana, translated beside him, though Teddy understood perfectly and the rest of us could have figured it out.

"*E a cada dia ele ia para a selva para encontrar jaguar,*" Paulo cried, his voice cracking.

"And every day he would go into the jungle to seek the jaguar," Sam said.

"*Mas quando ele não estava olhando a onça vinha por trás e tomava um de seus cães.*"

"But when he wasn't looking the jaguar would come from behind and take one of his dogs."

"*E ela o comia!*" Paulo exclaimed.

"And he would eat it!" Sam cried with jizz to match.

Paulo went on, buckling with laughter, as was everyone else by then, even Teddy—everyone but C, who was sitting on the edge of the bow looking out into the night—describing how the hunter went to the jungle a second time and lost a second dog, and then went a third time and lost another dog, and so on. Anticipating a punch line that would be riotous, Paulo's audience, all of us sprawled out on the deck, rolled and writhed, our heads thrown back, laughing so hard we could hardly hear Paulo talking and Sam translating as the dogs continued to dwindle.

"*Finalmente, o jaguar comeu o último cão,*" Paulo said.

"Finally, the jaguar ate the last dog."

"*E o caçador, ele estava louco...*"

"And the hunter, he was mad..."

"*E então ele foi para a selva para confrontar a onça-pintada...*"

"And so he went into the jungle to confront the jaguar..."

"*E ele repetiu a história toda para ela, como ele perdeu um, depois dois, depois três...*"

"And he repeated the whole story to him, how he lost one, then two, then three..."

Now even Sam was doubled over laughing.

"*E o jaguar ouviu atentamente...*"

"And the jaguar listened carefully..."

"*E quando o caçador estava terminando de falar...*"

"And when the hunter was done talking..."

"*A onça começou a chorar!*"

"The jaguar began to cry!"

Paulo sat down and sloshed his wet eyes with his fists.

"That's it?" Leon yelled in English over the chorus of laughter. "There's no payoff in that."

"No payoff in the jaguar's tears either," Sam cried. He repeated it in Portuguese for the others. Everyone laughed harder.

Our launch had gone out on coal, but after the first week our supply ran out and we had to stop every few days to gather wood. The wood-gathering slowed us considerably. There was always a dead tree to be found near the water's edge, and with so many of us to work at it, it took no time at all to hack it into pieces that would fit into the boat's furnace. But getting to the trees was a different story, for it meant cutting a path through thick foliage that was home to snakes and insects of every description. The simple act of pulling aside a vine or creeper could mean exposing a nest of wasps or hornets. Or disturbing some ants underfoot could mean being entirely covered by biting insects in seconds. You had to have eyes in back of your head, Nuno Bonito, who was always willing to make a joke at his own expense, liked to say.

And there was always some arseways incident that further delayed us each time we went ashore. The first time we stopped for wood, Leon was bitten by a fish at the edge of the water. No one saw what it was. We only saw the silver streak flashing in the murky waters near his ankle, and the next thing anyone knew he was crying out like a wee dote. We had medicines, but we had to find them amid the rest of our provisions before we could apply them and wrap the wound.

The second time we stopped, Gomez came very close to stepping on the tail of a caiman. No one had seen him there with only his eyes resting on the mud at the edge of the water. The thing whipped around fast as a fart in the wind and would have made himself a meal of Gomez's ankle—or mine, since I was right beside him—but Captain Sam had his rifle at his side, and before the gator could act, he shot him in the back. The gator fell back at once and rolled into the river. He wasn't dead; he was still thrashing, and he might have put up more of a fight and come back at us, but as his blood spread out in the water, blood-red piranhas appeared out of nowhere, hundreds of them, thousands, maybe, and began to attack his flesh.

It took no time at all for the fish to devour the gator—and I could not help but think it would have taken even less to devour the softer exterior of a man. C was the only one able to act over the mayhem, removing his shirt and using it as a net to pitch some of the attacking fish from the river onto the beach. The beached fish squealed like a room full of dotes and flapped around madly, biting at grasses or roots or whatever they could get their ugly gobs around, until Paulo finally thought to break off a branch and begin the job of clubbing them into silence.

We built a grill that day, by making a fire with some deadwood and then cutting four narrow green branches, each with a forked end, and standing them fork-side up to hold two horizontal branches, across which we placed several more green branches of matching length. We ate well afterwards, and the incident provided as lively a theme as we could want to accompany our fine meal. But it all meant that our traveling was done for the day, much earlier than it should have been. We were in a race against time now, a race against the coming of the rains.

However disagreeable and time-squandering our adventures on land were, eventually they became a welcome relief from the long days on the slow-moving boat. Except for a few fishing boats, we hadn't seen another human since we'd left the outskirts of Manáos to steam along the Rio Solimões—which was what the Portuguese called the Rio Amazonas after it passed through Manáos—and settled onto the Rio Purus. The weather was hotter than ever, and more humid. And as the river was not nearly as wide as the Rio Amazonas—it was downright narrow in places—we found ourselves very close to the shore and impacted by its presence. Sometimes the smell of blossoms was so strong it was almost sickening. As soon as the sun came up, the *pium* arrived, tiny flies that came in droves and left our hands and faces speckled with their bites. At night Sam found places to tie up and we slept aboard—either in the cabin with the windows open to catch the breeze or out on the deck—covering our hammocks with netting, but the mosquitoes and other insects found us anyway, and everyone awoke in the mornings with fresh bites. Paulo had the tips of two toes bitten by vampire bats the second night on the Rio Purus, and after that we all slept with our boots on—except C, of course, who didn't have boots and who was so unpleasant that the bats didn't bother with him anyway. And to make matters worse, now that we were closing in on our destination, the *caboclos* were becoming edgy and excitable, and they clacked on almost constantly about the perils of the jungle.

Paulo had been on the lookout for a *sucuruju*, the great snake that ruled the river, since day one. But now that everyone else had begun to verbalize their fears, he talked about *sucurujus* incessantly. He said a *sucuruju* could mesmerize a man. The first time he said it, the rest of us tittered and waited to see if this would turn into one of his foolish narratives. He knew a *sucuruju* could mesmerize a man, he continued, because his cousin had been out in a canoe fishing these very waters one day when a *sucuruju* as long as our launch appeared on a nearby beach, a *praia*. This cousin took up his rifle and went to shoot it, but he made the mistake of first looking it in the eye, and in that instant he went numb and dropped his rifle into the river. The *sucuruju* then slithered into the water and tipped the canoe and slogged the man down whole.

Some other men in another canoe witnessed the event. Fearing the monster would come after them next, the *patrão* on board gave his men orders to shoot, but without looking the thing in the eye. So they shot, but everyone was so afraid of accidentally catching its eye that they wound up looking at their feet and no one hit the monster. The youngest man on board took aim a second time, but this time he *did* look it in the eye. (Later he would say it was impossible not to. His gaze was pulled that way as soon as he lifted his head.) And he too was immediately mesmerized. But the *patrão* managed to shoot and kill the thing before it could attack, and once it was dead, the young fellow came out of his stunned state and was himself again. We laughed uneasily when Paulo was done, but he insisted it was the truth and nothing less.

Gomez, the only one of the four *caboclo seringueiros* who had some knowledge of rubber tapping and whose job it would be to instruct the other three, was more concerned with warning everyone to hide their rubber *pelas* once they got to work, because rubber was gold and there were always *seringueiros* out to steal it from you. You had to mark your *pelas* so that you could identify them if they were stolen. If you caught the thief, you had to shoot him, even if only in the arm or leg, because there was no such thing as law and order in the jungle, and only by making an example of him could you decrease the chances that more thieves would come to your camp. It was hard to imagine villains appearing in the jungle when we had seen no one for some time, but the *caboclos* insisted Gomez was speaking the truth.

Gomez also spoke with dread about the *selvagems* in the region where we were headed. There were rumors that *selvagems* everywhere were weary of tappers coming to bleed trees they thought of as their own. There had been uprisings in other areas, and if that happened to us, if we were attacked, the only solution was either to kill our attackers or make them into *seringueiros* too, by force if necessary. Otherwise there was no telling what would happen.

Gomez started this conversation one evening when we'd built a fire on a small *praia* to boil our water for the next day and cook our miserable famished selves a fish that C had caught. When Gomez saw the look on the faces of the four of us, he added that it was perfectly legal to do what you could to civilize the *selvagems*. In fact, it was preferable to make them work than to kill them because there flat weren't enough *seringueiros* to meet the rubber demands of the outside world. Paulo interrupted to say he'd heard rumors that there were people in the Orient growing rubber now, on plantations, and one day they would flourish and take over the industry. Everyone had heard that rumor and no one believed it. Gomez ignored his comment and went on, saying that one large camp of *seringueiros* somewhere in neighboring Peru had captured over six hundred female *selvagems* and was breeding with them to produce a new generation of *seringueiros*. They were thinking ahead, he said, and he admired that. He rubbed his plumbs and smiled salaciously, exposing his crooked yellow teeth.

Baxter and Leon and Ted and me listened to Gomez quietly that evening but the next day, we four found ourselves gathered near the port rail in the late afternoon, where we speculated on what we would do if our work was threatened by angry savages. I said I would never force anyone to work for me. It came out sounding self-righteous, I will be the first to allow, and the others looked at me with raised brows and Baxter said, "Ah, don't mind his grim ugly arse. He talks like that 'cause he thinks he kissed the Blarney Stone in his sleep and received the gift of eloquence, the wee fuckin bootlicker. Don't mean he means a word of what he says." But then Bax agreed that he wouldn't force anyone to work for him either, though he added that if the savages could be persuaded to work by an offer of a share of the money, that would be another matter. One thing our Da taught us good is you don't ask a man to do for nothing what you your miserable self wouldn't do for the same. Leon agreed with Baxter and added that he would be willing to breed with the women if they were beautiful enough. Bax and I had a laugh over that. Then Ted took his chance to speak. "I'd shoot them dead and be done with it," he said, shrugging. Everyone laughed, until we saw the stony look in his mud-colored eyes. He shrugged again. "They're savages, ain't they?" he went on. "They don't read or write. They don't know nothing about how the world works." He shrugged a third time. "They're just taking up space could be used for better things."

"The *caboclos* don't read or write either," Baxter countered. "You want to shoot them too?"

"Baxter don't read," I added, hoping some levity would offset the tension. "You want to shoot him?" Everyone looked at me, but no one laughed.

"You know who Darwin is?" Ted went on. "They talk about such things in Hoboken? You mean to say you'd let savages stop us getting rubber to make tires and stuff for hospitals and other important things? We're doing the world's work here. The world's got to have rubber and we got to be the ones to deliver it. The savages have nothing to contribute. That's why they're savages."

"Depends on the size of their skulls, don't it?" Bax said.

I spun around to look at my brother. It was the closest I'd ever heard him come to agreeing with Ted on any matter whatsoever. I couldn't help but chuckle, thinking what Nora would have said if she'd heard him. She would have bitten *his* head off, skull and all. But then Baxter smirked, and I saw he was only razzing the little mucker and not really thinking that way at all.

4

WE FELL INTO A routine. Each evening after we secured the boat, we four younger men would bathe while the older fellows beat the water with sticks to warn the fish and caiman away, and then we would do the same for them. One evening when we had finished in the river and were climbing the bank to prepare a fire for our supper on a beautiful white *praia*, I asked, casually, or so I hoped, about the whores in Manáos, just to see what the *caboclos* would say. They laughed at first, and teased me, and Nuno Bonito said I must have the horn and me own brother called me a miserable gash hound. But then Captain Sam got serious and said if I ever found myself back in Manáos and wanted a whore, I should see Fabiano, that his were young and clean and more affordable than the ones imported from Poland and France and other faraway places. Fabiano's whores were only local girls, but as a vagina was a vagina no matter where it originated, he didn't see it mattered all that much. Embarrassed to see where my question had led, I said I was going back to the boat for some whiskey. I'd only wanted confirmation that whoring was, in fact, what this Fabiano was about. The last thing I wanted was to hear the captain pipe up with details about Fabiano's whores' pussies.

When I returned the men were still talking about women, though no longer whores and their gashes. By now everyone knew that Baxter had a woman waiting for him, and everyone knew her name was Nora. The *caboclos* were all married (except maybe C; since he stayed outside these conversations there was no way to know about his personal life), and while Nuno Bonito and his wife had no children (Captain Sam said they were both so ugly, neither could get near the other), Sam had one and Gomez and Paulo had three apiece and Cabeça de Galinha had six. Yet they almost never spoke of their wives or families. It was Nora they all wanted to know about. Whenever we passed a red blossom or saw a bird with red feathers, someone would ask, "Is that the color of Nora's hair?" Or a Hyacinth Macaw would fly overhead and someone would say, "Beautiful blue feathers, just like Nora's eyes."

Baxter had great fun painting Nora to be a goddess for their amusement—though when they wanted to know about her freckles and where they were on her body besides her face and arms, he had the good sense to answer in such a way so as to discourage them from becoming any more *lascivo* than they were by nature. But it bothered me the way Bax talked about her. And then too it bothered me that it bothered me. I found myself wanting to add to my brother's descriptions, which were solely regarding Nora's appearance, to say how she liked to dance, and how she would hold the eyes of her partner and there'd be no breaking away unless she was the one who desired it; how she loved to laugh, and that even though I'd heard some of the older folks, including me own mum, comment that she laughed too loud for a lass, most people couldn't help but chuckle themselves once she got going. She was caring for Mum, yes, and she was a saint in that way, but there was the devil about her too. I remembered once again the way she'd looked that day as our ship pulled away from the docks. One minute she'd been ministering to Mum, telling her quietly to hush, hush, everything will be all right, and the next minute she'd turned back with her teeth flashing white, her eyes dancing with mischief...

But I could say none of this to the others, because they would think *I* was the one in love with her, and Bax would surely have a go at me, and I was too hot and wet and sticky to entertain even the thought of a brawl in the jungle or up on the deck. And anyway, and in spite of the fact that I could easily conjure up an image of a walking, talking, dancing, laughing Nora, ever since Manáos I had been thinking, almost constantly, of Bruna. There wasn't much to conjure regarding her disposition or her mannerisms, because I hadn't had the good fortune to observe much of them, but our near erotic encounter had left plenty enough fuel for my imagination. What if I had allowed her to remove her undergarments? What would she have looked like? I had touched her shoulder, and her skin was silk above her wound. If her shoulder felt like that, what would her wee diddies feel like? I remembered the feel of her hand in mine. I had held it loosely, so she wouldn't be afraid. She could have pulled away at any time. But she didn't. The first chance I got I intended to write to her. I would give the letter to Captain Sam, who would be turning the launch back for Manáos once he'd dropped everyone.

It took nearly a month to arrive at our first destination, which was called the Teacup camp because of the way the land jutted out just to the north of it, like a cup handle. This was the camp where the *caboclos* would be staying. It was also the place where the launches would come at the end of the tapping season to collect rubber. There were other *seringueiros* working in the area, Captain Sam explained, and they would have to find their way to the Teacup to deliver their goods and get their money and pick up their provisions for the next season.

Once the rubber was collected, the launches would carry it back to Manáos, and from there it would go to Belém and then to ports in New York and London. The delivering *seringueiros* would have the choice of staying at the camp, if there was still any room, or returning to their own camps to wait out the wet season. Most were starved for companionship after their first season tapping, Captain Sam said, and they were happy to share stories and play cards with others of their kind for a short while at least. Because it had to accommodate any number of *seringueiros*, a large house had been built a few years back, and with a bit of luck, we would find it standing still.

The *caboclos* were unusually quiet as Sam secured the launch to some trees in the cove. They were worried about how the season would go and whether they would bring in enough rubber to pay for their provisions and still have enough left to satisfy their wives and families waiting back home. Of late their conversations had shifted from threats from thieves, *selvagems* and *sucurujus* to stories of *seringueiros* who had failed to achieve the goals set out for them and had become little more than slaves to their *patrãos*. Gomez admitted that a friend of his had croaked from fever during the tapping season and his *patrão* had taken this friend's eldest son into service to pay off the father's debt. They all agreed that their own children were safe, that Abalo wouldn't go that far. But still it made them anxious. The four of us listened to Gomez and the others gripe, but when we were alone we reminded one another that we had youth on our side. We pledged once more to make it work for us.

But now there was something wrong with Ted. He'd had a fever the week before, and for a few days he lay in his hammock and ate almost nothing. Then he was fine again, just weak. But now he was down once more, and it was worse than the first go-round. We'd been giving him quinine powder, but it didn't seem to be helping. And he said it made his ears ring. The second or third time he beefed about his ears, Paulo piped up to say that his problem was more likely *curupira* than quinine. The *curupira* was an ugly creature, as ugly as Nuno Bonito, Paulo said, with three eyes and blisters all over its face and its feet on backwards so it could mislead anyone trying to track it. Its whistle, which only certain people could hear, was known to drive them crazy. Everyone laughed at the time—except Paulo, who believed in all sorts of mythical creatures, and of course Ted.

We left Ted on board to rest in his hammock and went off to help the *caboclos* settle into their camp. The house had been built up on a hill at a distance from the river, which would soon flood and spread out over its banks like some monstrous kelpie seeking to drown as much and as many as possible. Even though the shack had been occupied the year before—Sam didn't say what had become of the previous occupants and we didn't ask—the path leading up to it was already completely overgrown and had to be cut anew. We had brought along our *facãos* (machetes), and using a compass, C led us inland.

The jungle is densest near the river, where trees and vines and grasses compete for light. As we moved away from the river, the forest thinned some and the cutting went easier. But it was still slow going. A sapling could be cut with one quick blow, but when you struck out at a creeper it would only swing back at you. You had to hold it against a tree to chop it. And you never knew what would come down on your head along with the creeper itself.

Except for C and Sam and Gomez, none of us had ever ventured deep into the jungle before, and I at least was surprised to see how dark and dank it was. We walked gingerly on a carpet of decaying leaves, beneath which anything could have been hiding, continuously having to climb over the trunks of rotting trees. The only sunlight came from narrow shafts that somehow found their way through the thick canopy above. But where the light fell, its illumination was something special for fair. At one point, Bax stopped and waited for me to catch up to him. Three blue morphos were playing in a cone of light, chasing one another in circles. The color of the leaves on the tree whose branches they played near was emerald green. You could see tiny insects crawling on them. "Look at that," Baxter said. "This is why we're here, ain't it? This is what we'll take back with us...besides a sack full of moolah of course."

"Indeed," I mumbled. I was distracted, thinking about Ted back at the launch. I'd gone to check on him just before heading into the jungle, and I'd found him crying quietly in his hammock. "You all right?" I'd asked. Ted had turned to look at me, his brown eyes pleading. "I'm thinking of my mother," he said. On more than one occasion Bax and I had talked about Da and how much we missed him, and Ted had revealed that his mother had died about the same time, from a tumor growing in the stomach. He never said much more than that, and somehow the silence that followed the fact of her death always became the catalyst for another conversation. Not knowing what to say, I'd patted his shoulder and hurried to catch up with the others.

The three butterflies flew off and Bax started moving again. "You got your knickers in a twist over that booby," he said over his shoulder.

He'd read my thoughts again. I didn't bother to respond.

"Don't mollycoddle him, Jack," Bax warned. "He's a little fellow. I don't think there's room enough for two to climb up his arse, and he's got one up there already."

The dwelling was a large rectangular shack, built up on stilts to keep it safe from flooding. The roof was made of palm leaves woven together, and Sam was chuffed to see that it looked as though it had held just grand since he'd been there last. The rain would be the real test when it came.

The previous occupants had covered the windows as best they could with sticks tied together with vines, but insects had got in anyway. One was a beetle almost eight inches long, a *besouro gigante*, Cabeça de Galinha said. "Well, bugger me sideways," Bax exclaimed when he saw it, and we all laughed. But then Leon aimed his rifle and Cabeça de Galinha yelled out and slapped his hand over the barrel of the weapon and pushed it downward. If Leon had shot, he would have blown off his own stinkin foot. Cabeça de Galinha went to the corner where the beetle was lurking in fear and picked him up by his grand glistening shell and brought him outside and dumped him on the ground. The mucker bolted under the house at once. "You'd better be careful with that weapon," Cabeça de Galinha warned. Leon ducked, as if he'd been hit, and came up laughing, but no one laughed with him.

It took a few hours to clean out the larger insects, but we found no snakes or mammals. While we worked, Sam went out with his rifle and returned with a curassow, a grand dinger of a bird with a crest of curly feathers on its big head. Gomez made a fire and offered to prepare the bird straight away so that those of us heading back to the launch could first share in the feast. Except for the fish that C was sometimes able to catch, we'd been eating *farinha* daily, because it was the only thing we had in surplus, and we were fuckin sick of it.

While the bird was roasting, I went off to write my letter. There was no time to sit with the dictionary, so I wrote in English and hoped Bruna would have no trouble finding someone to translate. Since I didn't know who that someone would be, I took great pains not to say anything that could be piled up to appear intimate. I told her I thought of her as a new friend and hoped she'd allow me to visit when I got back to Manáos, which, I imagined, would be after two tapping seasons. What I really wanted to tell her was that she must escape this Fabiano. I remembered how her eyes filled with tears when she'd thought I'd wanted to buy her time. And her bruise. It disturbed me that she was made to suffer abuse at the hands of anyone with some dough in his pockets. I addressed my letter in care of Louisa at the home of Manuel Abalo.

When we returned to the boat that evening, Ted was awake, sitting up in his hammock for the first time in days, and furious because he'd been left alone for several hours. We'd brought some of the curassow back for him, but since he still had no appetite, that appeased him not at all. He said while we were gone a giant snake had appeared in the water, so long and so strong that it was able to lift itself high enough that he could see it peering at him over the edge of the bow. "He could have slithered on board!" he cried, his spittle flying.

We had seen our share of marvels in the jungle, but no one, not even Sam or C, had ever mentioned seeing a snake stand up that high out of the water. Even Paulo's *sucuruju* couldn't do that. "Could have been an *arowana*," Sam offered. We had seen plenty of *arowanas*, which were not snakes but eel-like fish that swam close to the surface of the water hunting for prey from above. *Arowanas* were excellent jumpers; they could leap six feet out of the water to grab something from an overhead branch. Leon and I had been on the bow once when one jumped just in front of the boat—scaring us half to our deaths—and took down a wee bird in mid-flight. "It was no *arowana*," Ted whined.

"Were your ears ringing at the time?" asked Baxter. "Maybe it was the *curupira* whistling sweet words to you and it was your fuckin pud rose up to salute it."

"Shut your mouth, Baxter. You're out of line," Sam spit. It was the first time I'd ever heard the captain speak harshly to anyone. Baxter regarded him for a long moment, then he shrugged and walked away.

With nothing more to say on the matter, C and Sam and my own discomfited self turned away too, to tie up our hammocks for the night. It was only Leon who stayed at his side. "Let it go now, Teddy," I heard him say.

It took another two days on the river before Sam announced we'd reached the mouth of the Rio Coregem, which was as far as it was safe to travel in a launch. Ted's fever had broken by then, but now he had chills, *seceoa*, Sam called it, and although everyone else was drenched in sweat, Leon and I had to wrap Ted in blankets to keep him warm. His teeth chattered continuously. He remained listless and unable to eat, but he said nothing more about the monster snake and he seemed calm.

While he rested in his hammock, the rest of us carried the remaining crates to shore. There was a small beach there, with higher ground beyond it. When our possessions were all out of the launch, Leon helped Ted to stand and climb down. At the last minute, after we'd said our so longs to Sam and as he was preparing to turn the launch for home, I hopped back on board and handed him the letter for Bruna and three others I'd written to me mum. Sam looked them over and agreed to post the ones to Hoboken and hand deliver the one going to the Abalo household. I was pleased to see he didn't laugh or tease me. But as I turned to depart, I bumped into Baxter, who'd boarded right behind me apparently, with his own letters. He smirked and nodded knowingly. I gave him a good shove and climbed down.

Me and Bax and Leon made the assumption we had arrived at what would be our camp and looked to the green wall behind us to consider where best to begin cutting a path. Ted was sitting on the ground, too miserable to take heed. But while we were surveying our surroundings, C was splashing around at the edge of the water just to the side of the beach, and when we turned to see what he was up to, we found him using a tree limb to dislodge something of size from under the thick grasses that overhung the bank there. C threw the limb aside and pulled at the thing with both hands. I half expected him to drag out a *sucuruju*. But what emerged was a canoe, a rough-carved dugout, seventeen or eighteen feet long. "We're not going anywhere in that, are we?" Leon asked.

C narrowed his eyes at us and sneered, a look by now all too familiar, and one that remained stuck on his face as he pulled the canoe to the beach and began to check it and the paddles and poles inside it for signs of decrepitude. Once he'd resolved the dugout was fit for travel, he removed his manky shirt and rendered it mankier by using it to wipe out the insects that had been homesteading in the boat. Then he dragged the thing back to the water and began to load the crates. The three of us groaned, but not wanting to be abandoned boat-less in the middle of nowhere, we got busy helping. But then Ted caught on what was happening and began to chant, "No more river; no more." Once everything was loaded, Leon carried the protesting Ted—who had lost so much weight he looked more like a wee boyo than ever, who kicked his legs just like a wee boyo would—on board and put him in a safe place between two of the larger crates. Then the rest of us climbed in and settled.

While the canoe looked like it would float all right, it rode high up on the water. It was as if we were sitting on the water's surface. It was unsettling to think we would be exposed to anything swimming beside us and anything in the forest too. "I hope we don't encounter Ted's snake," Baxter said. It was a bad joke. I shook my head in warning, but Bax was pleased with himself and he went on chuckling. He removed his derby and stood up carefully—the canoe rocking nonetheless—and put it in the crate that carried his personal possessions and reached around until he found the straw boater that was like the ones the rest of us wore. Perhaps he had regard for Nora's gift after all, I thought. We took up paddles and began to pull.

I had wondered what the wooden poles were for and I found out soon enough. The water was shallow in places, and within an hour we were grounded and C shouted for us to put aside our paddles and use the poles to push the boat forward off the sandy riverbed. "Isn't it easier to just get out and push?" questioned Bax, and without waiting for an answer, he jumped out of the canoe ready to take on the task all by his loogin self.

"Candiru!" C cried.

Bax jumped back in as fast as he'd jumped out, rocking the boat again in the process, causing Ted to scream like the booby he was and me and Leon to laugh and C to turn his ugly mug over his shoulder and give us all his snaggiest look. We knew about candiru from the *caboclos*. They were tiny fish, covered with both barbs and mucus, that attacked humans by swimming up their orifices. Once they were in the body, dislodging them was nearly impossible—or flat impossible, depending on which orifice they'd chosen. The *caboclos* said there were men who'd had to have their *penes* cut off because candiru had swum up into them while they'd been pissing. These men hadn't even been deep in the river. The candiru were able to swim right up their piss stream. "Fuckin things could have rendered me pud useless as tits on a bull," Bax lamented, and me and Leon laughed.

The river narrowed as we went on, until the trees made a nearly unbroken canopy overhead and the spiny palms and ferns and creepers and mosses and lichens along the banks all but caressed us as we slithered by. We had to duck constantly, left or right or forward, to avoid being slapped with branches. Only Ted was safe, slouched between the crates. It was as if we traveled through a long, low tunnel, a tunnel that was alive. All manner of insects crawled on the ferns and lichen and leaves, and it was no bother at all for them to hop from their residence into our boat when they were so inclined. We couldn't see them coming either; we didn't know they were there until we'd been bit or stung or taken one in the gob.

Sometimes the tunnel was so dense we could hear movement above and beside us but couldn't see a wretched thing. Other times we were able to glimpse the squirrel monkeys that seemed to be following us, and birds darting in and out between limbs in the trees. When there were breaks in the tunnel, we saw *cigano* hens diving for fish, and parrots and egrets and toucans. Lizards watched us dead-eyed and motionless from the branches on either side of our passageway. When the manky things felt threatened, they dropped into the water, making a loud plopping sound that startled everyone, except C. C told us to keep an eye out for wasp nests. If we disturbed one, there'd be no recourse but to go overboard and take our chances in the water, where we'd probably drown before it was safe to lift our noggins for air. We had to be alert at all times, looking in every direction—even when there seemed to be nothing to see. Ted, who was feverish again and who'd continued chanting—softly, for the most part—on and off throughout the day, jumped every time something made a noise.

By the time we stopped for the night, we were flat knackered, all of us rubbing our necks, which had gone sore from stretching them to look everywhere at once. We made a fire on a sandy beach and ate *farinha*. For the first time I thought I understood why C was so unpleasant. After the kind of day we'd had, what was there to be pleasant about? No one spoke at all. Thankfully, even Ted kept his gob shut. Sleep was the only respite left to us, and it couldn't come fast enough.

But sleeping out on the beach, I soon discovered, was for fair much different than sleeping in the cabin or on the deck of the launch. I drifted along on the surface of sleep without ever sinking into it. Noises that didn't bother me on the launch woke me now. There was a shrill scream sometime in the middle of the night, the scream of a large animal, I thought, but it was impossible in the total darkness to guess how far away it was or even the direction it had come from. I found myself listening for it to come again, so I could determine whether it was getting closer or moving away. I kept my hand on my rifle. When the sky began to lighten, I saw everyone else had slept with their guns at the ready too.

We spent six more days traveling in C's wretched canoe, and we were not always able to find a sandy beach to make camp at night. There were several times when, after a day of dodging massive tangles of underwater plants and pushing off sandbanks and ducking under wasp nests, we had to climb the high banks and cut through vines and trees and clear a place big enough to tie our hammocks. One late afternoon, when even C seemed knackered and ready to stop for the night, we came upon a passel of *capivara*, water hogs, feeding on the grass along the edge of the river. The river was not wide enough to get around them, so C stopped the canoe with his paddle and lifted his rifle and shot, not at them but as a warning to scare them out of the water. What a show they put on then, snorting and barking and splashing. Then all at once they ran up the bank, and, to my surprise, began to attack one another. "Now!" C yelled, and we put all our strength into paddling away before the *capivara* figured out the enemy was not among them. Me and Bax and Leon laughed, but our laughter had about as much spark as a hen has teeth. There was no denying we were quick losing our bucko glim.

By the time we got to the place that had been designated for our worksite, we had all lost weight, and with the exception of C, our movements were like those of old men. I felt feverish almost all the time, and I surmised Baxter and Leon did too as the quinine supply was quickly diminishing, but there was no point beefing about it. If C learned we were all sick, he would likely leave us for dead and head back to Manáos for a fresh batch of more vigorous men. So we did what we had to do, unloading the crates and helping C to cut a path into the jungle, but every step required exertion. The land rose higher as we went inland, steeply in places, making our progress even more challenging. And Ted was no help;

though his fever had broken once again, he remained too frail to contribute to the workload.

Bax and me had never shot a living thing. Da had always told us that hunting was more than killing a thing to eat it, that there was a level of alertness that was required in order to get the most from the experience, the same level of alertness that one's prey lived with all the time. When both the hunter and the hunted were mutually keen and attentive, the hunter became one with his prey, and by extension with all of nature, and it became a fair fight. Good hunting, right hunting, was a profound experience.

We'd gone hunting with Da on two occasions, up in the forest surrounding our Aunt Emily's house in the woods of New York. The first time we sat all day in a cold November drizzle and saw nothing. On the second occasion, a year later, a large buck with a ten-point rack appeared in our view, and Da nudged Bax, the first born and always his favorite, to shoot it. But Bax was gobstruck, so eager to hit it that he forgot to aim, and he missed his shot.

And then Da died, and we never got the chance to go back and do it right. So naturally we'd been looking forward to hunting in the jungle, but when we went out together, at C's command, to find something to eat the first night at camp, we were numb to the experience. How disappointed our father would have been. We sat side by side on the jungle floor, flicking the more dangerous-looking insects away from us and being grateful—or at least I was—for the interlude from the more difficult work taking place back at the camp. I didn't care whether we were successful or not; I felt so sick and so close to starvation that it hardly seemed to matter. Game was moving all around us all the time, but we were actually able to see very little of it. And if it was a large animal that crossed our path, it would only mean we would have to exert more energy than we had to drag it back.

But there was a shallow stream not far from where we were sitting (we'd had to follow it so as to be able to move away from the campsite without getting lost), and sure enough a tapir eventually appeared on its opposite bank. For all I knew the brown pig-like animal was a figment of my imagination, but I raised my rifle just the same, and my brother and me shot at the same time. The thing bucked and ran for several yards and then collapsed, its chest heaving as it struggled to breathe. We looked at each other, Bax and me, gobsmacked. Bax actually cracked a smile, first I'd seen from him in days. Maybe I cracked one too; probably I did. We got up and crossed the stream and moved to the spot where the thing lay heaving in its flat pool of black blood. I shot it once more, in the head, to end its misery. I thought to wonder if there were any humans—besides C and Leon and Ted—close enough to have heard our shots.

I was the first to awaken the next day, and having had a good meal the night before—we gorged ourselves almost to the point of puking—and not feeling as feverish as I had for the last several days, I was able to fully appreciate the beauty of our surroundings. Because the days were so hot and evenings cool by comparison, a thick cloak of fog covered the terrain in the wee hours, making it impossible to see more than a few feet in any direction. We'd experienced this phenomenon at times out on the river, from whatever boat we'd been on. But now, deep in the jungle, the unveiling—as the mist dissipated by degrees and the trees and plants revealed themselves one by one, enlarging the world incrementally—was a fuckin dinger like no other I had ever seen.

I grinned like the fool I was as I watched, my piss-pot eyes brimming with tears. And then I found myself remembering the lunar eclipse we'd seen a few years back; my eyes had pooled up then too. Me and Bax, we hadn't even known it was coming, the eclipse, but Nora had. She'd been across the river with her aunt all that day, and when she got back, late at night, she threw pebbles at our window, as was her way when she wanted us "after hours," and we awoke and went outside. Then the three of us ran down to the river and sat on the grass with our eyes all but popping from our heads as a blood-red shadow slowly overtook the full moon.

I'd never seen nothing like it. I was mesmerized. Sometimes it looked to be dangling, that moon, like some ninny had it up on a string, and sometimes, especially as the light dwindled down to a sliver, it looked like an eyeball, staring right at me, trying to relay a message. And in the gobstruck state in which I found myself, I began to imagine the message had something to do with Nora, that it was trying to tell me I must tell her how I felt...about her...in my heart, no matter that I'd always suspected she liked Bax more than me. But just then, just as the glim dropped off the edge of the moon, I saw with the corner of my eye Bax placing his hand over Nora's on the grass, and I knew my chance was gone, gone forever, that the blood red moon had a message for me all right, and it was clear what it was. What would have happened if I'd been the one to lift my manky hand and place it on hers first?

Once the mist had lifted, the sun broke through in narrow shafts, chucking spears of bright light on dew-soaked leaves and blossoms in such a way that they glittered like gems. Paulo had once said that Indian myth had it that the jungle was full of gold, if only you knew where to look for it. Now I thought it must have been this fine exhibit of dew-drop jewels that led to such legends. The others awoke one by one, and with the exception of Ted, they all seemed to understand that the moment was a blessing from nature. Even C nodded with satisfaction as he took in our surroundings.

We were able to complete work that day on a clearing large enough for the building of our shack and the smokehouse we would require to smoke the rubber. Since Leon had proven himself to be of more use to C than us Hopper boyos in the past few days, C sent me and Bax to cut palms for constructing the roof while he and Leon selected the trees from those they'd felled making the clearing to build the structures. Even Ted was feeling a wee bit better, and he was some help to C and Leon too.

Three days later, we were done. The shack was about fifteen feet square, just large enough to hold our hammocks and supplies. The roof was made of palms braided over bamboo, and the floor was made of split palms (*abacaba*, C called them), with the rounded ends facing up, fastened together with vines. The shack had been erected up on stilts, some five feet off the ground. It had been storming on and off for the last few weeks. Our clothes were never dry anymore. C explained that when it got this hot, the trees began to sweat, just as we did. So many trees meant a lot of sweat, which rose up and became clouds that returned as rain.

As if to demonstrate his lesson, not an hour after the completion of our new home, when we were still all standing around admiring our handiwork, there was a thunderous and torrential downpour and the five of us sat around the perimeter of the room looking upward to see if the palms had been woven tight enough to keep us dry. There was no leakage at all! And we were bloody amazed when the storm ended and we opened the door and saw how much rain had fallen in that short time. Water was everywhere, running in streams and rivulets all around and even under our shack. We'd set out tin pails to catch rainwater coming off the roof and they were all full.

With the shack construction behind us, C began to teach us how to tap for rubber. Now something approaching excitement—*arrah*, me Da would say—returned to us. After all our travails, here, finally, was the thing we had come to do. The dreams me and Bax once shared about returning home with pockets bursting, heroically, with stories everyone would want to hear, were dimmer now, but whatever was left of them bobbed at the surface and gave us the stamina we needed to follow C into the jungle each day between storms. Even Ted, who stayed on C's heels like he intended to become his shadow, seemed to chipper up a wee bit.

First we had to learn to recognize rubber trees. There were two kinds, one that looked a lot like the birch trees that grew upstate in New York near our aunt's house, and a taller one—maybe a hundred feet tall—with bark almost the same rosy color as the river dolphins. What both varieties had in common was their leaves. These were feather-shaped with lateral veins extending from the center, a deep green in color—which is to say they were not so different from many other jungle leaves. The trick, after learning to recognize the trees, was to be able spot them in the midst of vegetation so thick in some places you couldn't see two feet in front of you. But with C's help—and I will admit that while he had the charm of a toothpick, he was an excellent *mateiro*—we could soon identify the trees on our own.

Next we had to cut trails, called *estradas*, to access the trees we intended to tap. This meant not only cutting through the jungle but also cutting trees to build bridges to cross the streams that stood in our way. C showed us how to use our *facãos* to scrape the moss off the tree trunks and then cut

70

grooves so they wouldn't be slippery when we crossed them carrying all our tapping equipment. Once we got to a rubber tree, we had to clear the vines and thorny plants surrounding it. We learned to be alert, like C was, and survey the area for snakes and hornets before we began to cut. The trails—two of them, one to be worked by me and Bax and the other by Leon and Ted—would be looped, like figure eights. This pattern would allow us to reach a larger range of forest without the risk of getting lost. Because of the necessity of the configuration, not all the rubber trees within proximity of our camp could be included. "You'd think someone would think to clear some land and plant a lot of rubber trees all in one place, so we *seringueiros* wouldn't have to work so hard," Leon said once.

C shook his head. "They get sick when they all together like that." He smirked. "They like you boys. They don't like their own kind."

He laughed at his little joke, revealing gaps where he'd lost teeth in the back of his mouth. He laughed so seldom that it was a surprise to find myself looking *into* his mouth. No one asked what he meant, but I thought he must be referring to Bax and Ted. The tension between them seemed to grow daily. Ted, who still insisted his ears were ringing much of the time, would often test their condition by cupping and uncupping his hands over them. It drove Bax batty to see him with his hands on his ears, his bulging eyes swinging from side to side as if he was expecting the source of the ringing to suddenly manifest. Bax seldom beefed about it, but the faces he made—rolling his eyes and twisting his lips, and sniggering—revealed his disgust, and he went out of his way never to speak to Ted directly.

When we were done, several days later, each of the two trails contained about forty trees. Once the season started, C said, we would have to get up before sunrise and slash each tree on our *estrada* diagonally with our small tapping axes, our *facas*, and place the tin cups we'd been provided at the bottom of the slash to catch the whitish milk that would begin to bleed out; before sunset was the time the milk ran fastest. If the tree was wide enough, we could make more than one slash and leave more than one cup. With a very wide tree, we might leave as many as four cups. We would have to be sure to cut just deep enough to reach the vein without cutting so deep that we harmed the tree, which we would be bleeding again and again. And all the while we would have to keep ourselves from being bit by the armies of insects that traveled up and down the trees or the mammals that came to guzzle their seeds. "But how will we see if we set off in the dark?" asked Ted.

It was a good question, the first Ted had ventured. It made Leon smile and Bax scowl. During his tapping demonstrations C had amassed a quantity of rubber. When we were back at the shack, he took a small piece of it and made it into a ball and showed us how to split the end of a green stick and insert the ball into the fissure and light it to make a torch.

In the middle of the day when the heat was worst, C advised, we should return to camp to eat and rest. Later we would make a second run through the *estradas* to pour the milk that had collected in the tins into our large buckets, which were wider at bottom and smaller at top to prevent spillage. Then we would return to camp again, this time to the smokehouse to slowly pour the rubber milk over a limb held in place by two horizontal guides set above a smoky fire made from wood chips or palm nuts. Gradually the milk would coagulate into a yellow-brown mass. This was a slow process and worked best with one person turning the spit while the other poured. When the ball got to be about half the weight of your average-size man, we could move it off to the clearing and set it on some limbs to dry out. If we placed green leaves over our smoking fire, we could keep it smoldering from day to day and save ourselves the trouble of having to start a fire from scratch each time.

The wet season was going full force by then, and almost every night, and sometimes during the day, there were violent thunderstorms that downed branches and even uprooted trees. The humidity, even when it wasn't storming, had gone from bothersome to flat out suffocating. Everything was wet all the time. The jungle smelled of a mold that almost seemed toxic.

Inside was the same. The walls in our hut were wet; our clothing was wet; our hammocks were damp and smelt like cat piss. The books I'd bothered to carry all this way—the ones I'd read and the ones I'd planned to—were so full of black mold it was nearly impossible to separate the pages. Bax joked it was fortunate we'd learned a fair amount of Portuguese on our own, because his language dictionary had almost disintegrated.

We threw them all—his book and mine—into one of our cooking fires, and that was the end of that. The only book that remained thereafter was one that Leon had brought along. It was called *Report on a Journey to Pennsylvania and Regions West*, and it was more or less a travel guide for emigrating Germans.

Even though Leon's version was an English translation (rendered to extend the longevity of the wisdom within), Leon hadn't read a word of it. He'd brought it only because his grandmother had given it to him on her deathbed and told him to keep it safe. *Das ist magie*, she'd said when she'd pressed it into his palm. *This is magic*. And for her it had been.

It—the original, published, in 1827—was the book that had given her and Leon's grandfather the courage to climb on board what was to become a typhoid-infested ship and travel to America and start new lives.

And maybe there was some magic going on with the thing itself, because the pages weren't nearly as susceptible to mold as those of my books had been. Or maybe Leon just took better care of it, placing it near the candles we burned some nights to dry it out a bit.

During the first real weeks of the storm season we went out each day to walk the *estradas* with C to assess the previous night's damage. We brought our *facãos*, because almost always there was cleanup to be done. Often we found that one or two of our bridges had been carried away by a rushing stream, and we had to build new ones. We continued to work to widen our paths as well. In the beginning it had seemed unlikely the day would come when we would be able to see our way from one rubber tree to the next, but now it was happening: the *estradas* were looking like real trails.

The inevitable happened one morning after breakfast when we'd all gone back into the house to get what we needed for the day: C announced that he had done his job and would be leaving. His declaration was followed by silence. Then Leon said, "You're taking your canoe, then?" C nodded. Me and Bax and Leon nodded back at him. We'd expected as much. We watched as C took down and rolled up his hammock and stuffed his few possessions into his canvas sack. He was unceremoniously making for the door when Ted, who'd been sitting on the floor finishing a cup of coffee, jumped to his feet and cried, "I'm going with you." He turned to Leon. "I'm sorry I didn't say so before, but—"

C moved to stand between Ted and Leon, facing Ted, blocking his view of his gobstruck crony. He moved his head slowly from one side to the other. "You have to take me," Ted pleaded. He took a step closer. "I can't stay here. You'll need me to help pole through the river."

C, who liked his space, gently pushed Ted back from him. In his peculiar mix of languages he explained that he'd be traveling with the current now, and that the river was swollen from all the rain and there wouldn't be any need for poling. Getting back to Manáos on high water would take a third of the time it had taken to travel the distance before.

But Ted persisted, tears spilling from his piss-pot eyes. "I'm not staying here. I'll die. I know it. Bad things are happening. You've got to take me!" He glanced over his shoulder at the rest of us.

C turned, and without as much as a so long fellers, he reached for the door. But before he could open it Ted flung himself at his back, and C turned so quickly and sharply that I sucked in my breath. With one hand C lifted Ted high into the air, pinning him to the wall by his arm and shoulder, while the other hand positioned itself to encircle his scrag of a neck. But it didn't. C stared at him a moment, fire dancing in his black eyes, and then released him. Ted dropped to the floor like a ragdoll. Then C went out the door, into the morning mist. Me and Bax and Leon stepped around Ted to watch him disappear.

Eventually Leon turned to Ted, who was still sprawled on the floor, rubbing his shoulder and sobbing quietly. He squatted in front of him. Ted wiped his eyes and allowed his friend to help him up, but once he was on his feet, he went directly to his hammock and lay there, sniffling and staring at the ceiling. I could see my brother was working hard to keep from saying something he might come to regret. But it was there on his ugly mug if anyone cared to notice. The mist lifted and we went out to walk the *estradas*, but Ted stayed in his hammock, one foot pushing off the wall to keep himself in motion.

5

A FEELING OF ABANDONMENT slipped over me, and given the tart cast to their ugly mugs, I'd wager the others felt the same. As long as C had been there, there was reason to believe we would survive. No one imagined C would ever minister to our sufferings, but we all shared a belief that he at least would know what to do if something threatened us. He'd gotten us to our campsite, after all; never mind that we were half starved and ablaze with fever much of the time. He'd built our house. He'd taught us the secrets of tapping for white gold. And now he'd gone and taken the canoe with him, and until he came back for us at the end of the tapping season, we were as stranded as if we were in the middle of the ocean, in a boat without an engine or even a compass.

Nights were longer with C gone. The screams of the howler monkeys and other animals seemed closer. So did the trees that crashed to the ground, whether it was storming or not. Everything was magnified without C lying there snoring lightly in his hammock. If something were to attack us, whether a slew of *selvagems* or an army of ants, we had nowhere to escape. "I think I'm suffering from *saudade*," said Leon one day. It was a word we'd learned from Gomez, who'd professed to suffer from it all the time. He said it was a kind of sadness, but much more *profundo* than ordinary sadness. Nuno Bonito said there was no real way to explain it; it was untranslatable. But once you experienced it, you never forgot it, ever.

Me and Bax and Leon went out hunting, though we seldom spotted any animals to kill. We shot at monkeys sometimes, but more often than not we missed, and no one liked preparing them for roasting anyway because their anatomy was too close to human. It was like skinning a scraggly dote! Worse, when you shot at one and hit it, all its cronies screamed too. We were a bunch of miserable sons of bitches, but we still had hearts beating under our shriveled gray skin. We put forth the effort only because we couldn't stand *farinha* anymore, and our canned goods were dwindling fast, and no one wanted to starve to death before the fuckin bloody tapping season even got started.

Quare enough, the less we had to eat, the more we clacked on about food. It was our preferred topic of conversation. Me and Bax described the stew Mum made so many times I could near taste it—the potatoes and carrots she threw in, how she let the meat simmer, so it would be so tender it would melt in your mouth, the hearty breads she baked for dipping. Leon was big on desserts, cabinet pudding being his favorite. Teddy didn't say much during any of our conversations, but he had even less to say when the subject of food came up. I supposed it put him in mind of his mum.

Even though his physical health was improved, Ted stayed behind from our hunting expeditions, and Leon agreed that was best, that he should rest up so he'd be ready to work on the *estrada* when the rains ended. Once, when we were alone, I asked Leon if he really thought Ted would be up to the job, and Leon admitted he was worried. "We'll figure it out," I reassured him with a slap on the back. "If it comes to it, Bax and me will take turns helping you on your *estrada*. But maybe he'll pull through." I could only imagine what Bax would say if Ted failed to participate in the work when the time came. I was so distracted with the possibilities that I almost failed to see a *capivara*, a wild hog, when it crossed my path a while later. *Almost.* I aimed and shot and I hit it! We smoked the meat that night over a grand fire that would have lasted till morning had not the rain come fast and hard and put it out. That was a damn swell night nonetheless.

But three nights later the *capivara* was gone and the tension began to rise again, and, as always, it was Ted who was at the center of it. For a bucko so rawny in stature, he could cause a stink when he cared to. For the most part he didn't talk, true enough, but sometimes he would lower his head and mumble, low enough so no one could hear exactly what he was saying. When he did that, my eyes would shoot direct to Bax, whose dislike of Teddy was so great now you could actually see it become manifest in the quickening of his breath and the way he pressed his lips together and rolled them in and out of his ugly gob. If I looked away fast enough I'd catch Leon watching Bax too. Then me and Leon might share a glance, as if to agree it was only a matter of time before Bax reached the end of his rope. If we'd been back in Hoboken, Bax would have called Ted a fuckin asswipe and got himself away so as to gather his wits; Bax was never one to go after someone that much smaller than him. But there was no walking away from anything once the night closed in around us. The hut was our prison, and the dark outside— with its insects and animals and falling trees and sudden downpours that could spark streams strong enough to carry a man straight out to the river—were our prison guards.

That night, when there was a lot of sighing going on to begin with, because we were all bored as dry shite, Ted started in with the mumbling again. Sure enough, that look came over Baxter's face, fierce and tight as ever. The mumbling went on for a minute or two and then Leon said, "What'cha mumbling about, Teddy?" though he was looking at Bax when he said it. He said it almost sweetly, the way a lass might. Then his smile disappeared and something evil flared in his eye. He was trying to get my brother's goat; any loogin could see it. Leon didn't usually mess with Bax, but he didn't stand down from him either, and in this moment at least he was as bothered with Bax as Bax was with Ted.

"You coddle him he'll only keep it up," Bax said flatly.

"Kiss my fat German arse," Leon replied, almost as flat. "You ain't the boss of anyone."

Bax and Leon stared at each other, eyes blazing, Bax's lips slightly parted in astonishment, Leon's twisted into a smirk. "You're pulling me wire here," Bax said finally, "and I won't have it."

We were all sitting on the floor with our legs extended straight out in front of us, except for Ted who was in his hammock. Bax was leaning against the east wall, doing nothing, because there was nothing to do. Leon was catty-corner to him, leaning against the south wall, and I was a good yard off from Leon, almost to the door. Between Leon and me a candle burned in one of our tin cups, making our faces even more grotesque than the moment itself could provide for.

My brother's hand moved, from where it had been resting on his thigh to the floor just beside his hip. He flattened his palm, the way a man does when he's planning to push himself to standing quickly. When I looked at Leon, I saw he'd done the same. They were nearly spitting images of each other, both staring hard at his opponent's face, chewing their lips and flaring their nostrils like the kinkers they were. If you discounted the wind and rain outdoors, it was dead quiet in that moment. Even Ted had gone mute as nails now that he'd stirred the stew.

Leon's fingers began to move, inching along like he was hitting notes on an invisible piano. Unless I was imagining, they were making their way toward the candle. In my noggin I saw how it could unfold if he picked up the candle and threw it at Bax. They'd jump to their feet and come to blows. The candle would roll across the floor. It probably wouldn't burn down the shack because everything was wet as water to begin with, but it might get things smoking if I couldn't get to it quick enough. And for what? Because Ted was mumbling and Leon got a rat up his arse and decided to play the mucker for once, commandeering a role that Bax thought was his alone.

I checked Leon's hand. It was still inching along, like he didn't think anyone would notice, or maybe he was only still deciding. His book, the one his grandmum had given him about how to find your way in America once you got off the boat, was behind the candle, standing on its edge. Leon had gotten in the habit of thumbing the page edges every so often while we sat around watching the minutes crawl by, like you would a deck of new cards.

My hand was going for the candle now too. Leon didn't notice because he was still staring at Bax. I only meant to slide the thing out of Leon's reach, but when my fingers arrived at their destination, they shifted direction and reached for the book instead.

I can't say I gave it much thought ahead. For fair, it didn't seem I was thinking anything at all; it's just what happened. I picked up the book and I opened it to somewhere in the middle where the pages happened not to be too black, and I cleared my throat and began to read, aloud, from a paragraph about how to avoid runners upon first arriving in New York. "What in fuck are you doing?" Bax shouted.

I reached for the candle and slid it close. I felt giddy for no good reason I could think of. *"These unscrupulous men,"* I read, *"may claim to be agents of boarding houses and offer to find you a suitable room. But once you hand over your deposit…"*

In my peripheral vision I saw Teddy's head pop up and disappear again. The story was about as interesting as a bag of spuds, but that didn't matter a quid to me. It was good to be saying words that had no place in the jungle, some of which— *boardinghouse, runners*—I remembered from back when I was a wee boyo, sitting late at night in the kitchen, guzz-eyed from too much stew, while Mum and Da clacked on about the bad old days and how it was for them coming to America.

Bax went on blasting me, but he didn't give it his all and I didn't pay him attention anyway. I only made my voice louder to be heard above him. Leon put forth a crack or two as well. But no one pulled the candle away or went for the book. Nor did my brother or Leon go for each other.

I read at first against a backdrop of pounding rain and snapping branches, and then, when the rain stopped, against the sound of rushing water from newly formed streams carrying away debris and working hard to rearrange the landscape. I read descriptions of the soil a German immigrant might expect to find in Pennsylvania, the crops that could be expected to grow from it, and even the birds he might encounter. *"The flowers in my cornfield attract those harmless little fellows called hummingbirds, which, I can report, tolerate human scrutiny at close range better than most of our feathered friends."* In the back of my noggin I heard old lady Sullivan, my teacher that last year in school, saying, "Mr. Hopper, could you try it with some expression? Your voice is as flat as a flounder."

When I finally stopped, an hour or so later, I found my brother had fallen asleep, his head tilted back against the wall and his gob open to catch any winged creatures that might be flying about. Leon was awake, but with his features gone soft, as you might expect from a man contemplating the home he'd left behind.

I read the next night too, before Ted even got a chance to start with his mumbling. And I read again the night after that, taking us through one of the worst thunderstorms we'd ever experienced, and we'd experienced many. For fair, a tree crashed so near us that night I stopped reading when I heard the crack and didn't begin again until the thing hit the ground and we could all breathe again.

And so it came to pass that soon I was reading most every night, sometimes for hours and sometimes, when I was feeling muzzy me own miserable self, for only ten or fifteen minutes. Before long I'd read everything in the book that could be deciphered through the mold, and then I started in anew, reading the same stories of raising chickens and keeping horses in the great state of Pennsylvania.

No one said a word when I read. It was like the words, all the talk of farm animals and weather variations and corn stalks, cast a spell on all of us. We were transported from our miseries and our boredom for some short pocket of time. Even Ted behaved—and we slept better for my efforts afterwards.

One night while I was reading a tarantula appeared in our shack, and Leon went for his rifle just as he had when we'd seen the *besouro gigante* at the Teacup. This time there was no one to stop him, and he shot at it—and missed, leaving a small smoking hole in the palm flooring. Disgusted with him and everyone else just then, I put Leon's book on the floor and pushed my loogin arse of a miserable self to standing and captured the thing in my boot. When I opened the door to dump it outside, I saw, to my bloody and fuckin amazement, a jaguar standing there staring back at me, its enormous yellow eyes reflecting the candlelight from inside the shack. "*Jay*sus," I whispered. The jaguar opened its mouth, its lips pulling back to reveal its fangs. It looked about to growl, or maybe pounce. I wouldn't have cared either way; it was that beautiful a sight. I was as mesmerized as the fishermen who'd come upon *sucurujus* in Paulo's stories. But it didn't leap; it turned instead, and in a flash it was gone. By the time Leon and Bax got to the door, there was nothing to see.

"Jaguar," I said. The word barely dropped from my mouth, so boggled was I.

"Speak up," demanded Leon.

"Four feet away."

"Me arse and Katty Barey! I thought only one of us was off his nuts," Bax chided, jerking his head toward Teddy, "but you've got him skinned to the teeth."

They had a right to doubt. All this time in the jungle and we'd only had a glimpse of a jaguar once, when we were still on the launch. It had been moving behind a thick curtain of trees and C'd had to point it out to us or we never would have noticed. And what we saw even then was shapeless, a flash of gold moving behind a tangle of green.

Leon turned to see if Ted had heard Baxter's jab, but he was in his hammock, staring at the ceiling. "Next you'll be saying you saw the holy mother of God sitting out on a tree limb," he said, trying to outdo Bax in his sarcasm.

"Most beautiful thing I ever seen," I whispered. I was still staring out into the dark hole that had swallowed him, hankering for his return. "You can fuckin believe me or fuckin not, don't matter a fuckin bag of fresh shite to me."

"Then why didn't you call to us?" asked Leon.

I shrugged. "He would have only run off faster," I said. "Tomorrow," I added, "I'm going to hunt him down. His hide'll make a fine rug to bring back to me mum."

"Sounds lovely," said Leon. "Your ma should like a nice spotted rug like that under her dogs."

Bax laughed. "Let us know if you need some help. Or, second thought, don't."

In truth, I would never kill a thing like that, but I had to say something, so that's what I said. "I'm not believing this myself hardly," I mumbled. I turned from the door to look them in the eye, first Leon, then my brother. The gobsmacked looks on their faces assured me my own piss-pot face was still aglow from my encounter. "If only you'd seen him," I went on. "His fangs were enormous, long as my finger. He drew his lips back when he saw me and then he lowered his head into his shoulders like he was going to attack and—"

"And then a change come over his heart and he slunked off," Bax finished for me. But *his* heart wasn't in it now. He stared at me a beat longer. "You really seen him, didn't you, you shite-faced ugly beggar!" He thought it over. "A jaguar! At our door step. Something good on the horizon. That's what Mum would say. Nora too. A jaguar. Fuckin shite."

"You think it's been living nearby all this time and we just never even knew?" Leon asked, all curiosity now that Bax had opened the top of the kettle and tasted the tea.

"They stake out a fairly large territory," Bax answered, back to his all-knowing self, "but it's possible. It's possible he'll come again."

"Should we be worried he might attack, you think, now he knows we're here?"

"Nah, just because we have no jammy hunting don't mean the same's true for him. The jaguar is the hunter supreme, his excellency, thank you very much. Plenty of critters for him to eat without stalking anything as ugly as any of us. More likely he heard the shot and came to investigate."

I looked beyond them. Even Ted had turned his head in our direction. "I say this is cause for celebration," I declared.

I went to the crate where my things were stored and found a bottle of whiskey. When Bax saw what I was doing, he cried, "If you wait long enough..." and me and Leon finished along with him, "...something worth celebrating will assert itself!" Our laughter was like a bolt of light tacking fast through a dark tunnel.

We'd been rationing for a while, so that the liquor would last until the end of the season. We didn't lose any skin over it because most days we were too sick to bother. But if ever there was a right time to indulge, this was it.

We got our tin cups, the same variety we would soon be using to catch us some white gold, and guzzled and clacked late into the night. At first we talked about the jaguar, speculating more on what its appearance at our door might portend—something auspicious, we agreed—and then, as we became less sober, about how different this jungle world was from home, how it would be impossible to describe it to anyone who hadn't experienced it for themselves, how beautiful it was, in a sinister sort of way, and how we doubted we could stand to stay much longer than two tapping seasons. And finally, when Ted's snoring assured us he was asleep (he'd had a bit of whiskey too), we talked about him—or at least me and Leon did—about how we understood what he was suffering because we were shook up too. Somehow Ted just wasn't equipped to function over his fears. "Everyone has a breaking point," Leon said, and we both looked to Bax for a reaction, but he had none.

6

FINALLY THE RAINS BEGAN to let up. Because we had been diligent about minding our *estradas*, we looked forward to a prosperous season, especially now since our visit from the jaguar. Ted was back with us too to some extent, or at least he was able to get up from his hammock and out onto the *estrada* and physically help with the work. He seemed to have shut down mentally though; he seldom spoke, and when he did, it was either mumbled gibberish or he made references to conversations we'd had days earlier, giving his opinion about wee problems we'd already solved, as if he'd been pondering them all along. And though he didn't say a word about the ringing in his ears, he continued to cup and uncup his jug handles to the annoyance of all the rest of us. His rhythm was off, Leon said to me one morning when we were out together readjusting the poles that held up the smokehouse, but at least he'd stopped beefing about every wee thing. And he'd get better now that the rains had let up and we'd be kept busy. "He'll succeed," Leon predicted.

"Success comes to those too busy to be looking for it," I said unthinkingly in response.

"Who's that?" Leon asked. "Someone famous?"

I laughed. "I have no bloody idea. It just landed in me empty head out of nowhere, like the lizards plopping into the river from the tree limbs overhead."

Hours later, when I was out on the *estrada* with Bax and Leon and Ted were out on theirs, it came to me. I put down my tools and stepped away from the tree I was gashing and cupped my hands around my mouth and shouted as loud as I could, "Thoreau!" And I laughed like a fellow as mad as a box of frogs when I saw Bax looking back over his shoulder, flummoxed for once and for certain.

The work was grueling. Our hands were sore from hacking into the trees with our *facas*. The buckets we returned to camp with at day's end were heavy, and as we also had to carry our rifles and all our tools in sacks hanging from our shoulders, our arms and shoulders hurt all the time. Smoking the rubber was the worst. In order to do it successfully, the fire had to be smoldering and the smoke had to be thick. Inhaling it made us dizzy. Me and Bax, having lost our father to smoke inhalation, were especially aware of the dangers. We tied our shirts around our gobs, but we coughed up gunk anyway. None of this would have been a hardship on the strong young buckos we once were, but we were near starved and still taking turns getting and recovering from fever. It was an endless cycle of severe discomfort and it left us feeling weak so often that weakness had become our normal state—just as it had long been normal to be covered from head to toe with insect bites.

But we stuck to the routine that C had laid out for us, and that gave us purpose, which, I discovered, was just enough to keep a body going. We marked off the days on the wall of the cabin, counting down until we could expect the wet season to begin again and C to return with the canoe. We hid our dried rubber *pelas* in a thicket near the house where they would not easily be seen but where we would be close enough to hear if someone came to steal them in the night. There was a time when the notion of some cady seeking out our remote camp for the purpose of fleecing our stash seemed laughable. But if we had learned one thing, it was that the jungle was full of surprises.

There wasn't a day that passed when we weren't startled by something unexpected. One day it was a swarm of bees, and if we hadn't been near enough to the shack to gain shelter, that might have been the end right there. Another time Leon went to shoot a tapir but before he could pull the trigger, the thing came rushing at him, and Leon had to drop his rifle and climb the nearest tree. The tree was full of ants, but he didn't dare jump while the tapir remained below, snorting and barking and stamping the ground with one paw. Ted finally figured out what was happening to his partner and shot his gun in the air, scaring off the animal. But for all his talk of killing *selvagems*, he didn't think to shoot the thing—and thus it was canned meat and *farinha* once again that night (and me and Leon trading looks attesting to the fact that we could see Bax was well off his nut and we would have to jump him if he got up sudden and went to murder Ted).

On another occasion, perhaps the most surprising of all, I awoke one morning to find a boa constrictor in my hammock with me, lying along the length of my body with its head nuzzled into my armpit, as snug as any of the mollies who visited me in my dreams. There'd been a breeze the night before and we'd left the door open in the hope of some relief from the heat and humidity. Baxter, who awoke at the same time, whispered, "Get up and get the fuckin thing out before *he* wakes up," and he jerked his head toward Ted.

C had warned us about snakes curling up with sleeping men to enjoy their body heat, but I for one had not believed him. I got up gingerly and lifted the thing, which was about five feet in length and surprisingly heavy, and keeping my hands as far from my body as possible, pitched it outside. It was only when the thing was slithering away that I was able to take a deep breath and admire it, the saddles running down its back all orange and yellow; it was actually beautiful.

Quare enough, I thought of Nora in that moment. I had not thought of her in some time. Now I saw myself telling her, *One night a boa constrictor crawled into my hammock with me.* I could almost see the glim appear in her eyes and hear her laughing and saying I was spoofing her and me saying, *You think so, huh? Well, then go and find our fellow Bax and ask him and we'll have the truth, won't we?* And then we would all be laughing, the three of us, and it would be good as gold all over again.

Baxter, I realized, was at my shoulder, watching the thing slide out of sight. "Quare how the exotic critters seem to gravitate to you, ain't it?" he said.

One day in the middle of the season Ted felt too ill to work the *estrada* and stayed in the shack in his hammock instead. I volunteered to work with Leon for the first part of the day and planned to work with my brother for the second. Both would get less done, but it was a better solution than having Leon work alone through both shifts.

While me and Leon were going along the path with our tools, Leon confided that he was more worried about Ted than ever. "What do you mean?" I asked him. "He don't say much, but mostly he's been keeping pace. Amn't I right?"

"It's not about pace," Leon said.

I stopped walking and turned to face him. It was still dark and we were both carrying torches. "What is it then?"

Leon looked around, as if he half expected to find Ted had followed us out. "He says we're being watched," he admitted. "He says there's enemies surrounding us, that he's seen them, and that they're getting ready to attack. Mad talk, or maybe not so mad, but either way… Then he clams up when you and your brother are around, tells me not to say anything to you. He's making me mad too, Jack. He never shuts up. He's got me looking over my shoulder for things coming out of the trees."

"What kind of enemies?"

"Some days it's *selvagems* and some days it's rubber thieves…"

"He could be right for all we know. Some days I get to feeling we're being watched too…"

"Let me finish."

"Go on then."

"Most days he says it's ghosts, or *curupira*. He blames them for his hearing problem. What do you think of that?"

"*Curupira*! Preparing for a mass attack?" I chuckled in spite of myself.

"I'm serious, Jack."

"You should have said something before now, Leon. We'll need to convince—"

"There's no convincing him of anything, I tell you. I've tried everything. I wear myself thin thinking of ways to convince him, or at least to fuckin shut him up. I'm really the only friend he's got in the world, and sometimes, well… I don't know. I don't know what I'm talking about I guess."

We separated briefly so Leon could slash into one tree while I cut one further along. After we'd set our cups we began to walk together again, not side by side, because the path would not allow for that, but single file, with Leon in front. "There's something else you should know," Leon said, talking over his shoulder. He took a breath. "Remember Ted said his mum died of disease of the stomach?"

"Tumor, wasn't it?"

"Not true. He lied about that."

"How'd she go then?"

"Did herself in."

"Me arse!"

Leon stopped walking and turned. "No one's sure why. She didn't leave a note or nothing. Might have something to do with Ted's old man. That's what my ma said at the time. Anyway... Ted don't have brothers or sisters, so he was alone with it, and his old man, who never liked him much to begin with, best I could ever tell, started smacking him around worse than ever after that, making fun of him for not being more manly, if you know what I'm saying. 'Cause of his size and all. And him getting agitated like he does. It's why we're here, if you want God's truth. I read about men coming out here to work as *seringueiros*. And then in the *Pittsburgh Gazette*, the article about Carnegie... I thought it might be the answer for Teddy—and me as well, because I was looking for something more out of my meager life too." He barked a wry laugh. "I guess I was wrong on all counts."

I didn't know what to say. I put my hand on his shoulder. "No wonder the poor bugger sees *curupira*. We'll figure it out, Leon. We're all brothers now. We made promises, didn't we? Promises mean something. Maybe they mean everything. Let me talk to Bax. Maybe we can mix it up, change partners every few days, so Ted will have to be with me or Bax some days. Maybe there's a solution there."

Leon turned and began to walk. "He'll know I talked to you, and Bax don't like him as it is."

"I don't see another way to look at it. Let me talk to Bax. I can get him to listen to me."

"Well, I've put it out there now. But listen, don't let on to Ted I told you about the suicide. Not ever. Talk about promises, he made me promise that. About a hundred times. You can tell your brother, 'cause that might soften him some. But tell Bax this too: if he spills the beans one day in the heat of anger, I'll murder him, I swear it." He turned to let me see his expression, which was eerie in the torchlight.

We worked in silence after that. Daylight came, or what passes for it under the canopy, and we put out our torches. But I couldn't stop thinking about all Leon had said, and towards the end of morning, I put down my tools and approached the tree where he was working and said, "Mind if I ask how she done it, his mum?"

Leon turned from his work and looked me in the eye. "Blasted her brains out with the old man's pistol. In her bedroom. Ted was the one found her. One of her eyes was dangling, from a string of goo, hanging halfway down her face."

We had our midday meal and our all-too-short rest back at the house, and when it was time to go back out again, Ted got out of his hammock and went to Leon's side and stood there defiantly, as if he was jealous that Leon had spent the morning with me. Leon and me exchanged a quick look. I was already pondering how I would frame my argument to convince my brother that we needed to change our work pattern for Ted's sake. We took two torches, one for each team, because it would only just be getting dark by the time we returned, and headed out on our respective paths.

Me and Bax were just about done collecting when I caught up with him and told him about my conversation with Leon. Bax listened without interrupting, wincing when I said how Ted's mammy had done it. When I was finished, he said, "I don't know, Jack. Seems like the right thing to do. But top of the list is, Can he keep up with me? Or you? We're here to collect rubber, not mollycoddle one another. You might have to face the fact that you and me and Leon could likely get the work done faster without him."

"You don't like him one bit, do you?"

Baxter narrowed his eyes to slits, until the only thing shining through was his dander. "And you can kiss me sweet Irish arse, Jack Hopper, if you try to tell me you do." He looked down at his feet and then up again. "Remember we joked once about me marrying Nora and bringing her along? You think Nora would carry on the way he does?"

I couldn't remember the last time I'd heard him say her name. "Nora was never made to open a door and see her mother lying dead with her brains splattered over the wall and her eye popped out of her head. Or have her father rough her up afterwards, as if to make out it was her fault."

Bax chuckled as he bent to pick up his bucket. "You know what, Jack? You read too many fuckin books. Da always said so and he was right. You're making connections where there ain't any."

"Books ain't got nothing—"

"Listen to what I'm saying!" he shouted over me. "This ain't about poor old Jack don't have his books anymore. This is about fuckin Ted and how he's not pulling his weight. And don't give me any excuses for him either, 'cause I seen your face tighten when he starts up. You just like playing Holy Joe. That's you all right. The good brother. The tolerant one. Anything to make out I'm the bad egg. But I know down deep in your clackers you like him just as well as I do, maybe even less. You're a fuckin fake, Jack."

I opened my gob to say my piece, but he hurried on before I could do so. "That's the real difference between us. And regards Nora, she mightn't have been through what Ted has, but she ain't had it easy either, growing up with that queer hawk of an aunt, who'll have left her on her own by the time we're home again. And she may not have seen her parents croak, their blood splattered all over the walls and their eyes popped out and dangling, but they're still dead, ain't they?"

"Listen to you, you fuckin blowhard," I shouted, but I didn't go further because just then we heard screaming, coming from the direction of the camp, and we both turned to look in that direction and then back at each other. We dropped our tools and took off running. Baxter had the torch, so I slipped the rifle strap off my shoulder and readied my weapon.

When we got to the clearing we found Leon sitting on the ground, holding his leg, crying out loudly, rocking in pain, the features of his face clenched as tight as a fist. His bucket was overturned, and the sticky white sap had run out all around him. It was Ted who was doing the screaming of course. He had a torch in one hand and his bucket in the other and he was screaming full out like the meater he was, hardly stopping even to breathe. Baxter went right to Leon with his torch. "What happened?" he shouted over Ted's screeching.

"Wandering spider, I think," Leon managed.

Me and Bax looked around. Whatever got him was gone. We'd seen a wandering spider back when we were still traveling on the launch. When we'd gotten off the boat one evening to make our fire on a nice white *praia*, we brought an empty pail along, because Gomez thought we might find some turtle eggs, *tracajá*. There hadn't been any eggs, at least not that we could find, but when we went to leave, we found a wandering spider had crawled into the pail, and Gomez and Paulo began to argue over who was going to dump it out.

In the end it was C who stepped forward, and lifting the pail, sent the creature diving into the river. The thing had a radius of five or six inches, I observed as the current swept it away. C warned us to be mindful of them. He said wandering spiders were so called because they spent the night hunting for prey instead of building webs and waiting for prey to come to them like any proper spider. They weren't afraid of humans either. When they came into contact with them, they threw their front four legs up in the air and sat back on their back four in a defensive posture, to give themselves momentum for an all-out attack. Depending on how much poison they released, their bite could be fatal.

"Let me have a look," Bax said, and he got down in the puddle of spilled sap and pried Leon's hands away from his injured leg. Peering over his shoulder, I was shocked at the size of the bite on Leon's calf, at the dark ragged edges that remained around the flesh that had been torn away.

"Where'd it go? Maybe it wasn't one," I cried hopefully. I had to yell because Ted was still screaming, getting shriller by the minute.

"Shut up!" Bax yelled, but Ted didn't.

"Look, Ted, we've got to figure what to do," I cried, trying for diplomacy.

But he still kept it up.

Finally it was Leon who yelled out, angrily, over his pain. "Shut up, goddamn you, Ted. I can't take it no more!"

That shut Ted up all right. He stared at his friend for a half a minute, his gob hanging open. Then he dropped his bucket, adding to the puddle of spilled sap, and took off running, running and screaming again. In the blink of an eye his torch light became a mere speck. "Holy Mary mother of God, help us all," Baxter said, getting to his feet. "I'll go after him. He won't get far. Try to do something with his wound."

He picked up his torch and began to run. And then his light too was swallowed by the pitch-black night.

I got Leon inside, got his wound cleaned and bandaged, but the pain must have been excruciating for he was still cringing and moaning. I had him stretched out on the floor, his leg, which was red and already swollen to twice its size, elevated on a pile of blankets. I couldn't help but notice he was chubbed up. I thought it must be hurting him something awful, because his hand kept going towards his pud and then pulling back again. It had to be an effect of the venom. I was trying to get him to drink whiskey from one of the tin cups when the door burst open and Bax marched in. We looked at each other. Then he shook his head, confirming he had come back alone. A lot of thoughts had run through me miserable noggin in all the time he'd been gone—including that Bax and Ted were having a tête-à-tête about Ted's behavior—but that he would come back alone was not one of them. It wasn't possible. "You couldn't find him?" I shrieked.

Baxter went for a cup. He poured himself some whiskey from the bottle on the floor and slogged it down in one big gulp and poured more. I noticed he'd hurt himself too. His left thigh had been scratched, likely by thorns, and it was bleeding good. The wound was exposed—our cacks had all become so badly ripped that we'd long ago cut them into short pants—and blood was pouring down his leg into his boot. But as Baxter wasn't paying any attention to it, I didn't mention it either. "How can that be? You went running right behind him!"

Leon was rolling his head from side to side, crying in agony. There was no way to tell how much of his suffering was about Ted and how much was his pain.

"I don't know what happened, Jack," Bax said calmly. "He disappeared, torch and all. But I could hear him screaming, so I followed the sound. Then his screaming stopped. It was like someone plucked him out of the jungle. I was lost myself by then. I wandered for a long time calling out to him, and then I turned to come back...and realized I didn't know where back was. Somehow, by accident, I stumbled onto our *estrada*, or I never would have found my way."

"What'll we do? We can't just leave him out there!"

"Then you go, Jack," Bax said, his voice loud and tight. "*You* go out and *you* look for him."

I got to my feet at once. I grabbed my rifle and headed out. But as I closed the door behind me, I saw that there was nothing but darkness—no moon, no stars, just black and the sounds of the jungle. It would be the death of me to head out in any direction.

I was back in the house a moment later. I could feel my brother watching me, hard, but I didn't look back because I didn't want to see his ugly mug just then. I hung my rifle back on its hook and sank down beside Leon, who was sobbing now, sobbing and gasping and clawing at his throat, as if he couldn't get enough air. He was still chubbed up too, God help him. I hung my own ugly mug, and for the first time since Da died, I began to cry.

Bax and me drank ourselves to sleep that night, it being the only way to get there. Leon had his share too, but no matter how much we gave him, the pain would not abate and he continued to gasp and struggle to breathe. We managed to get him up into his hammock, and not long after we passed out dead drunk in our own hammocks. When I awoke in the morning and all was silent, I knew right away that the unimaginable had happened. "Bax," I whispered. "Bax, wake up."

Bax woke up, and seeing my expression, he froze for a moment and a shiver ran through him. He used his foot to gently rock Leon's hammock. "Leon?" he called loudly. "Leon. Leon, my man, you asleep?"

Leon didn't answer.

"He's passed out, from all the pain," I offered, hoping it might be so.

Baxter was already on his feet, reaching over to feel Leon's wrist. His furrowed brow made it clear he wasn't finding what he wanted. He shook Leon, gently at first, then harder, but Leon had already gone stiff. "What are we going to do, Bax?" I cried. "This is a man with family who love him. How will we even get word to them? How can this be happening? Maybe we didn't go about it right. Maybe we should have amputated..."

The look on Baxter's face when he turned sobered me fast. "We're going to bury him," Bax said in the same flat voice he'd used the night before, almost as if he was reading his words out of a book. "That's what you do when someone has croaked." His voice was so low it was almost a growl. "Then we're going to try to find Ted. If we find him, and he's dead, we'll bury him too. If he's alive, well and good; we'll try to keep him breathing and half sane until C comes for us. If we can't find him, we go right back to the *estradas* and pick up where we left off. That's why we're—"

"But you—"

"But me nothing!" he shouted. "Dry your arse, you fuckin booby! Can you even hear how you sound? We work both *estradas*. We work them day and night. We work them till we're half dead ourselves. We'll bring in more rubber than anyone anywhere ever imagined two scrags like us could ever handle. We'll collect our dough, and then you can make up your mind what you want to do next. I can tell you I for one am done. I'm going home, if I have to swim there. I'm going back to the docks and my girl waiting for me, if she'll still have me, and I never want to see this jungle, or any other, again, long as I live."

"But what if—"

"Shut up!" Baxter shouted. His hands went to his ears, almost the way Ted's did when his ears were ringing. I had never seen him look so fierce. "Get up. Why are you sitting in your hammock like someone's mott? We got work to do."

7

UNDER THE WATCHFUL EYES of several bald-headed black vultures, we carried the remains of our friend Leon along the muddy path leading to the river. All the while there were noises escaping me, which I hoped only sounded like I was huffing due to the load or due to the fact I was slipping and sliding and having to deal with vines reaching out for my ankles on either side every step of the way. For fair, I couldn't say if I was blubbering on account of Leon or in consideration of me own miserable ball of shite life. I couldn't see my brother's face—I was ahead with Leon's feet, Bax behind with his shoulders—but I pictured it pinched up tight, in the scowl he'd previously used only for Ted.

We wrapped Leon's body in a blanket and buried him as deep as possible, because—I think; we didn't discuss it— we suspected if animals found him, they'd acquire a taste for human flesh and come looking for more. I mumbled prayers and farewells over his gravesite while Baxter looked aside, buggered because I was wasting time, and then we set out to search for Ted.

We spent the rest of the day wandering as far from the camp and the *estradas* as was safe without risking our own worthless lives, calling out Ted's name. But we didn't find a trace of him, not his torch, not even footprints. He'd flat disappeared.

It was astounding that this could happen to Leon and Ted, half our crew, and I felt the call to talk about it, but every time I opened my gob, Baxter shut me up. We'd had disagreements all our lives, and I'd never hesitated to argue with him before, but there was something so cold and so foreign in my brother's vulture eye that I found myself without the will to antagonize him. I wondered if maybe Baxter was losing his mind too, if he'd wind up like Ted, running off mad into the jungle night, if this is what the jungle did to square men over time. I imagined it; I imagined myself the last man standing, waiting alone when C came back in his dugout. The thought made me heartsick.

The day after Leon's burial we cut down Leon's and Ted's hammocks and buried them too. Then we went through their other possessions. Neither kept a journal, but I found a photograph among Leon's things, a woman sweeping outdoors in a wide intersection in front of a three-story building. She wore a tattered apron and a dark-colored scarf on her head. She was smiling in the picture, her face turned, looking not at the camera but at someone standing off to the side. She seemed too old to be Leon's mum, but too young to be his grandmum. I put the photograph between the pages of Leon's book—the only shelter I could offer the sad bit of a thing. Then me and Bax sorted through Leon and Ted's clothes—though Ted's were too small and Leon's were just as ragged as anything we owned—and their food supplies. Then we went back to work.

Baxter took over the role of leader now, pushing us both beyond the limits of human endurance. Each day we worked both *estradas*; each night we smoked the rubber from both. We slept only three or four hours a night, and then, well before the sun was up, we were at it again. We ate mostly *farinha* and what was left of the canned food, because there was no time to hunt. Our clothes were falling off us. When our belts disintegrated, we tied vines around our waists to hold up what was left of our cacks. Our beards hung long on our chests, scraggly and crawling with tiny bugs we no longer paid heed to. Baxter's thigh was swollen bright red and white with infection, but he didn't say a word about it. One day when we were heading back from our *estrada*, I happened to glance at his leg and I thought I saw some movement in his wound. When we reached camp, I said, softly, so as not to provoke his miserable self, "I think you got some maggots running circles in there." Baxter shook his head in disgust and didn't answer.

We'd all had parasites under our skin at one time or another. And usually tying a piece of meat over the wound was enough to persuade them to sally forth and surrender. Later that evening Bax opened one of the last of our meat tins, and after shoving a fistful of gray slop into his ugly gob, he set a strip on his wound, but from what I could see from across the room he had himself no jammy with it. For fair, the movement in his wound seemed worse the next day, as if the maggots were all jizzed up now and ready for a shindig. Whatever was crawling around in there liked it fine and intended to stay.

Once, on a day when I had worked for hours with fever and had come back so knackered and sick I could hardly stand, I said to Baxter, "Maybe we should shoot each other and be done with it." I thought of Ted's mother, her eyeball dangling on her cheek. It didn't seem so shocking anymore.

Baxter barked wickedly. "Don't be a chancer, Jack. I'm too tired to whale your fuckin arse right now, but I will if you force me." He climbed into his hammock.

On I went, because I had reached the point where I missed having the last word. "Maybe that's what he wanted, Da. He wanted us to have an adventure and croak so we could join him up there on the other side where things are quiet and uncomplicated."

"Another word along those lines and I'll make you sorry you opened your fuckin gob," he said. He turned his head, so that he was facing the wall.

"Ha!" I cried. "What will you do to me, Bax? Make me suffer? How? I'm hardly human anymore. I push myself to get the work done, but hardly a thought finds its way in or out of my noggin. And never an emotion. What is a man if he don't think or feel? A machine, that's what! I'm no more than the engine that powered the launch that brought us to the Coregem."

I climbed into my hammock as well and willed him to jump out of his and plant his brute hands around my throat and squeeze the piss-pot life blood out of me. But he didn't do more than turn his head back in my direction. "That's the goal, you sap puss. The goal is to work and not to think, because there's nothing worth thinking about. Not while we're here living in this nightmare. Just don't get like Ted on me. If you lose your mind and run off mad into the jungle, I won't even look for you."

"That's quare, Bax, because that's what I've been worrying about you, that you might be the one…"

I trailed off. If Baxter said anything more, I'll never know.

A few days later we squabbled again—because I realized after our last twist I very much preferred arguing with Baxter to the days on end we'd spent in silence, wandering back and forth on the *estradas* like different breeds of caged animals. I dreamed of Leon at night, groaning in pain, and sometimes I awoke thinking I'd heard Ted screaming for help from deep in the jungle. Then it would take several minutes of hard listening to convince me miserable self that it was only a monkey or other animal exercising its lungs. For all I knew, Bax might have been right; I well might be losing me fuckin mind. If I was, I didn't know how to stop the trolley from going off the tracks. I only knew fighting with Bax was the closest things came to the way they were before...before we'd ever set foot in the jungle. At least it made me feel alive.

Accordingly, I came out of the house one day after our afternoon break wearing Baxter's black derby, the one Nora had given him. Bax hadn't worn it himself since we'd gotten off the launch and into the canoe on our way to the site. He kept it at the bottom of his crate, under his extra blanket, as if he thought by covering it he could keep it safe from vermin and humidity. It had lost its shape and something had eaten away the edge of the brim all along one side. Baxter had been out behind the house earlier that morning, having himself a nice long shite, when I remembered the derby. It took only a moment for me to imagine the mayhem my wearing it would beget, and less than that to locate it in Baxter's crate.

I bent to retrieve my empty bucket, which was under the shack, and my rifle, which was leaning against it. Bax already had his gear and was waiting for me at the foot of the trail that led to the first *estrada*, the one that had once been Ted and Leon's, about fifteen yards away. He was looking aside, lost in thought, or maybe he'd heard some animal, so at first he didn't notice I was wearing his hat. He glanced at me and looked away and then his head snapped back my way again. "What do you think you're doing?" he cried.

"Looks good on me, yeah?" I grinned; knowing what I'd set in motion filled me with perverse pleasure.

Baxter dropped his bucket and tools and rifle and jumped into a boxing stance, his dukes up and his jaw clenched. He came at me like that, hopping sideways like a scraggly crab, a hateful low growl burning in his throat. When he reached me, he threw his whole body against mine and we both went down. I used what wee bit of strength I had to flip him over, and in a moment I was on top. I hammered him, but I was so weak I couldn't even get his ugly camel toe of a nose to bleed. Then next thing I knew, he was up on me, pinning me to the ground with his good leg, his bad one leaking pus against my side, and probably maggots too, punching me with both dukes while slobber dripped from his ugly gob.

Between the two of us, we weighed less now than what one of us had before, back in the days when life was great *craic* and worth the living of it. We were all bone, and loose skin hanging down where muscle had once reigned. We continued to roll each other over and to shout and pummel, but our slugs were so lag that half the time our fists missed their mark and slid off the other's manky body. Our struggle seemed to be happening in slow motion.

Like two old boozers on a spree, we gulped for air. But as neither of us wanted to be the one to back down, we kept at it, rolling and striking out futilely. Once, when I was the one beneath, I happened to glance up over my brother's bone of a shoulder, and damned if I didn't see two squirrel monkeys up above, cuddled together in the crook of a palla tree, their fingers stuffed in their mouths like they'd never seen anything so fuckin arseways in all their lives. I almost laughed.

After several minutes we'd knackered ourselves out. Baxter rolled off me and lay on his back panting, his legs open and his arms out at his sides. He even chuckled a little. I chuckled myself. It was a good moment, a familiar moment. Many times in the past our brawls had ended just so—with exhaustion and laughter. We were brothers, after all. We were blood. Maybe everything would be all right after all, I thought. Then I remembered the derby and sat up to see where it had rolled to. That's when I learned we were surrounded by *selvagems*.

There were four of them, standing in a semi-circle about ten feet off, all buckos about our age, and except for the fact that one was wearing Baxter's derby—and that they all wore multiple strings of ornaments around their necks, wrists and ankles, as well as pieces of bark fastened over their puds— they were stark naked. Their faces were painted with lines, black and angled, and two of them had whiskers as well, thin sticks protruding from the flesh below their snoots, as if they were playing at cats, trying to look like the jaguar I'd seen that one night before everything fell to muck. They carried wooden spears, presently (thankfully) at their sides. One of them also had some sort of vine-woven bag over one shoulder, like a lass heading to market. And the one wearing the derby wore a woven sheath, such as would hold a *facão*, tied to his side with the same vine that held his pud plate in its place. Whether their expressions revealed curiosity or amusement, I could not determine.

As I regarded them, I was surprised to find myself mostly fearless. It was almost as if I'd expected it to end this way. It solved one problem; at least I wouldn't have to do it myself, with me own stinking weapon, like poor Teddy's mother.

"Baxter?"

"Shite-faced beggar?"

I smiled. It was almost an endearment after everything that had passed between us. "Are your ugly piss-pot fish eyes open at this arseways moment in time?"

"I'm at rest. Leave me be."

"There's something you ought to know though. Someone has taken your hat."

Baxter didn't move at first. If anything, his panting ceased and he grew stiller. Then he sat up slowly and looked first at the wound on his leg, which was oozing rivulets of blood and some foul-smelling yellow liquid. Then he looked up, into the tree overhead, taking in the same two meaters I'd noticed minutes before. Finally he aimed his gaze at the Indians. "This is your fault," he mumbled.

"I beg your pardon," I said, my eyes on the one wearing his derby.

"They're going to kill us, you know." Baxter sounded calm too.

"It's a better end than what happened to Leon—"

"Maybe Ted was right, saying we was being watched. They've probably been watching us from the moment we arrived. Maybe it was them snatched him out of the jungle."

The thought was a great relief to me, because my rag of an imagination had offered scenarios far uglier. "Maybe."

One of the cat-faced Indians spoke, not to us but to the one wearing the derby, the leader no doubt. Derby nodded in response. Then the four of them began to shake their spears and chant—three syllables sounding like Ebonbay...e bon bay...e bon bay..., over and over again. The bracelets they wore around their wrists made a rattling noise, background music. The chanting was so unexpected, so unlike anything I knew in life, that I had to make an effort to keep from laughing out loud. They stopped all at once, and Derby jutted his chin in the direction of the jungle.

"I think they mean for us to go with them," Bax said.

"I think you may be right." We watched as the two cat-faced Indians went in two different directions to retrieve our rifles and then returned to stand with the other two. Derby said something and one of the whisker boys, the one wearing the woven bag, went off once again, this time into our shack. I thought he would be ruffling through whatever was left in our crates, but he came right out and rejoined his friends.

As we were getting to our feet, Derby jumped in front of Bax and contorted his face and put his dukes up in the air. The others began to chuckle immediately. Derby dropped his pose and chuckled too. Even I chuckled. Only Bax remained grim-faced. "He's mocking me," he mumbled. And in his anger he reached out to take his hat back from Derby's head. But Derby's reflexes were much faster, and the next thing anyone knew, Bax was on the ground again, on his back, the point of Derby's spear quivering just over his heart. Then it began to move, and as I watched in horror, Derby guided it slowly across Baxter's torso and over his hip until it was positioned right above the oozing vermin-filled vile volcano on his thigh.

"Fuckin asswipe," Bax mumbled as he lifted himself on his elbows to have a look at what was happening. He glanced at me, his expression as aggrieved as I'd ever seen it. Finally he looked at his assailant and nodded, as if to confirm he'd had enough and wouldn't be trying a number like that again anytime soon.

Derby hesitated a moment, staring him down, then he lifted his spear away by degrees and replaced it at his side, its tip pointing skyward. Baxter got to his feet again, gingerly, his wound gushing a river of yellow muck. The other whiskerless Indian spoke to Derby, who nodded and then removed the hat. I thought he would give it to Bax after all, but he turned and handed it to me. "He thinks it's mine," I said to Bax, keeping my eyes on Derby. "He thinks you tried to take it from me." I thought a second. "I'm going to give it back to him, a gift. It might mean the difference between them killing us outright or torturing us first."

"Do what you must."

I extended the derby to the Indian. When he didn't take it, I held it higher, towards his head. He understood and bent his head and allowed me to put it on him. When he straightened, there was a wide grin on his face. He said something to me, which I took to be an expression of gratitude. He bowed his head, and I bowed back to him.

We set off into the jungle after that bit of ceremony, along a path we'd never noticed before—even though it was not that far from the second *estrada*. As the four Indians walked ahead, we might have made a break for it at any time, but what was the point? There was nowhere to go and no way to defend ourselves from either our captors or anything else that was likely to pursue us.

Though we both had fevers, Bax was worse off by far. His leg was sickening to look at, black now around the circle of bubbling skin, and you could smell the foul odor it emitted from three or four feet away. I took his arm and stuck it over my shoulder and wrapped my arm around his twig of a waist and dragged him along. He groaned miserably, not liking the arrangement one bit.

Watching our captors moving in front of us, four sleek bucks making a holy show of their muscles at work just below their naked brown skin, I found myself vexed they didn't bother to help. Still, I had to admit they were quarely accommodating in other ways, such as when they saw us faltering not long after we'd started off, they stopped and found a place to wait until we caught up. Mostly they stood in silence, looking out at the forest. They didn't seem to be annoyed.

Before long I was all but carrying Baxter. I had to hold onto his wrist to keep his arm from sliding off my shoulder.

His feet were moving on their own, but more arseways than straight; he was nearly a dead weight along my side. I could barely keep my own ailing self upright and in motion. But as the Indians still made no move to help—probably because he smelled so bad—there was no choice for it.

The path we followed ran more or less parallel to the river, and every now and then we had the chance to escape the hovering trees and walk out on an open beach. Sometimes we would come across a caiman or a snake, and one or another of our captors would say a word, in a whisper, and I'll be a shite-faced beggar for fair if that one whispered word didn't tell the others exactly where to look and what the danger factor was. Or sometimes one would whistle, one or two short bird-like chirps, to the same effect. It was almost as if the greater part of their communication happened without sound.

And they had a certain beauty about them, truth be known. They were smaller in height and bone structure than us—or than we had been back when we were men and not the slags we'd become, hunched over like half-dead monkeys with our bullocks hanging empty as our heads—but they were well proportioned and had almost no body fat. They also had little body hair.

When it began to get dark, we found a clearing and the Indians built a large lean-to with limbs and vines that Derby cut with his *facão*. Still, I hardly slept that night. At first I wondered if the Indians would kill us in our sleep, and then I wondered if they might conclude we weren't worth the bother and simply leave in the morning before we awoke. If it had to be one or the other, I hoped for the former. Fatigue had rendered me amenable to a quick death.

In the morning we walked again, and after about an hour, we rested on some downed trees. When it was time to move on, Derby stood up and said to us, "Gha-ru." He swept his arm to indicate his companions.

"What's he clacking on about?" Baxter slurred. He was burning with fever and his eyes were red and unfocused and bulging from his gray face.

"I think it's what they call themselves. Gha-ru." I looked back at Derby. "Gha-ru," I confirmed. I thumbed my chest and then pointed to my brother. "American," I added.

Derby mumbled something, perhaps repeating what I'd said.

The Indians carried no food, and they seemed not to be hungry. Baxter, of course, was too sick to be thinking of food, if he could be said to be thinking at all. But my fever had abated during the night, and I could think of little else. Imagining large chunks of boiled beef or poultry seemed to make it easier to endure my brother's weight and the horrid grunts and gasping sounds he emitted continuously, not to mention his rank odor. I thought Baxter might be dying, and I wondered if our scrap back at the camp had contributed to his decline. But each time my mind drifted in that direction, I forced it back to boiled beef and kidney pie. I could not contemplate losing me own stook of a brother—no matter what he'd done to ruin things between us—and still have the strength I needed to drag him through the jungle.

When we came across several banana trees clumped together on a rise, I thought I'd lost my mind for fair and was seeing things not truly there. Dragging Bax along with me, I moved toward them as quickly as possible to find out for me own starving self. I hadn't had fruit of any kind in longer than I could remember. We hadn't known where to find it. There were no fruit trees on the *estradas*.

The bananas were real, and so I broke off two with the hand that had been clasped on Baxter's wrist and peeled one with my teeth and slogged it down whole. When I turned, I found the Indians watching me curiously. I laughed, my mouth full of banana, the nutrient strings entwined in my beard. I peeled another and held it in front of Baxter's ugly gob. He nodded, so I shoved it in, and if I'm not mistaken, a twinkle appeared in his piss-pot eyes, as if he were having a snicker too, on the inside at least.

I remembered Da taking me and Bax to the ocean for the first time, to Sandy Hook in the grand state of New Jersey, and how gobsmacked I was when I ducked under water and opened my eyes: so many cheeky fish swimming right there where I was standing! That's just how it was when we arrived at the Gha-ru *maloca* (in Portuguese the word meant both an entire camp as well as to indicate any of the individual structures within it). Me and Bax hobbled through some brush expecting to see yet more forest and instead came up into a large clearing full of people going about the business of living their lives. The Gha-ru gaped too as we came into view behind our captors.

There were women working in gardens at the edge of the clearing, women sitting on the ground weaving vines together, all of them chanting softly, until they saw us at least; men sitting on tree stumps, whittling pieces of wood; children... Everyone was stark naked, except that the women wore woven aprons over their private parts. As we approached, the women stopped their work and the children ceased playing and everything became silent and still, eyes shifting from our faces to Baxter's leg, which was oozing like a pissing monkey at that moment. Derby said something to those within earshot, and some of them nodded and went back to their work. Others continued to stare.

There were three dwellings in a row, all made from limbs and palm leaves, far grander than the one we'd built with C back at the camp, and as the land was high here, they were on the ground and not up on stilts. Our Gha-ru captors marched us toward the largest of them, which was also the one closest. It had a pitched roof that was about forty feet high at center. Paintings on animal skins hung on the outer walls on either side of the door, figures of men, or maybe gods, probably to protect the dwelling. I'd read somewhere that some tribes used juices from fruits and vegetables as paint.

We had to bend low to get through the doorway because it was only about four feet high. The people were smallish, but not that small. I wagered their strategy was to make it harder for enemies to enter undetected. Pulling Baxter along at my side, I followed our captors to the center of the dwelling. A hole had been cut into the roof there, allowing light in and smoke from the fire pit below it out, though there was no fire at the time. It was a large space, large enough for many families. There were hammocks all around the perimeter, where the glim hardly reached. There were no partitions between the sleeping areas, but the posts that held the roof up served to define each section clearly enough. I could see mats or rugs hanging along the walls, and animal skins. I thought I saw jaguar. As my eyes adjusted I made out a few older men in some of the hammocks, working on something, maybe arrows. They had to have keen eyesight for fair to be able to do intricate work there at the edges of the *maloca*. A few spider monkeys perched on crossbeams looked down at us with curiosity. They seemed to be pets. As a precaution, I made certain not to get beneath them, for they were known to go out of their way to relieve themselves on an intruder, and we'd been pissed on—or worse—in the past. There were parrots too. As my eyes adjusted even more, I could see there were a few boa constrictors, to keep away mice and rats I guessed. Maybe they were pets too. Although it was hot and humid outside, it was comfortable within.

The four of them, the Indians who had brought us there, sat down around the fire pit. Following their lead, I helped Baxter to the clean-swept earth floor and then I sat too. Baxter stretched his leg out in front of him and we all had a good look at it. It occurred to me that if we made it back to camp alive, I would have to amputate it. It made me sick to think what that might be like. But as I doubted we would return, I didn't stay long with the thought.

An old feller came into view, emerging from the darkness against one wall like a ship sailing out of the fog. He wore a crown of blue feathers, macaw, and he had feathers inserted into his ears too—and thin sticks protruding from the skin beneath his nose like two of our captors. His face was etched deep with age lines, but also painted lines going in different directions. He wore even more necklaces and bracelets on his wrists and ankles than the other fellows.

He sat in front of us and looked us over. Meanwhile our captors, the ones who'd been carrying our rifles, handed them over to his majesty along with the woven bag the one fellow had taken into our shack. The chief dropped his gaze from our ugly mugs to the rifles and ran his hands up and down the barrels. He knew what they were; he'd had contact with guns before. When he was done caressing them, he barked an order and an older woman, likely his wife, emerged from the darkness at the edge of the *maloca* and took our weapons and disappeared with them. Then he opened the woven bag and peeked in. I leaned forward—I couldn't guess what the whiskered fellow could have taken from our hut in the short time he'd been in it—but the chief sensed me looming and looked up quick and gave me the stink eye and I fell back.

But then he had a change of heart and reached in and pulled forth, of all the freaky things in the world, Leon's book on how to come to America from Germany and set yourself up farming in or around Pennsylvania. I almost laughed. Did the Gha-ru have plans to travel then? I looked at Bax, but he was in a daze, his head lolling from side to side like he was about to lose consciousness. When I looked back at the chief, he nodded. Then he slipped the book back in the bag like it was something precious, and right on cue the woman who seemed to be his wife came out of the dark and took it away.

The four of them, our captors, spoke, each in turn, with Derby, who now held his hat on his lap, going first. The chief stared at us the entire time, expressionless. Sometimes he nodded. When they all began to chuckle, the chief included, I knew Derby was telling him about the fight me and Baxter had had. I laughed too. I thought I must be delirious to find myself with a light heart.

The chief called to the old woman again and she brought him some kind of hollow bone that was U-shaped. Then she handed him something else—it looked like resin, a glob of reddish resin—and he stuffed it into one end of the U-shaped bone and placed that end in his gob and the other far up his nostril and blew hard.

He shook his head once, hard and fast, like something had just exploded inside his blue-feathered noggin. His eyes were wide open one second and squeezed tight the next. The mugs he displayed for the next several minutes suggested he was in excruciating pain, but no one seemed troubled by it. Finally he stilled. When the bone fell to his lap, the old woman came out of her secret hiding place yet again and took it away. The chief seemed to be in a trance. His eyes remained closed but his lids fluttered, and he was rocking slightly, back and forth. His lips were parted, and every now and then I thought I heard him make a sound, a grunt, as if in response to something only he could hear.

Bax was fast asleep by then. At first his head dropped onto his chest, but then his whole body slid to one side, with his head coming to rest not an inch from the chief's thigh. No one paid attention to him. We were all watching the chief.

After what seemed like hours, the chief opened his eyes, and when he saw Bax asleep beside him, he poked his arm with one rigid finger and Baxter sat up at once in a daze. He looked around. He seemed to have no idea where he was or what he was doing sitting amongst a group of *selvagems*. For fair, my loogin brother was smiling; he must have thought he was asleep and dreaming what he saw. The chief nodded to the younger Gha-ru, and without a word the four got to their feet. Before I knew what was happening, two had gone behind Bax and the other two got in front, and they put their hands on him and held him still while the chief leaned forward and prodded his wound with the same rigid finger. Baxter cried out in pain, but he was too weak to struggle against the eight hands holding him and I was at a loss of what to do to help. And then it was over. The chief withdrew his finger, and holding it away from him—disgusted no doubt by the slime on it—he got up and left. Just like that. The other four let go of Bax and left too. Baxter lay back down and fell asleep at once, leaving me alone to contemplate our situation. In fact, it seemed we were the only ones now in the entire *maloca*. If there were still old men in their hammocks on the perimeter, I could no longer see them. Only a few curious monkeys remained, watching us from the beams overhead.

Eventually a woman came in carrying a gourd that had been painted with some sort of black sap and glazed. It was beautiful, not what I would have expected from people living in the forest. More importantly, it was full to the brim with food. The woman smiled as she placed it in front of me. She seemed to have no fear of the two ugly white strangers—not that we were particularly intimidating in our present state. I considered that maybe the kindness we were being shown was because me and Bax—especially Bax—looked about ready to croak. Maybe making the soon-to-be-dead comfortable was a cultural tradition. Maybe his majesty thought we might relay some message on to the other side once we got there, put in a good word for them with their ancient gods. But the food: boiled yams and pineapples and cashews and fish. I wanted to guzzle everything at once, and I admit I tried me honest best, but my stomach cramped after the first few bites and I realized with dire regret that I wouldn't be able to eat much at all. I still hadn't digested the banana from earlier. It had turned to brick in my gut. But I made the effort, taking wee bites and chewing slowly, hoping it would somehow go down. Bax awoke, and to my astonishment, he was able to eat more than me, though he too nibbled his way through rabbit-like, all while maintaining his horizontal position.

Later the same woman came and took the gourd, which remained nearly full, away. Bax was still awake, but he was on his back now, staring upward, and he hadn't spoken a single word. He seemed to be concentrating on his breathing, trying to keep it steady. It had gotten darker in the *maloca*, and soon it would be too dark to see. I looked around. I hadn't seen anyone other than the gourd lady in hours, but then the Gha-ru were so stealthy they were almost invisible. For all I knew Bax and me were surrounded by fellers wielding spears.

After a time I realized I was hearing chanting coming from outdoors. I shook Baxter and asked him what he thought we should do. I didn't really expect an answer, but Bax, being lucid in that particular moment, said we should go outside and see what was going on. I helped him to stand, almost toppling over myself in the process. By then it was nearly completely dark. I went forward with one arm outstretched, half expecting to run into someone who'd planted himself flat in front of door for the purpose of scaring me senseless, the other dragging my brother to my side.

The Gha-ru had been waiting for us, or so it seemed. Why hadn't someone let us know? They were sitting in a circle in front of the hut, maybe a hundred and fifty men, women and children. Torches burning on poles behind them lit the clearing. Their chanting got louder when we made our grand entrance. Two of our captors, one of them being Derby, got up quickly and pushed me away from Bax and took over the job of carrying him—which worked out just fine as I was about to drop him, through no intention of my own—and brought his manky arse right into the center of the circle. There was a banana leaf there, and they lay him down on it as gently as if he were the king, this shindig being for him apparently. A young girl appeared and led me to a space between our other two captors, the cat fellows.

A woman approached Bax with a basket. She squatted over the edge of his banana leaf and began to remove items: several piles of wet leaves and a bone that had been carved sharp like a knife. She separated the leaves out into piles, four of them. When she was done, she got up and the chief went to squat in her place. He looked at Baxter and then he looked up and lifted his hand. The chanting stopped immediately. It was if we'd entered a vacuum.

The chief took the first pile of leaves and tried to shove them into Baxter's mouth. Bax resisted at first, but the chief mimed chewing, and Baxter finally parted his lips to take some in and began to chew. They were smallish; I thought they must be coca leaves.

Baxter chewed and then turned his head to the side and spat. He'd been up on his elbows, but after a few minutes he lay himself down and seemed to relax. Meanwhile, the chief lowered his head so close to Baxter's wound that at first I thought he was going to suck on it. Almost as quare, he began to whistle—an odd sort of whistle that was all discordant and punctuated with clickings of his tongue; it brought to mind an image of clucking chickens. And by God's ivory bones, wouldn't you know that within minutes one of those slimy maggots showed its manky head and the chief was able to pull it out!

In my excitement I gasped, but when I looked around I saw that no one else had moved a muscle, not even any of the children sitting with the women behind me. The chief continued with his whistling and clicking, and the maggots came marching forth like wee putrid soldiers reporting for war. In no time they were coming out so fast the chief had to signal for one of the women to come and help him. She gathered the maggots with the edge of her hand and flicked her hand so the maggots went airborne and landed somewhere beyond Bax's banana leaf. When the wound was clean of them, the chief took up another of the leaf piles and separated the leaves and placed them one by one over Baxter's thigh. Then another women brought him, the chief, a drink, in a cup made of clay, all painted finely and glazed like the gourd had been. Everyone sat quiet and watched him drink it down. As far as I could tell, Bax was just lying there, unconcerned about what was being done to him, looking up at the stars, pleased as Punch.

After a while the chief, who seemed to spend a lot of time visiting secret corners in his own noggin, began to rock and chant, more vigorously than when he'd snorted the resin earlier. Then everyone else began to rock and chant as well.

The fellow next to me looked at me in a way that made me think I was expected to join in, and so I did.

A long time passed, maybe hours, maybe not. I cannot say for the simple reason I lost track of me manky self. *Finally, I thought, I have escaped the jungle, and so what if I done so by going out of my mind!* I was somewhere, but where I hadn't a clue. I only knew I felt as quare as a three-sided rectangle, no longer a part of my surroundings. Then the chanting stopped and more minutes passed, and we all watched the chief, who was sitting with his eyes closed. When he opened them he nodded a few times, again, as if to some inner voice, and then removed the leaves from Baxter's leg and took the bone knife and began to cut into Baxter's wound.

Bax grit his teeth and arched his back, but the men on either side of him grabbed him and held him still. The chief dug in deeply. I could see the river of fluids—pus and blood, and maybe a surviving maggot or two—pouring down the side of Baxter's leg. But he never cried out: Bax wouldn't. He'd sooner die than let it be known he was capable of pain or sorrow. He was moaning, but not what you'd expect for what he was going through. Or maybe it was something about the leaves…that they contained some sort of natural anesthetic. When the chief was done cutting, a woman brought him a bowl of water and he dipped another kind of leaf into it and gently cleaned the wound. Then someone else approached, a girl, and handed him a second smaller bowl and he extracted something from it, something so small I could not see it from where I sat some five feet away, and applied it to Baxter's wound and immediately Baxter screamed out in agony, but it was brief and then he was quiet again.

The chief repeated the process several times over, reaching into the bowl and making a careful application of whatever it was. Then the girl took the bowl away and the chief used the last of the leaves—they were huge when they were opened, like water lily leaves but more pliable—to cover the wound. He placed one after another, until Baxter's whole thigh was wrapped in greenery two inches thick. When he was done, the same woman came back with another bowl and poured water over the leaves. It must have been hot for I could see the steam rising off it. But the leaves were thick and she was careful and Baxter didn't seem to feel a thing.

The woman went off and returned once more, this time with Leon's book. She came right up to me and pushed it in my face. When I didn't take it from her, she pushed it up to my chest and actually hit me with it. I looked to Baxter, but he was asleep now, or nearly so. I looked to the chief. He was staring at me, waiting. I looked all about myself. Everyone seemed to be waiting for me...to what? Read?

It was too dark for my weak eyes. I would either have to get closer to one of the torches or fake it. I decided to fake it. Even though I hadn't read from the book since the night before Leon died and Ted ran off, I had read the paragraphs on the least damaged pages so many times I knew them by rote.

I began, droning on about hummingbirds in the cornfield and what kind of soil was best for planting tomatoes, and when I finished one section I turned the page and began again.

I could not guess why I'd been ordered to put on this performance. My voice was low and flat, but I could not get myself to speak any louder. Behind the words I was reciting, I was thinking hard, trying to put together how the Gha-ru had even known about Leon's book. Leon had handled it with care; it was precious to him, and now it seemed it was precious to the Gha-ru too. Or was it the reading of it that meant something?

We'd been spied on; that was certain. But how? I found myself imaging Derby sitting under the house with some sort of periscope—like the ones they used on submarines—looking up at us through the hole Leon had shot into the floor when he'd tried to kill the tarantula. But how was that possible? Maybe they'd made their own hole along one of the walls. That would be easy enough to accomplish now that I thought about it.

Finally the chief grunted, and I took that to mean he'd heard enough for one night and I ceased reading at once and took in a deep breath. The woman who had brought me the book appeared and reached out to take it back. I was only too happy to hand it off to her.

The show, whatever its purpose, was over. Everyone began to get up. Derby caught my eye and gestured to me that Baxter should remain on the banana leaf. The others motioned for me to follow them into the *maloca* where we had been earlier, but I was reluctant to leave Bax alone. When they figured that out, one of them went behind the *maloca* and returned with another banana leaf and I lay myself down beside my brother. There was at least half a chance animals would smell Bax's spilt blood and come for us in the night, but I was knackered silly and dizzy with questions and went straight to sleep anyway. And I'll be dashed if it wasn't the best night's sleep I'd had since I'd left me own sweet cot in Hoboken.

8

WHEN I AWOKE IN the morning, the *maloca* was quiet, no one to be seen at all. Since it didn't seem likely the Gha-ru were late sleepers, I guessed they'd gone somewhere together. I went back to sleep, and when I awoke a second time, a woman was bending over Bax, examining his leg. She had unwrapped all the leaves and put them aside. Baxter was not awake, but he was snoring lightly, so I knew he'd survived the night. I was hoping he'd wake up, because I wanted to tell him about how I'd been made to read from Leon's book the night before, and I wanted to see his reaction to the fact that the woman's diddies were swaying back and forth above his pud, like two grand pendulums. I imagined we'd share a chuckle, and truth be told I was hankering for some confirmation that I was still in his good graces. But he did not awaken.

I sat up to look at his leg and learned at once what the chief had been applying to his wound, the thing that had caused Bax to cry out. They were sutures, but I recognized them: ants. The *caboclos* call them *tucandeira*. *Tucandeira* were large, maybe an inch long, and could easily kill a person with their stingers. But the ones the chief had used on Bax had had their stingers removed—and their heads too, for that matter. Of course they couldn't reach across the entire breadth of the wound. But the chief had sliced some of the skin above and below the wound to make it easier to dig out the muck. Where it was a clean edge like that, he'd used the ant sutures, the *tucandeira*, to hold the skin together on either side. I guessed they were alive when he applied them, that he had pressed the pincers in where he wanted them and then pulled their heads away, leaving only the pincers behind.

I was so intrigued I almost forgot to look at the wound itself. Amazingly, it didn't look too bad. It was deep; there was definitely a hole in Baxter's leg now, a gouge big enough to fit a small apple. But already a very thin scab was forming in its crater. You could see his blood beneath it, but no pus. And the black on the edges looked like it was fading. The Gha-ru had saved his leg, maybe his life. Probably his life.

I awoke once again when the sun was above the tree line on the east edge of the clearing. I couldn't remember the last time I'd slept so much. I was hungry; I'd been hungry since we'd come to Amazonas, and for fair I'd gotten used to going about half starved. But the wee bit of delicious food I'd picked out of the gourd the day before had set me off somehow. Now I could have eaten the arse off a horse if I had me one. I looked around. I was surrounded, much like the day before when we'd first arrived. They, mostly women, were hard at work everywhere, weaving, pounding on bark or leaves, or off in the garden. A few older men were whittling or working in what appeared to be a separate garden just for coca trees, or maybe just for men.

I checked Bax to make sure he was sleeping and not dead, and then I got up and went to have me a piss behind a huge Kapoc tree. After that I had me a walk around the edge of the *maloca*. The young men who I thought of as our captors—

now I didn't know how to think of them—seemed not to be around. I wagered they were off hunting or fishing. I tried not to think about the work Bax and me were missing back at the camp, and how we would never get home if we didn't bring in enough rubber. But truth be told, in my weakened state my connection with my old life hardly seemed real to me anymore.

I went to the garden where the women were singing—not to each other but, far as I could tell, to the plants. When they saw me approaching they stopped and shooed me away with hand gestures. But once I'd backed up a few yards, they went back to their work and their songs. Nobody seemed to mind that I hadn't moved off altogether, which left me free to stand in place and observe.

How could *selvagems* in the middle of the jungle have such a large and orderly garden? Who had taught them such skills? I saw yams sprouting up from the ground, manioc plants, tidy rows of tall sugarcane stalks, clumps of vines I could not identify—all surrounded by a network of what appeared to be drainage ditches, or irrigation ditches. I began to walk around the perimeter of the clearing, passing a small grove of banana trees, and then a row of cashew trees, the nuts hanging down from the bottom of plump yellowish-red fruits that looked like bells. I reached for the fruit, but a hand appeared out of nowhere and cut me off. The elderly woman it belonged to shook her head at me, and I continued on my way, past peach palms, with their golden fruit, past palms bearing what looked to be pineapples.

As I walked back toward Baxter, I encountered several women mashing up blue corn, from ears that must have been two feet long. They were mixing the mush with water in a huge urn that seemed to have been carved out of a tree trunk. Some of the younger girls were chewing up corn from a second pile of ears and spitting the bolus into the mix. That must ferment it, I realized, and while I knew the fermentation process must take time, I pointed hopefully to the brew and then to my stomach. Bolus or not, I was fuckin starving. But the women shook their heads and the girls laughed at me, and I was denied again. Why would they save Baxter's life if they planned to watch me starve?

In the time I had been gone, someone had erected a lean-to—a mat of braided palms set up at a slant with two posts at its entrance—over Baxter, to keep the sun from beating down on his mick-white skin there in the center of the clearing. As it was big enough for two, I crawled in beside him. Baxter was asleep but still breathing normally. I entertained the notion of having a little kip myself—I knew if I lay down, sleep would come for me quickly—but I couldn't bring myself to give in to the desire there in the center of the *maloca* with activity going on all around me. I felt like an animal in a zoo as things were.

After a while an older fellow with very long hair and red paint over most of his face emerged from the main hut and went to stand before two hollowed-out tree trunks hanging from a crossbeam about fifteen feet away from the side of the hut. I'd noticed this structure before and had thought it was ornamental because of the elaborate designs painted on the two trunks. But now the man picked up a stick, which featured a ball of crude rubber at one end, tied in place with a network of vines, and he began to beat the trunks slowly, one, then the other, then the first one again. The deep booming sound—it was almost more vibration than sound—was at once familiar. We'd been hearing it all along, ever since we'd arrived at the camp! We'd thought it was distant thunder, or waterfalls, or rushing creeks somewhere. Or howler monkeys. Or simply the jungle taking a nice deep breath. In the jungle, it's almost impossible to distinguish one distant sound from another at certain times of the day. Now I saw it was a code. The man replaced the drumstick at the foot of the structure and returned to the dwelling. Over the next hour boys and men emerged into the clearing from every direction. The drumming had called them home.

Our four captors emerged together, like a pack of wolves. Two of them carried huge leaves tied at both ends with vines. They dropped them off at the front of the big hut and then all four came to the center of the clearing and moved aside the lean-to and gestured to Baxter, as if to ask me how he was managing. I shrugged. What did I know? Derby (he wasn't wearing the derby now) squatted down and shook Baxter gently. Bax opened his eyes. You could tell by his expression that he was startled again to see a naked *selvagem* with a painted face leaning over him. But then his face unfroze and his eyes softened, and when Derby indicated that he was going to peel back the leaves on Baxter's leg and have himself a peek, Bax nodded and got up on his elbows.

As I watched I couldn't help but think about how *seringueiros* had been tapping rubber in the area for only a handful of years. If their garden was any indication, the Indians had been here much longer. If there was any truth to what the *caboclos* had said on the boat, that the *selvagems* were fighting back against *seringueiros* working on what they thought of as their land, then the Gha-ru were an exception. Or maybe they simply didn't think of the camp as part of their land. Or maybe all this civility was part of a plan I hadn't deciphered yet. After all, they had succeeded in removing us from our work at the camp. Maybe that alone had been their goal.

Derby removed the last leaf and everyone leaned in to see. For fair, the wound looked better than it had only hours before. "Does it hurt?" I asked.

Baxter shrugged. "Not like before. How do you think they did it?"

"Can you walk on it?"

"I guess we'll see, because I'm about to shite me cacks, here in front of Katty Barey and anyone else who might care to take a gander." He chuckled uncomfortably.

I pointed. "I've seen a lot of them go off in that direction."

Baxter looked where I was pointing. So did the Indians. They realized at once what the issue was. Two of them reached down to help Bax up, and off they went, all five of them, the two with their shoulders under his armpits so that his feet hardly touched the ground.

They came back laughing, all of them. Once they'd lowered Bax to the ground and covered us over with the lean-to, they turned and left and we were alone again. The moment was dreamlike. "Now if only you could get them to feed us," I said, and I looked over at the women who'd gathered at the nearest hut. They had unwrapped the leaves the Indians had left there and were preparing the fish that had been in them for the fire. At the second hut, women were preparing some large birds, maybe curassow. I couldn't see what was happening at the third hut, but women had gathered there too. In front of all three huts the women were animated, smiling and singing softly while they worked. "They took Leon's book," I said.

"Did they now?" Bax looked at me. He seemed amused, as if I was telling him something he already knew. I figured he must have awoken when I was reading, or pretending to read.

"What do you think they would want with a book?"

He shrugged. "What does anyone want with a book?" He shook his head, as if to point out that only a loogin would ask such a question, but he didn't say anything more and I didn't either.

While the women oversaw the food preparation, the men, including our four friends, disappeared into the huts, to rest, I guessed. In no time the smell of the cooking meat and fish permeated the air. Everything that was happening seemed not simply unlikely but downright impossible. As far as I could tell, these people didn't even have guns—except, of course, for the rifles they'd taken from Baxter and me—and yet they were able to go out into the jungle for a few hours and return with an abundance of food. Some had *facãos*—further proof they'd had some contact with other non-Indian peoples—but you couldn't hunt with a knife. I thought of all the times I'd taken aim at something while on the *estrada* and missed, all the times we'd gone hungry because no one had seen anything in days, or we had, but our shot had only managed to frighten away the prey.

After the cooking was completed and the fish was cool enough to handle, the women working in front of the big hut gathered all the fish together in the same leaves that had been carried in from the jungle and brought them to the center hut, where the birds were still cooking. The women from the hut in the distance gathered there too, some of them carrying baskets on their heads. When the birds were cooked and cooled, all the food stuff was torn or cut (some of the women worked with bone knives, others only with their hands) into pieces and divided onto smaller leaves, which were then folded over and bound with thin strings of vine and brought to a large palm mat that had been at the side of the center hut. Three women got on one side of the mat and lifted the edge and dragged it right up to the center of the clearing, which is to say, right in front of where I was sitting and Baxter was sleeping. Then they retreated.

I couldn't take me piss-pot eyes off that mat. As soon as I thought no one was looking, I got up on my haunches and waddled over to it and snagged me one of the tidy leaf packages. But before I could waddle me skinny arse back and under the cover of the lean-to, a young girl started to yell out and point at me, and next thing I knew several of the women were running at me like I was some chancer plotting to plow me way through all the riches of their whole swanky village. One of the women pulled the package right out of my paw and replaced it on the mat, hard, and gave me the stink eye. Then off they went, chirping like birds, back to their chores. I would have made a second attempt but they left the young lass behind—my own personal guard. I could see by the set of her mouth and the way she packed her arms over her flat chest that she was a cooch who wouldn't stand for any hokum.

She watched me and I watched the food and time slithered by like a snake shedding its skin. Out of one manky, dusty, long-uncluttered corner of my brain there came a recollection of a myth concerning a feller who was made to stand beneath the boughs of a fruit tree just out of his grasp, in a pool of water that receded whenever he went to drink from it. I liked learning that sort of thing back in me school days. I couldn't remember his name, this feller, but he was me and I was him, and there was no denying it.

Oh, but my mind was dull now, as dull as dry shite. *And so what?* I asked me miserable self. What good was book knowledge to the likes of me anymore? How quare that it had once seemed so all important—what I thought separated me from other men, truth be known. Now the jungle had revealed me to be no better than any other man it had slogged down and shat out. The only difference between me and Ted or me and Leon was that I was alive, though barely, and for how long? I thought of the time I'd yelled out into the forest, to alert Leon to the fact that I'd remembered the name of the author I'd quoted to him earlier. I'd amused myself that day. And I thought I had me one over on Bax as well. Now I could remember neither the quote nor the author, and moreover, I didn't give a bullocks.

As soon as the sky began to darken, torches were lit—though not the same ones used the night before. These featured some kind of resin that cast a strong red flickering light, and as the people emerged from the three huts, their shadows were long and vivid and scarlet and chilling. Everyone sat in two large circles, the men and bigger boys in the inner circle and the women and younger children behind them. Me and Bax, who had finally awoken from his stupor, didn't have to move an inch. Two of the Indians removed our palm lean-to and then sat down on either side of us, and the circle continued out from there. At one point we Hopper boys looked at each other, really looked at each other, maybe the first time since the night Ted disappeared and Leon died. Then Bax shrugged, as if I'd asked him a question and his answer was, Search me!

The chief was the last to come to the circle. On this night of nights he wore a veil of crimson macaw feathers, beginning at his head and trailing behind him all the way to the ground. Two of the women had to jump up and grab the end of it so he could sit without crushing it. Around his neck, in addition to his bead necklaces, he wore one strand of huge fangs from some large animal. The teeth glistened in the torch light. The lines painted on his face were thicker and blacker and more dramatic than they had been the day before. They were jagged and sharp, like lightning bolts, cutting in and out of the deep wedges that were his wrinkles. Now I thought I knew what people meant when they said someone was *larger than life*. His presence was almost beyond human. In his grand headdress, under the flickering red torches, he seemed to be twice his normal size. When I squinted, I saw he was not a man at all but an enormous bird of prey.

Once he was settled the chief began to chant, softly and then louder, and soon the others joined in. Just like the night before, the chanting went on for a long time and I found myself carried away from my concerns and my doubts and even my hunger. When the chanting ended, one of the women got up carrying a large clay bowl that she'd been holding on her lap. She handed it to the chief. I thought it must be the same drink he'd had the night before. But whereas he was the only one to drink then, now he drank and handed the bowl to the fellow beside him, and then *he* drank and passed it on. I wondered if it could be some kind of mind-altering concoction, but then why was it being served to boys who were maybe only five or six or seven? The only males who did not drink were the babies and toddlers in the outer circle with the women. As I waited for the drink to come to me, I observed that it was impossible to tell which of the toddlers belonged to which of the women, because they went from one lap to another, as if all the women were their mothers, and they seemed to receive the same measure of affection wherever they landed.

I drank the bitter golden red-brown torch-lit liquid with gusto—so eager was I in my thirst, not only for its own sake but to see what would happen. I passed the bowl, half empty by then, to Baxter. For a while I sat calmly watching the bowl as it moved through the remainder of the circle, listening to the women talking to each other softly behind me, thinking of nothing beyond the quareness of the situation. But then all at once my stomach began to lurch. I made to get up, for I did not want to puke right there in the midst of so many people, but the Indian beside me clamped his hand on my arm and stilled me. After a few minutes the retching ceased and only then did the Indian, feeling the tension go out of my body, let me go. I concentrated on my breath, trying to keep my stomach from lurching again. Now I thought I knew why no one had let me eat any food. Eventually I began to feel calm.

The chief was chanting again, and shaking a branch of dry leaves. The leaves sounded like tiny bells, hundreds of them. Thousands of them. I felt myself in the grip of the mood the chief was evoking. The bells, the whispers of the women, the jungle sounds beyond, the breeze, the full moon rising above the tree line... I realized I felt joyful, almost giddy with joy. Even so, I was slightly dizzy and still a bit sick and I wanted to lie down. A great physical heaviness had come over me, and it occurred to me that this must be what death felt like. Maybe I *was* dying. If so, I didn't much mind. I looked around to see what the others were doing. For fair, many of the men were stretched out, some of them with their heads on the laps of the women sitting behind them.

I was melting, and it was beautiful. I turned around and found myself looking at a young woman, a bit older than myself. It took a while to bring her into focus, but when I did I saw that she was lovely, with long black hair falling over her small breasts, her smile relaxed and inviting, as if she had been expecting me to turn and find her. I edged myself back until I was very close to her. She was sitting with her legs bent to one side. She guided me to rest my head on her thigh. I lay there, looking up at the moon from the comfort of her body.

Soon I could feel her touching the sides of my face, not in a sexual way but almost maternally, the way I had seen some of the women touching the wee dotes. Her touch was so light it could have been the breeze; it was possible I was only imagining it. Still, I was overcome with love, a sense of *being* loved. For the first time since I had left the port at Hoboken, I felt safe, physically helpless—I was sure I couldn't have stood if my life depended on it—but otherwise safe for fair. The paradox made me laugh out loud. And hearing my own laughter made me laugh more. I knew I must be making a fool of myself, but I was helpless to rein in my outbursts.

The young woman didn't seem to care. She was chanting, singing the same words the chief was singing. No sooner did I begin to listen—I mean *really* listen—to her voice when a man bent over me and I was gobstruck to see that it was none other than my da! I was dreaming, surely, but quare enough, I continued to be aware of my surroundings. What was I to make of this?

I could hear the young woman; I could feel her touch on the sides of my face; I could hear the chief, the sound of the bells I knew to be leaves. So how could this be my father? But there he was, and when he bent closer, I could smell the scent of his cigars—White-Cat, what he always smoked. "You're doing fine, lad, you'll be okay," Da said, nodding. I wanted to answer. I wanted to say, *I know that, Da*—though I knew no such thing, and I couldn't get the words out anyway. My vocal chords had closed down on me. I told myself this was more proof that I was dreaming. But then Da put his hand on me manky knee and gave it a squeeze—a gesture as familiar as the odor of the White-Cat. He smiled. Then he winked. Then he vanished.

I braced myself to feel my great loss all over again, but grief didn't come. Every bone in my body was rejecting discord. The quare thing was that I began to remember everything that happened that night, with great clarity, as if it were happening again now, but without any of the pain or emotion I'd experienced the first go-round.

Murphys' backyard. Mrs. Murphy with her stomach as big as a wash tub. Gifts piled up on a table outside, for the baby who would soon arrive. Then Baxter pulling me off to the side, where we wouldn't be heard. "I've done an assessment, and I'm here to tell you Mulligans' fence has some boards missing near the back end," Bax had said.

I looked in the direction of the Mulligans' property, next door. "So?"

"Here's what's so. We get the younger folk to cross over into Mulligans', through the opening in the fence, and have a shindy of our own."

"Mulligans should love that."

Bax laughed. "That's the beauty of it, Jackie boy. Mulligans ain't home! They left last night for Pennsylvania, some relative's funeral. All five of them. Won't be back until mid-week."

"You're looking for trouble. As usual."

"Aw, don't be such a wet blanket. We'll get everyone over there, and if we turn things arsewise, we'll go by in the morning and clean them up. Who's going to care?"

"And if the adults start noticing their offspring disappearing?"

"Look around. Who's going to notice anything?"

I looked. There had to be a hundred people in Murphys' backyard. My eye fell on several men off in one corner, drinking, and some women, no doubt their wives, close by, keeping watch on them, making sure no one got too rowdy. Piano music was playing, and some couples were dancing on the patio.

I followed Bax to the end of the yard, where the shrubs were thickest. Sure enough, three slats were missing from the fence that separated Mulligans' from Murphys'. One more would make a space big enough for an average-size person to slip through, and the slat to the left of the gap was already loose. It only took a moment for us to wiggle it free. Several nails were still protruding from it. I carried it down to the end of the yard on the Murphy side where it wouldn't be a danger to anyone. I figured we could use a rock to hammer it back into place later, no one the wiser. Bax was right. I was a wet blanket, though that was never my intention. I walked back to where he was standing, on the other side of the shrubs.

"Your next job," Bax said, thumbing at my collar bone, "is go around and get all our gang and direct them over to Mulligans'. Don't tell any of the wee ones, or we'll have parents down our necks in no time."

I pushed his hand off my chest. "You do it, beggar."

"I can't, bigger beggar," Bax said. He smirked and looked off to the right. I followed his gaze. Both our sets of eyes fell on Nora, standing amid a group of girls, a big green bow at the back of her head. She was clacking animatedly and the others were hanging on her every word, but she must have had a psychic sense, because she looked up all at once, directly at Bax and me, and she smiled broadly and winked. The girls in her group turned at once to see who she was looking at. One of them, Susie, a small dark-haired girl, smiled shyly when she saw me. I forced myself to smile back.

Having got Nora's attention, Bax jutted his head toward the place where the fence was broken and then disappeared into the gap. A minute later Nora followed. I knew my brother hoped to steal a kiss or two in privacy, but Nora's friends lost no time lining up behind her. By the time I returned to the opening with my first recruit, a boy named Willie Brown, Bax was at the center of the circle, amusing all the girls, and Nora was at his side, her little finger looped under his suspender like she owned him, a big wide grin on her face.

Word spread and before long, everyone over thirteen (and a few who were just under) was over at Mulligans'. The exception was Frankie Jones, who, at age fifteen, was carrying some two-hundred pounds on his five-foot three-inch frame and couldn't get himself through the gap. He was there, on the Murphy side, wrestling with the next board over, but it wouldn't loosen.

I peeked through a knothole to make sure I hadn't missed anyone. The adults were still having a grand old time, singing and laughing and drinking lemonade—and likely, much stronger—and eating the cakes and the cookies the women had baked. Music seemed to be coming from everywhere. I could still hear someone playing the piano in the Murphys' house. But even louder was the Victrola, with its large flower-shaped brass horn—which someone had set up on the table with the gifts. It was blasting "Coax Me," and several of the ladies had linked arms and were singing along at the top of their lungs, swaying to the beat.

I turned away from my peephole and observed that there were young people in Mulligans' yard who were not even from the party next door. Word had gotten out; it had traveled through the neighborhood, apparently, and beyond, because some of the German kids were there now and also a few Italians. Billy Ramons was there with his fiddle, and though he was still playing around with the strings, Tommy Quarters was already lining up the Mulligans' wash tub and any other pails he could find in the yard that could be drummed on.

Bax came over with a leather flask I'd never seen before and offered me some of its contents. "Where'd you get that?" I asked as I took it from him.

"If you wait long enough, something worth celebrating will assert itself," he said. He winked, and I thought, *I'll be dashed if it doesn't always turn out to be true—for him.*

I took a good slug and shuddered as it streamed down me gullet, but I didn't give the flask back until I'd gone a second round. Bax laughed and poked me in the stomach. I poked him back twice as hard, and we both laughed. Then Nora appeared, crying, "Come on! Billy's starting playing! We're all going to dance." She noticed me staring back at her, my face as dumb as a donkey's, surely. "You too, Jack," she said. "Come on, all the girls want to dance with you!"

I didn't believe her for a rat-arsed minute, but I was glad she'd said it anyway. I followed Bax and Nora over to where the other young people were gathering. There was so much noise I could hardly hear myself think. Or maybe it was the drink wearing down me senses.

The music started up, Billy with his fiddle and a few of the boys banging along on pails, with their hands or sticks or both. There had to be as many people in Mulligans' now as there were in Murphys'—boys clowning with boys, slapping one another's backs, girls all but jumping up and down in their excitement, boys and girls coupling off—but my gaze returned, as it always did, to Nora. She was dancing in a circle with her friends. The faster the music got, the higher her knees went. When she began to toss her skirts up over her knees the other girls got bold and did the same.

Once, when I was but a kid, I said to Da, "What if Bax has something I want?" Da looked at me for a long time. "You could ask him for it," he said finally. "What if it's something he's never going to give up just 'cause I asked?" I said next. And Da answered, "Then you'd have to fight him for it." I began to walk away, thinking I would do just that, punch him square between the eyes and kick him hard in the plumbs and declare myself the victor, when Da yelled from behind me, "What's wrong with you, lad? Find your own fuckin girl. Ain't nothing so special about that one, is there?" I turned to look him in the eye then, and when he broke our stare I thought maybe he'd answered the question for himself.

Bax appeared at my side. "So what do you think, little brother?" As if I might not know what he was talking about, he jutted his chin in Nora's direction.

"She's fuckin brazen," I said.

Bax went on smiling, pleased with my assessment. He had a bottle now. He offered it to me. I drank deeply, until he pulled it away.

I wiped my mouth on my sleeve and watched as Bax handed the bottle off to Carl, who was a church-goer who dreamed of the priesthood and could be trusted not to drink from it. Then Bax approached the circle of girls and took Nora's arm and pulled her away from her cronies. And off they went, laughing and dancing, skipping across the yard without a care in the world. The dance area got wider after that, with lots of buckos and lasses finding partners.

My mood soured and I began to pity myself. Why couldn't I find a girl like Nora to fall in love with me? Why was there no one I wanted to dance with? Suddenly the future felt locked up tight, like nothing would ever change. Like Nora, I had finished school the year before, and I had work at the docks, like Baxter and Da. I figured the docks would take up the bulk of my life, and sleeping and eating the rest of it. I saw Susie looking in my direction, and I got to thinking someday some girl like her—she was seventeen like me, but she had the body of a twelve-year-old—would coax me to marry her, and we'd have a few kids and then I'd croak...and that would be that.

I was mulling over these grim facts when suddenly there was a whoosh and then the sky lit up orange. In my rat-arsed state I thought at first it must be part of the festivities, that the fireworks were yet another Murphy extravagance, like their piano and their Victrola and their fancy garden. But then it hit me that it was coming from somewhere near the docks, where Da was. I looked over my shoulder for Bax, and when I saw him on his way, I began running as hard as I could.

There had been a horrendous fire down at the docks only a few weeks earlier. It had begun on one of the Delaware, Lackawanna and Western Railroad Company's ferry boats, and before the boat could be cut free from her slip, the whole fuckin terminal was ablaze and the train station as well. Bax and me had been there that morning, loading freight. When we saw the flames, we ran straight for the pier where Da was working. Once we were close enough to see him wave that he was all right, we ran back towards the flames, shouting, in case there was anyone in harm's way. We were able to rouse several men from Duke's place just before that structure caught fire. Later Da went around telling anyone who would listen that his boys were heroes.

Two ferries were lost in that fire, and several structures, but no one hurt. The folks who had been in Hoboken five years earlier, when the Pier 3 fire broke out and some two hundred people were burned to death, said it was a miracle no lives were lost. Da said the recent fire was a blessing in disguise, because there were plans on the table to build a new ferry station but no one could figure out how to demolish the old one without interfering with the coming and going of the ferries and trains. Now the job would get done. But Mum disagreed, saying the horror of having to live through another blaze at the docks could never be a blessing, not when there were so many widows in town who were still mourning their losses from the earlier fire. She said the only thing worse was coming over from the homeland, all the people that died over the years just making the crossing.

And now there was another blaze, though as Bax and me got closer we could see that it wasn't on the docks. It was a boarding house one block west of the docks. We cut through lots and hopped over fences and snaked our way toward the four-story building like the fire was burning under our own manky feet. A crowd had already gathered by the time we arrived. People were yelling over the sound of the fire bells.

Fire was shooting upward from two windows on the south side of the first floor. Smoke was pouring out of the windows on the second floor. In the windows above, heads appeared and then disappeared when the smoke got to be too much. "At least we know he's all right," I shouted at Bax as we ran up close.

"The German lady lives up there," Bax shouted back at me.

We heard the clatter of wagon wheels and horses' hooves behind us, and the voices of men shouting orders. Within seconds we were part of a lineup of men working to pull a heavy hose out from one of the fire wagons. Other men were running towards the building with ladders.

Once the flames had been put out at the door, men began racing into the building and bringing people out. Some of the ones coming out were coughing fiercely; others were crying; some couldn't walk on their own. As we worked, dousing the front of the building, I kept hearing my own words—*at least we know he's all right*—and my brother's—*the German lady lives up there*—repeating in my head.

I tried to remember what I knew about the German lady, but my noggin was thick as planks with smoke and a dark feeling that something, besides the fire, was amiss. I remembered only that once Da had mentioned her—she was a nurse, I recalled, and she'd bandaged Da's hand when he'd hurt it at work—and Mum, who was standing at the table, slicing an onion, went quiet, and then Da crossed the room and slapped her on the arse and said, "Come on, Maggie. No need to be jealous. *Tá tú mo chroí.*" *You have my heart.* But Mum looked skeptical when she turned her head to look at him over her shoulder as he was walking away. I was sitting nearby, doing schoolwork, and I happened to catch her glance before she went back to her cutting board. Her eyes were wet, but that could have been the onion.

Suddenly I was as certain Da was in that burning building as I was my name was Jack Hopper, and I was certain too that he was in there with her, the German lady.

I dropped the hose and began to run for the entrance. Men came running up behind me, grabbing at me, screaming for me to stay back, but I shook myself loose and threw myself forward. I landed on my knees in the foyer, from where I could still hear Bax calling me to come back.

The smoke was dense and I couldn't see a fuckin thing. I began to cough. People were still coming out, escorted by firefighters. I was in the way. People were knocking into me.

I took a deep breath and pulled my shirt up to cover my mouth and nose and found the railing and hoisted myself upward. I gained the first landing in time to see a flare-up of flame at the end of the hall, only somewhat visible through the thick smoke. People were rushing towards me, most of them screaming, one man with flames on the sleeve of his shirt. Someone bumped into me and I went down on one knee. As I pulled myself up, I felt a strong grip on my wrist, and I knew by the weight of it, the feel of it, that it was Da, even though I couldn't see his face. I turned and we hurried down together, Da and me and someone else, the person he had on the other side of him. He was leaning with the weight of her, just about carrying her.

Bax was right there at the entrance. He grabbed Da and led him away from the smoke and the crowd, yelling, "Are you okay, Da? Are you hurt?" I couldn't hear nothing of how Da responded.

The lady Da had been helping was beside me, hunched over, choking. She seemed to be about to slide to the ground, so I grabbed her from the back, even though I was coughing hard myself, and tried to hold her upright. She slipped to the ground anyway, gasping for air. "Help," I yelled. "Someone, help!" I got to my knees and rolled her from her side onto her back and began to crank her arms up and down, up over her head and then down and crossed over her chest, the way I'd seen people doing with smoke victims during the fire at the docks. I couldn't help but notice she wasn't wearing nothing beneath her dress. If there'd been a corset or a chemise, I'd have felt it. Someone grabbed my shoulder and pulled me back. I was only too pleased to go. I watched from a distance of a few yards as other men worked on her. Then one of them stood up and shook his head.

When two men came with a stretcher to carry her away, I allowed myself to look at her face. She was young, much younger than me mum. She was beautiful. And she was dead. I was glad when one of the fellows pulled a handkerchief from his pocket and covered her face.

Ambulances came, and I saw some men lifting Da into one of them. He didn't seem to be conscious, but no one had covered his face either, so I had hope. I ran over, thinking to jump into the wagon with him, but the men gathered there said they needed the space for other injuries and I could find him later at St. Mary's.

I wandered into the crowd, looking for my brother. I kept bumping into people; my balance was off. The fire was out now, though a blanket of smoke still hung in the air and puddles were everywhere, glass fragments glittering from them like precious stones. The crowd was even larger than it had been, now that the danger was over. Everyone was telling their story, where they'd been when they first heard the whoosh, what they'd been doing. People were saying the word was that everyone who lived in the building was accounted for; there'd only been one death so far. But a lot of people had suffered smoke inhalation and the number would likely rise.

I wondered if I was suffering from smoke inhalation, if that's why I felt so lightheaded and unable to breathe right. I was still milling around, wondering whether to go directly to St. Mary's or find Bax first, when someone slapped my shoulder. I turned with my dukes up, but it was Bax. "Where the blazes you been?" I shouted.

"I went to tell her."

"Went to tell who what?"

"Mum, you dumb beggar! Who else? She's gone to St. Mary's."

"Did you tell her about the lady?"

"What lady?"

"He came out with a lady. Was it her? The German lady?"

"Why would I know where the German woman lives?"

"But you said the German lady lived there!"

"You're nuts! Leave it alone, will ya?"

"But why else would he be there? He said he had to work."

"He was saving lives, you snaggin arsewipe! He was on his way home when he saw the smoke. If you say anything about the German lady—"

"If he was with the German lady, she has a right—"

"Shut your gob, Jack," Baxter shouted, and he threw a punch that landed square on my jaw.

I was as tall as Bax and almost as big, but with my chest full of sandpaper and my head flying in circles, I lost my footing and went right down. Then someone—it was Billy, the boy who had been at the Mulligans'—appeared and got between us before I could get up and sweep the ground with my brother's ugly noggin. "You're needed at St. Mary's," Billy cried. "My mum said your mum is crying her heart out."

Mum was in the waiting room being comforted by some of her cronies. Until she could control her sobbing, one of them told us, the nurses didn't want her going in. But we were to go in right away. We hurried along, me thinking Da must have been asking for us. But when we'd assembled ourselves at the side of his bed, it was clear he didn't even know we were there. "Morphine," Bax whispered.

His face and head were covered with bandages, only his eyes and nostrils and mouth showing. Every breath had to be causing him excruciating pain, because his face stayed set in a grimace that tightened on the exhale. His big black vile nose hairs—which Bax and me always teased him looked like antennae from a long-horned beetle (and which he had always joked we'd have ourselves one day if we turned out to be that jammy)—were gone. The little bit of skin that was exposed was raw looking, but not charred the way I'd been afraid it might be. I refused to believe he could die. It wasn't possible. Then again, the German lady hadn't looked badly burned at all, and she was dead and gone already. "They should let her in to see him," I said. "He won't know she's crying."

"It's for her, beggar," Bax whispered. "They don't want her worse upset than she already is."

Later, one of the nurses did bring Mum in to see him. She began sobbing again as soon as her eyes fell on him. He was struggling less with his breathing now. He almost looked like he might go to sleep. There was no indication he knew Mum was there. A priest came in from Our Lady of Grace and proceeded to anoint Da with oil. The procedure upset Mum even more. The priest rushed through it, and the minute he was done with his mumbling and his hand gestures, the nurse announced that Da's rest was of primary importance and ushered all of us out of the room.

Mum and Bax and me slept on chairs in the waiting room, in various versions of sitting up. About three in the morning Mum awoke. "What was he doing in that building?" she blurted.

Bax and me struggled to wake up at once. Neither of us had understood her question and she had to repeat it. I'd wondered when she would finally get around to asking. I glanced at Bax and saw his gaze focused on me and sharp as the blade on a razor. "He was on his way home from work," Bax said in an even voice. "He saw the smoke and he ran in to save—"

"How do you know that?" I interrupted.

"He told me so," Baxter spat. "I'm the one who was with him once he came out. He told me right before he collapsed."

I stared at him, wondering if it was really possible that the man who was dying in the other room would have thought to explain himself before he blacked out. Mum snapped, "And you, Jack Hopper. Why weren't you with him too?"

I looked at her, then back at Bax. "There was this lady," I said slowly. I could feel my brother's eyes slicing through my flesh. I looked at my lap. "She came out of the building choking and I tried to save her."

"Why? Why weren't you with your father?" She was almost screaming now.

I looked from Mum to Bax, and I didn't know how to answer. But before I could decide, the waiting room door flew open and the nurse marched in. She stood before the three of us and squared her shoulders. "He's passed on," she said.

For a long moment no one said anything. Then Mum screamed, "Just like that?" She stood up and Bax and me jumped to her side to steady her. "Just like that?" she cried again, leaning out towards the nurse as if it were all her fault. "Nineteen years and now you're telling me, just like that, you're saying? After everything we been through? Is that what you're doing here?"

I came drifting back to the present. The leaf bells were still ringing, and there was still chanting, but it was thin now, only a few people participating. The breeze was blowing cooler; the moon was higher in the sky. The Indian girl bent herself over me and looked right into my eyes. Her own eyes were full of sorrow. Her hand was flat against my cheek. I was thinking, *You know, I don't know how, but I know you know*, for it seemed to me that she had absorbed me, taken me over in some sense and traveled with me back in time, that she had stood at my side as I watched my father dying all over again. I closed my eyes. There was more to remember; I needed to go back. And I did.

I awoke that next morning to the feel of someone's weight sinking the edge of my cot. I turned over, and to my amazement, I found myself looking up at Nora. I thought I must be dreaming. Otherwise how could it be that the object of my secret passion was sitting on the edge of my cot smiling down on me like an angel? Then all at once everything flooded back. I remembered that Da had died, that me and Bax had spent painful hours holding back our own grief so as to get Mum calmed down and home to bed. I began to cry. I covered my face with one hand and sobbed behind my spread fingers.

Nora made hushing noises and brushed my hair back from my forehead. Then she got up to get a handkerchief from the folded pile on the bureau. I blew my nose, but I couldn't stop crying. I turned my head to look at Bax, but his cot was empty. I wondered where he was, if he was crying too, somewhere in another part of the house. Until the night before, I'd never seen my brother cry. He liked to say he'd never been a crier, even as a wee tot, that I was the only crier he knew of. I'd ask Da, "Did Bax ever cry?" and he'd always say, "Never as much as whimper, that boy." But I never knew if he was saying it because it was true or because he was out for setting me a higher goal.

Nora sat patiently, saying not a word for several minutes, until I was all cried out. I was surprised to find I wasn't ashamed to have blubbered in front of her. If you had asked me day before, I would have said she was the last person I would ever cry in front of—Nora, who, like Bax, never cried herself, or so Da always said—and if I couldn't help myself, I'd never look her in the eye again. But that was just what I was doing, looking her in the eye, waiting to see what would happen next. I felt drained of all emotion, depleted of thought. Someone else would have to carry the moment forward, if it was to be carried forward at all.

"Are you all right now, Jack?" she asked gently.

I nodded.

"That's good, because there's something I need to say to you, dear."

She'd never called me "dear" before. Only me mum called me that. If not for the sorry state I was in, I would have laughed.

She took a breath and looked around the room. Her gaze came back to rest on me. "Sometimes, Jack, the truth is less important than the well-being of the people we love."

In my dull state, I did not have imagination enough to realize what she was talking about. I found myself thinking how Nora had always got on so well with Da. Da didn't hold with her ideas about socialism. He believed imperialism was a manly pursuit appropriate for a manly nation. He insisted annexing the Philippines made good sense as it was the surest way to get to China. "The cost was lives though," Nora reminded him once, when she'd come to the house to play dominoes with Bax and me.

I remembered holding my breath, thinking Da might say something hurtful to her. But he only said, "Now why's a pretty girl like you worrying about the cost of progress?" He was smiling. Nora was too. She could do that; she could talk about things she was red hot passionate about and make it seem like normal conversation—or even like she was flirting. She quoted Mark Twain to him, saying, "We have pacified some thousands of islanders and buried them; destroyed their fields; burned their villages, and turned their widows and orphans out of doors..." Da only chuckled. He said she spent too much time in the bookstore. He told her to get him a book on survival of the fittest, "that Darwin fellow," when she could. *That* he might read, he said. She winked and said she'd do just that, and she'd read it herself when he was done. Then he got up from his chair, his copy of *The Wall Street Journal* tucked under his arm, and bent to peck her on the cheek on his way out of the room. When he was gone, Nora said, "You don't hold with any of that, right?" Baxter laughed. "Sure I do," he answered. She slapped his arm playfully. Her eyes twinkled like stars in the dark night sky and she slapped him once again. And we went back to our dominoes.

At the time I figured Nora probably didn't care one way or the other what *I* thought about imperialism. The quare thing was I agreed with her, mostly, though I never would have said so even if she'd asked me outright; I never would have gone against Da like that. But what troubled me was the way she'd slapped Baxter's arm, as if imperialism was a subject they'd discussed at length, a subject about which she already knew very well where he stood. I had never heard my brother speak about imperialism or socialism or any other ism. Not one single word. I'd always assumed he would follow in Da's footsteps. Or, in truth, I figured he had no opinion one way or the other, that he'd never given it a thought. But the way she'd slapped his arm... It seemed remarkable that Bax could have a side to him I knew nothing about. It made me uncomfortable, though I couldn't say why.

"Bax and I don't know if it was the German lady or not," Nora said.

I blinked at her. So that's what she was getting on about.

"It may have been, but then again... He's gone now, and so is that lady, if that was even her, so it can't matter to either of them. The only one it can matter to is your mum."

"And me," I said softly. I didn't know where she was heading with all this.

"And you and Bax, yes, of course. And me too, because I loved him like he was my own father. My heart is broken too, Jack. But our lives are all ahead of us, and whether or not your da had...a lover...is not going to bump up against our futures all that hard. But your mum's future? If she thought for a minute your da might have been with that lady? You think about that, Jack. She'll have lost your father in two ways instead of one. Being a lady myself, I can tell you truthfully the second way—thinking she'd lost his love and he'd been deceiving her—would be even more painful than his passing. She couldn't bear it, Jack. Her life would be as good as over."

I thought about this for several minutes. "What if she reads about the German lady in the paper?" I asked at last.

"I doubt she knows the German lady's name. None of us do."

So it was more than just politics she and Bax discussed when I wasn't around. I stared at her calm face, as patient and pale as a saint's, though I doubted many saints had freckles. She was a scamp for fair, like everyone said, though when it came to knowing right from wrong, she always had her strong opinion. But this couldn't be right, because it was a lie—or it was likely a lie. "A lie," I hissed through my teeth.

I don't know whether she heard me or not. "This is a chance for one woman, a woman we all love, to have a good life, for whatever years she's got ahead," she said.

I looked at her a while longer. "All right," I said finally. "I see what you're wanting from me. I guess there'll be enough pain to go around without me adding to it."

She placed her cool palm against my damp cheek. "That's the spirit, Jack. But I must have your word. Can I trust you to keep this our secret for all time? Right up until your last dying breath?"

Once I answered, I knew, she would get up and go away. I put it off as long as possible, the two of us staring at each other like we could cross the border between us onto the other side. "You have my word," I mumbled finally.

After she was gone, I admitted to myself I'd wanted to say, had almost said, *Tá tú mo chroí, You have my heart*, the words Da had said to Mum that evening when the subject of the German lady came up. Only, apparently, Da hadn't meant them.

And I was back again—the chanting, the bells, the moon, the young woman cradling my head and looking down on me like we had been together since birth and maybe even before then. Time passed with nothing to offer and nothing to withdraw, and yet I could have stayed as I was forever, without a single thought in my dull noggin. But then all at once I realized that some "thing" was coming into being before me very eyes. I forced myself to focus on it, though it seemed like too much work. At first it was a swirl of dark fabrics, but then three women in dark-colored dresses emerged from it, one of them with wild red hair tied back with dark ribbons. It was Nora and me mum! And was that a raven? Nah, it was another woman, an older women with a hooked nose and a hat with black feathers. Clementine, the teller of fortunes. The three sat in a circle, leaning towards one another.

Despite the hag's presence, I was beside myself with joy. I tried to sit up but I couldn't manage. How long would it take, I wondered, for them to turn and see me? If Da could see me, they would be able to too. I wondered what they would make of the fact I was surrounded by savages, my head resting in the lap of one of them. But they went on clacking as if I wasn't there.

The hag was saying, "No, no, I don't eat potatoes. Ever." Her head was high; her attitude snooty. She gestured with her hand, as if to push something away from her. A plate. A plate Mum was offering. I could see it! I could smell the fuckin nutmeg! Potato cookies! They'd be moist, filled with honey. I could just about taste them. Mum put the plate down on the center of the table and lifted her hand to her heart. I knew the gesture well. She was shamming being stunned; she was having one over on the hag. "What? You don't eat potatoes?

How can that be? Everyone eats potatoes!" Nora had her head tipped down, but I could see she was chuckling, caught up in the moment's merrymaking.

The hag lifted her chin higher and regarded the plate with aversion, and Mum, keeping her gaze glued to the hag, slid it from the center of the table off to the side. Nora covered her mouth to stifle a laugh. The hag closed her eyes and shook her head, and Nora and Mum took the opportunity to exchange a smile.

Mum was doing swell. And Nora too. I'd been worried they would languish, with Bax and me declining in the jungle. But they were stronger than that. They had each other. They were mother and daughter, in spirit if not in blood. I kept hoping they'd turn to me, even as they began to blend together, the three of them, even as they became a murky gray cloud, already floating away. I remembered Bax then and turned to see whether he'd seen them too. But I couldn't see my brother clearly. I saw only the shape of him.

Then I was lost, neither here nor there, floating without the bother of a body, comfortable and unconcerned. When I found my way back again I realized with a start that everyone was eating. I sat up at once. The young woman who'd traveled with me through my past had somehow extracted herself from my weight. She was eating too, a stranger to me now. Even Bax was eating. "Why didn't you wake me?" I asked him. He was just biting into the wing of a bird. He looked at me but didn't answer. I realized I was pouting when I saw one of the older women laughing at me. Through her chuckles she gave orders to a girl of seven or eight. The child got up at once and slipped between Bax and me to get to the mat, where she retrieved a leaf package, the last one, and quickly brought it to me. I opened it greedily. The food was still warm. There was white meat from one of the birds and a piece of a fish and a turtle egg and a half a yam and pile of something green and mealy, maybe mashed heart of palm. I devoured the yam within seconds, generating more laughter from the women nearest. I turned to look at them, my cheeks as full as a chipmunk's. I had never been so happy in me whole miserable life.

I awoke on the banana leaf beside my brother, the little palm tent overhead. I had no recollection of the end of the festivities, of people leaving or torches being extinguished, but every sign of the event was gone, leaving me to wonder if I might have dreamed it. Bax awoke soon after and said he was going to try to walk on his own. I wanted to tell him I'd seen Da and Mum and Nora, and the hag, and about the memories that had come flooding back to me out of nowhere. It's true the memories were mostly concerning Da, and therefore sad, but I had also glimpsed us, the buckos Bax and me had been not so long ago, before we'd come to the jungle. I wanted to ask Bax if he'd seen things of that sort too. But it didn't happen. Baxter simply said he wanted to walk, and not long after he got up and limped his way around the perimeter of the *maloca*, as I had done the day before, taking in the gardens and the fruit trees. When he came back he slept. Later one of the women came to look at his wound. There was nothing left but the long jagged purple concave scab that had formed over the hole.

9

IN THE MORNINGS EVERYONE awoke before the sun came up and gathered in the clearing. They sat in one big circle, men and women and children, with those who wanted to taking turns speaking, addressing themselves to the chief primarily but to the others as well. I felt certain these conferences were about dreams, because sometimes one of the speakers would hesitate mid-sentence, as if searching his memory, and invariably he would become animated, his expression revealing that he was describing a moment of fear or confrontation or epiphany.

I wished the Gha-ru could understand my language, or me theirs, because I wanted to share my dreams too. The dream sharing seemed so intimate. No one who wanted to speak was overlooked or rushed, not even the children. For fair, everyone stretched forward a little when a child spoke, and there was always plenty of commentary afterward. Those who had something harrowing to describe were comforted during the dream sharings, often by the stroking of their arms or heads or even legs by those sitting nearby. Though I did not drink the magical brown liquid again after the night of the ceremony, I had been dreaming vividly ever since. My waking moments felt more vivid too. It was as if my perception of the world had shifted. I felt alive. More than alive.

After the dream sharing, the older women told stories to the children, their narratives peppered with refrains the children were familiar with. I guessed it was their way of passing down their beliefs and stories of their ancestors. They seemed to have all the time in the world.

Some days when they were done, the Gha-ru went together, the entire village, to the river to bathe. To get to the water you had to grab hold of a vine and shimmy your arse down a steep bank that flared out at the bottom, making it unsafe to try for a jump. But while a sandy beach would have been more convenient, the water was deep and fast-moving, and no one was bothered by any blood-thirsty fish or other river creatures. Once you were in the water, it was only a few strokes to reach a cove that was almost entirely concealed by the thick foliage surrounding it. There you could relax and take your time.

The Gha-ru rubbed pieces of some kind of bark together to make suds. It worked just swell; after my first bath I felt clean for the first time in months—too clean to put me manky shredded cacks or my near-rotted boots back on. Baxter didn't dress either. And while we were sitting on the high bank waiting for the others, Derby showed us how to tie a piece of bark to a vine fiber to make a cover for our private parts.

When we returned to the *maloca* the first time after the bath, we had our faces painted by Derby and one of the whisker boys, who worked with red (using seeds from the *annatto* shrub) and black (using a dye the women made from the *genipapo* plant). Bax, who Derby worked on, looked like a jaguar afterward, a jaguar with a long beard; I guessed they'd painted me the same.

Their artwork was only the beginning of the many ways they used their knowledge of plants. When a small girl became sick with a high fever that same afternoon, Bax and me went with Derby and the other three deep into the forest and gathered leaves from two different plants. Back at the *maloca*, the two branches of leaves were given to the chief, who held first one and then the other to his chest. He sat with his eyes closed and nodded once or twice, receiving his communication, as always, from the grand beyond. When he opened his eyes, he tossed one branch away from him and gave the other to the woman who was waiting, probably the girl's mammy, and she took it aside and mashed the leaves with ashes and fed it to the child. Within hours, the lass was back working with the other children in the garden.

We learned to help the Indians gather *cumare* palms, the fiber of which the women rolled on their thighs to make into cords which were then woven into hammocks. They worked quickly, and one afternoon when we returned from our daily outing with our new boyos, two of the women presented us with hammocks of our own. After that we slept in the main hut at night, the chief's hut, in our own small space along the north-facing wall.

We went with the Indians to gather other plants too, including one the women added to a liana that grew in the garden to create the magic drink that had brought me glimpses of my loved ones. I went to touch a leaf when Derby was showing it to us, but he jerked it away quickly. Nor were we allowed to touch the bark that was used to make the resin (which the women boiled and then pounded and mixed with ashes) we had seen the chief snort. These trance-inducing plants were clearly sacred.

We were on hand one day when the chief, who was sitting outside the door of the hut on a three-legged stool, called for his snuff, this time to share it with a man of about forty who might have been his son. Since there were two of them partaking, instead of the U-shaped bone, they used a straight reed and blew the stuff into each other's nostrils. They both grimaced in pain afterwards, then went into a stupor, and when they emerged an hour or so later, they spoke together in an earnest manner before calling a meeting with some of the other men. Their tone made it clear some of their discussions were about grave concerns that had come to them, direct from their gods. They seemed to have some sense that some evil was coming their way, and I hoped it had nothing to do with Bax and me.

We learned to make blowguns. Every male had one, even the youngest boys. Some of these guns were as long as ten feet. They were made from cane and had a mouthpiece carved from wood. The darts, which were carved from palm wood, were dipped into a poison syrup of one kind or another; they seemed to have several ways to make almost anything. One of the poisons came from a frog. Bax and me watched as the men stroked the ugly critter's sides until it excreted a thin black liquid which the women then mixed with boiled leaves. We'd seen this frog before, back when we were traveling on the river. Captain Sam had said to stay away from it, because its poison was so strong it could kill a man in a matter of minutes. Another time we helped to gather the roots of a vine that grew near one of the many nearby creeks. Back at the *maloca* the women crushed them and left them sitting in water. The residue from this procedure was eventually scraped into shavings with a bone knife. Then the shavings were mixed with a pulp from another vine. The mix went into an earthenware pot and was simmered with large black ants—the very same ones from which Baxter's sutures had been fashioned—that had been gathered up in leaves by the children. When the liquid got thick, it was ready to be cooled and put in the pouches the men carried when they hunted. How could they know how to make such things?

Bax and me went out hunting whenever they—our four friends—went, which was every other day. I sorely wanted a blowgun of my own, but I was not offered one, and when I signaled to Derby that I'd like to try his, he made a X with his hands in front of his chest, a gesture I knew to mean, *Don't ask again, bucko.* And that was that.

But what a performance the Indians put on. They shot at birds I couldn't even see, birds that proved to be at a great distance once they'd fallen and the Indians had gone to fetch them. They almost never missed. If time passed and they didn't see any birds, they imitated the call of the ones they were hoping to entice…and the birds fuckin came! It was magic, nothing less. When they killed something they became animated, in their quiet way. Yet they always bowed their heads over the dead thing, silently thanking it for giving up its life for them, is my guess.

Nor was it only birds they hunted by imitating their cries. One day they made some squealing sounds and along came *porcãos*, wild pigs, two of them. They came running at us so fast that Bax and me took to the nearest trees and shimmied out of reach, causing the others to laugh more heartily than I had seen since the day of our capture, when they'd had one over on Bax. Derby and the one who seemed the youngest of the four used their blowguns just in the nick of time, and that night there was a grand feast back at the *maloca*.

We also learned their secret for catching so many fish. One day we helped them to gather a particular liana, which we then beat the bark from with clubs until it was soft and pliable. The mysterious bark was put into a basket and suspended in the river by a vine tied to a tree on each bank. Within minutes fish were bobbing to the surface. They floated as if dead, but I soon realized they were only stunned. The Indians used a trap made with palm sticks to retrieve them before they could come back to life. I couldn't help but wonder if C, being part Indian, knew of such skills, and if he did, why he hadn't bothered to share them. It was pure bullocks that we'd nearly starved to death when the jungle was blazing with food, as well as plants with the power to cure every possible ailment—including homesickness.

They loved their lives; that's what I gathered. They were never bored or moody that I could see. The quare thing, to me at least, was that they didn't seem distinct from one another. They were like separate parts of the same body. I wondered if Bax and me seemed like that to them too.

One morning towards the end of the dream-sharing ritual, when the chief was looking around to see if there were any holdouts who still might have something to say, who speaks up but me very own trickster of a brother. "I dreamed my skin changed," he began excitedly. Every head turned to look at him, yet no one—other than me—seemed gobstruck to hear him. He slid his hands up and down his arms. "It got smoother, almost hairless, like yourselves." He touched his face, rubbed his long straggly beard. Then he looked off to the side, upward, towards the trees at the edge of the clearing. "And there was this bird. Beautiful bird..." He drifted, lost in thought. Then he straightened and looked directly at the chief. "You were there. You were wanting me to see something, but I couldn't make out what it was. I didn't want to muck me hand, but I couldn't bring it into focus. That was it. That's all I remember."

To my further amazement, the chief responded just as he did to the others at these ceremonies. He spoke at length to Baxter, looking him right in the eye and talking in his soft monotone, pausing between commentaries to consider his words before he went on again. And even more amazing yet, Baxter nodded encouragingly each time the chief said something, as if he knew exactly what the chief was getting at. Well, bugger me sideways, I said to me miserable self. Ain't this one for the books!

Fourteen days we were with the Gha-ru, the last four of them spent building a canoe which was to be a gift for Bax and me. When we first saw what was happening, Bax tried to explain, with hand signals and pantomime as well as words, that we wouldn't need a canoe, because we would not be returning to our camp after the tapping season ended. But the Indians didn't understand.

Heck, even if Bax could speak their language they wouldn't have understood. While they had to be aware of other people coming and going on the river, how could they conceive of someone going so far away as to be *off* the river? To have no connection to it and so no need for a boat? It was a marvel, how much they couldn't possibly know about the world. New York City, the North Pole, baseball. They'd probably never seen a horse, let alone a bicycle or a motorcar. Finally Baxter gave up trying and bowed his head low, the gesture for thank you very much. I bowed too, and we went back to work.

We worked near the river, building a fire on top of the cedar tree they'd cut, and as the fire burned, using sticks and *facãos* to scrape at the sides of the burned area and hollow out the trunk. When the opening was wide and deep enough, we forced cross pieces into the hollow to keep the trunk from shrinking. We worked day and night, stopping only to sleep in shifts and to eat the food that some of the young girls brought us twice daily from the *maloca*.

When the canoe and paddles were completed, we went back to the *maloca* for a final celebration—though Bax and me didn't know at the time that it was to be our last night. This time there was music, both men drumming and boys playing a kind of flute. And there were dancers, men wearing balsa wood masks painted to look like animals, stepping high and spinning in frenzied circles before us, the guests of honor. There was singing too, loud and discordant, from the men and women alike. With the red resin glim of the torches, and the deep red shadows they cast, the scene was extravagant and otherworldly. Later there was wrestling, and our four boyos participated, as well as a few of the other males. The group picked partners and they wrestled all at once, being careful not to really do one another harm. If they'd asked me, I would have jumped in too, because by then I was feeling near myself again. Maybe Bax felt the same; he didn't say. But no one asked us so we remained spectators.

The following morning Derby approached our hammocks carrying our rifles. "What's this?" Bax said.

"They're sending us back," I said.

"They're not," Baxter replied defensively.

We left the rifles near our hammocks and attended the dream sharing and then went with the others to bathe. When we returned, we found someone had filled a large basket with food and left it near our guns, and Bax conceded I was right; we were being cast out of paradise.

Derby led us back outdoors, where the men who were going out to hunt had gathered, and each of them in turn came up to say his so long, which consisted of some Gha-ru gibberish and a palm raised and pressed against each of our foreheads—a kind of blessing, I thought it must be. Then Derby led us around the *maloca* so that the women and girls working in the garden or weaving on mats in the clearing could say their goodbyes. Next we followed Derby back into the main hut. The chief was in there, standing near the fire pit, Leon's book in his hand. He looked us over carefully and then opened the book and began to mumble, as if he were actually reading it. His measured cadence confirmed he was imitating me. Though he hadn't asked me to read again after that first night, he had apparently picked up everything he felt he needed to know about reading, if you don't count knowing the words and what they meant. He went on for as long as it would take a real reader to get through a page, then he closed the book and looked around for his wife, who came out of the dark to take it away. I remembered that Leon's photograph was somewhere in the pages, but I couldn't see the point of trying to explain that to the chief. For fair he'd be a better caretaker for it than would I. The chief spat into his palm and rubbed the spittle onto the tops of each of our heads, an even greater blessing than what we'd got from the others, I thought, and we both bowed low to show our deepest gratitude and respect.

We'd never had a reason to visit the other huts, so I was gobstruck when we entered the second hut, and after my eyes adjusted to the near dark, I saw to my right perhaps a hundred shrunken heads, hanging from dry vines tied to the overhead crossbeams. Bax was already bowing low to have his forehead touched by one of the older women. I didn't think he'd noticed. As I myself was bowing, I whispered, "Look right." Baxter shot me a glare, to razz me for speaking during the blessing, but a moment later I heard him whisper, "Bugger me," and I knew he'd seen the display too. Our

Indian companions must have known we were unnerved, for nothing went by them; they watched us like hawks.

There were eight or nine people in the hut, all of them elderly women, some of whom took quite long to get up from the mats where they had been sitting and make their way to us. I snuck another look while one old woman was slowly approaching. There were fibers hanging from the heads, from where their eyes and mouths had been sewn shut. One had wood pins skewered into the skin around its gob. Another had a huge spider clinging to its mug. Their features protruded comically as a result of the shrinking process, but it was still possible to tell that the majority belonged to other Indians, other tribes. A few looked to be *caboclos*.

Me and Bax bowed for a final blessing and turned to follow the Indians out. I saw Baxter take a last look as he was bending to go through the doorway. I did the same— and what I saw almost brought me to my knees. But as I did not want my own head to be added to the collection, I sucked in my gasp and kept moving. I dared not say a word to Bax either, at least not then. But I couldn't wait to get a moment alone with him. I was both horrified and relieved— horrified to think the same Indians who treated Bax and me with so much kindness would murder an innocent, if highly disturbed, young loogin—and relieved, deeply relieved, to know for once and for all that Bax had nothing to do with Ted's disappearance. I hadn't let myself think too far along those lines, but it had been there, solid as a rock at the back of my noggin.

We returned to the river and slid the new canoe into the water. All six of us got in, with Derby riding on the edge of the bow and Whiskers perched on the stern. We'd made four paddles and we took turns using them as we headed in the direction of our camp. We were on the cusp of the wet season; there had been a few humdinger storms and the river was already rising up over some of the lower banks. It took only about two hours to reach the camp by water.

Once we arrived at our destination, the Indians got into the water to find a place where the canoe could be tied in such a way that it would be entirely concealed beneath shrubs and grasses growing over the edge of the bank. It didn't take them long. There was overgrowth everywhere. When they were done, we walked up to the shack. Immediately Bax and me went behind it, to the place where we'd stored the rubber we'd collected. Nothing had been touched.

I expected the four would leave and head back on foot to their *maloca*, and when they didn't, I assumed they were waiting to start fresh in the morning. We shared the basket of food and then the Indians went into the shack and stretched out on the floor to sleep. Me and Bax made a display of insisting that two of them take our hammocks, but they refused. We slept in our own manky hammocks for the first time in many days.

Morning came and still they did not leave. After we ate what was left of the food, they gestured toward the *estradas* and then gathered together our tapping tools. Baxter let out a breath that was almost a bark. "They mean to help us," he cried. "Look, they know where everything is and what's needed."

"Of course they do," I replied. "They've been watching our every move since we arrived." I wanted to mention Ted right then, but I checked myself. Seeing Ted like that, suspended in the dark hut with, presumably, other Gha-ru enemies, had blunted the spell the Gha-ru had cast over me.

Over the course of the next seven days, three Indians worked with Bax and me gathering and smoking rubber while the other fished or hunted and prepared food. In this way there was always something to eat when we returned from the *estradas*. With the help of our new friends, we were able to accumulate more rubber in one week than we had in all the time between when Leon died and Ted disappeared and the Gha-ru first approached us—and this in spite of the fact that the rains had begun in earnest by then and on two occasions the latex had to be thrown out because too much water had mixed with it. On the eighth day, Bax and me awoke to find ourselves alone. We went outdoors and looked around, but there was no trace of them. The blowguns, which the Indians kept tied to crossbeams under the shack at night, were gone.

We waited awhile, but when they didn't appear we ate the food left from the day before and set out on the first *estrada* to work. Baxter led the way. "They could be watching us right now," I said from behind him.

He turned around to face me. "And you could be a ballsack disguised as my brother!" He began to walk again.

"Someone's a wee bit narky today," I mumbled.

He turned abruptly. "They saved my worthless ratbark of a life, and yours too. They treated us like we was one of them. Or two of them, as may be the case." He grunted.

"Did I say they didn't? All I said was they could be watching."

He held back from saying more, but I could see in his eyes he was thinking it. I had been leading up, once again, to ask him if he'd seen Ted's head dangling there with the others—what he made of the fact that we'd been treated like royalty and here Ted had been trounced—but when I saw the outrage on his face, I thought it best not mention it just then. And as the days passed, I began to doubt it myself. Maybe it hadn't been Ted after all.

10

THE DAYS THAT FOLLOWED lost their magic quickly, for me at least; I could not hang on to the sublimity I'd experienced with the Gha-ru. Me and Bax had tried to find the tree with the bark that stunned the fish long enough for capture, but either there was no such tree near the camp or we'd already forgotten its identifying features. And there was no time to dwell on it, or to attempt to make blowguns. Within a week, we were losing the weight we'd gained. And though we couldn't say why it should be different at our camp than it had been at the *maloca*, we were getting bitten again by every sort of insect. We went through our things to find clothing to cover up as much as possible.

Me and Bax came back from our work one day—by this time it was storming too regularly to tap but we still went out daily to maintain the *estradas*—and there was C, rolling a ball of rubber from where we'd hidden them behind the shack to the path that led to the river. Three *pelas* had already been moved to the head of the path.

He must have heard our approach—because I had shot at a curassow not a minute before, and having missed, Bax had called me a fuckin vexing dork to which I replied that he was a fuckin doodle who could kiss me skinny arse if he thought he could have done better—and yet C continued working with his back to us until we were standing right on top of him. When he finally turned, he looked us up and down, possibly surprised we didn't look as sick as when he'd left us; you could never say for sure what C was thinking. But all he said was, "Others?"

We had not taken the trouble to decide what C should be told and what was best unmentioned. We had started to discuss the situation once a few days before, but the conversation had ended badly. Baxter had said, "If you blow the gaff and mention the Gha-ru to C or anybody else, I'll kill you, I swear. I'll drag you over the jungle floor with your hands tied behind your back, and if the insects don't eat you alive, I'll throw you in the river for the piranhas." "Why would I do such a thing?" I cried, stung. "Look how you tried to ruin Mum's life," Baxter retorted. I had to think for a full hour to figure out what he was getting at.

I was counting on him to come up with something now. He was the shrewder of us two by far, as he was so fond of reminding me. He was the one who was always seeing the grander picture while I concentrated on the details there in front of me. Still, the moment stretched, and I did not like it. Nor did I like the eager gleam in C's eye as he regarded us.

Once he finally stepped forward, Bax seemed to have no problem filling the air with his falsehoods. Clever as he was, he made it sound as if the double tragedies had happened only the week before. If he'd told the truth, I realized while he was *not* telling it, he would have had to account for why we had as much rubber as we did. C did not seem surprised to learn Ted had lost his mind and run off and Leon had succumbed to a spider bite. Nor did he seem to care.

When Bax was done, C said he was going up to the house to rest and that we should roll the remaining *pelas* to the head of the path. Tomorrow he would teach us how to build a canoe, and between the two canoes, his and ours, we would float the rubber up to the base at the mouth of the Coregem, to the Teacup camp. Abalo would be there to pay us. There would be a launch to take the rubber to Manáos where it would get loaded onto an ocean-going vessel. Meanwhile, we would have to find our own way back to our camp to prepare for our second tapping season, because C would be working with new recruits. When C went off to the house to sleep, Baxter elbowed me and said, "Why didn't you answer him directly? Your hesitation showed him we're hiding something. I could see it in his fuckin eye."

"You're the one that's known for lying!"

"You fuckin bootlicker. Ain't you supposed to be the smart one?"

"That's right, beggar. I'm smart enough to know he's half Indian himself and if he had a thought of bringing any harm to the Gha-ru, surely it would have already happened."

"Don't matter he's half Indian. He's working for the white man, beggar. How can you be so naïve? Be sure you don't blow the gaff regards the canoe. In fact, you'd better get down there now and make sure it's still well concealed."

"You can go to blazes and kiss me bony Irish arse if you think I'll take orders from you."

Our disagreement was no more than a second from moving on to blows when I happened to glance up and see C standing in front of the shack, looking in our direction. "He's watching us," I whispered.

Bax glanced over his shoulder. "He can't have heard from there."

"No, but he was trying."

"Then we've both made a bullocks of it. Let's get down to the river and hope he don't think to follow."

It took eight days to build the canoe, which was half the length of the one we'd built with the Gha-ru in four. The storms were coming steady, and even though we were working under the thick jungle canopy, the torrential downpours found their way through and kept putting out our fires. C had brought some canned food with him, so at least we were able to eat. We still had *farinha* left too, though Bax said he'd rather suck arse juice from a dead pig than eat *farinha* more than once a day, and I had to agree with him there.

By the time the canoe was finished, the river had come up to within thirty feet of where we'd been working. We'd known the river would swell—it had swollen the year before—but not like this. Much of the floor of the forest was submerged now, making it easy to slide the new boat into the water. I wondered what would become of the other canoe, tied and hidden under a bank that was no longer visible.

We divided the *pelas* into two groups and then tied them together with ropey vines that we attached to the boats. "Make them tight," C said of our knots, and Bax and me exchanged a look; if there was one thing we knew from our days as longshoremen, it was how to lash a knot.

We set out on the river for the Teacup, me and Bax in the new canoe and C in his old one. It was much easier traveling on the swollen water, even dragging the rubber behind us. The current carried us in the right direction, for one, and it was not necessary to travel through the green tunnel we had come through on our way down to the camp; for fair, it would have been impossible. The tunnel was gone, submerged like everything else. There were floodplains everywhere— *várzeas*, C said—and thus we were able to navigate between what were now islands of tree canopies that extended beyond what had once been river banks. Sometimes we were even able to take shortcuts—*furos*, waterways that crossed right over whole regions of land.

Traveling along the *furos* and *várzeas* was eerie and beautiful. When it wasn't storming, the water was glasslike. The reflections from the trees and branches and even the sky were almost more intricate than the things themselves. You couldn't tell where the reflection ended and the real thing began. Nor could you see the horizon line much of the time, only deep dark forests everywhere reaching out in two directions, up and down. Occasionally we were held up by debris. There were plenty of birds' nests and leaves and branches floating around, even trunks of trees, and the *pelas* would frequently get caught in them. For the most part though, we moved along quickly, using pails to bail water when it rained.

We were unable to make camp at night—because there was no way to get to dry land without going far out of our way—so we tied our canoes to branches in the canopies above the flood. The launch would only be at the Teacup for a short time, C said, and if we were late arriving, it would leave without our load of rubber, as it had been near full to capacity when C left. That would mean waiting at camp until it returned to pick up the next load to get paid. And getting paid was top of the list. Though we didn't talk about it much between ourselves, all we were wanting was to get ourselves home.

The launch was still there when we arrived some four days later. As we tied up the canoes, the two men up on the steamer's deck began counting the balls of rubber as they floated into view. Then three other men appeared and began hauling the rubber on board with the help of fish gaffs, one *pela* at a time. C told Bax and me that it would take a while for the rubber to be weighed and our pay to be calculated. So we took our rifles and headed up the path to find Abalo.

We could hear the voices of the *caboclos* right away, because the path was only half the distance it had been before the wet season. They sounded weaker, drained. Even so, I was gobstruck when me and Bax came into the clearing and Paulo and Gomez and Cabeça de Galinha looked up at us from where they sat in a circle with a half a dozen or so unfamiliar men around a small fire they'd started to keep the bugs away. They looked abominable. The straggly beards on some of them reached down to their puds. They were one and all bitten and scarred and thin as rails. Their copper skin had gone gray. Their clothes, which were in tatters, hung on their skeletal frames. Their eyes protruded from their heads. "*Dia Uas!*" I whispered through my teeth.

Baxter laughed sharply. "You think you look any better, beggar? We look just like them."

But I knew we didn't look just like them. We were thin and bruised and gray, but not the way these men were. Even though it was some weeks now since we'd been with the Gha-ru, we had still not returned to our former state of frailty. And in that moment I knew that C knew it too. Our hesitation when C had asked about Ted and Leon would only have confirmed what was already obvious: we'd had help; we'd made contact with someone, or someone had made contact with us.

If the *caboclos* noticed that we looked relatively healthy, they said nothing about it. They had other matters on their minds. They had not lost any men, they said, but Nuno Bonito had tried to hang himself and would have succeeded except the vine he chose was an epiphyte and it fell to the ground with his weight, what wee bit there was of it. Cabeça de Galinha found him hours later. He was covered over with ants; some had even begun to eat his eyeballs. "He's uglier than ever," Gomez said, but it wasn't a joke and no one laughed.

Paulo said Nuno Bonito was in the hut if anyone cared to have a look. He was worthless now, almost dead, but he was reluctant to let go for fear Abalo would take his wife into labor to pay off his debt. "He should have thought about his wife before he tried to hang himself," Gomez said. Paulo barked a laugh, but there was no pleasure in it. "Have you seen his wife?" he asked no one in particular. "She's as ugly as *tucunaré* and has a worse disposition," he went on, referencing the aggressive river fish. "Abalo wouldn't let the likes of her through his front door. Nuno Bonito's got nothing to fear there. He should just give up and let himself go. He stinks something awful, like he's been dead a week or more already." Paulo turned his head to the side and spat.

Having given their report, the *caboclos* thought to ask where Leon and Ted were. Baxter spoke up right away this time. The men were all ears. They were especially interested in the fact that Ted had lost his mind. Such tales of jungle mayhem made them feel just a wee bit better about their own ordeals.

I had not heard my brother clack on so much in a long time, and I was comforted by the lilt there in his banter. But when he began to tell them how Ted's mother had killed herself and how Ted had been the one to find her, I interrupted. "That was secret," I said in English.

Baxter turned to look at me. "He's gone, beggar. What difference does it make?"

I looked around at the other men, the ones Bax and me didn't know, *caboclos* from other camps. Though otherwise as skeletal as any of the others, one of them had a huge abdomen; it fell over his lap and hung almost to the ground. Dropsy, I thought. Another looked leprous, with raw spots around his nose and mouth where the flesh had been eaten away. One had removed his boots, probably because his feet were swollen and cracked, and there was blood oozing between some of his toes. Baxter was right. What difference would it make? Still, I found myself fuming to think he would use the information in an entertaining way, and it was all I could do to keep from whaling him one.

Once Baxter had satisfied their curiosity, I spoke up, to ask about Abalo. C had said he would be there—and unless he was out alone in the forest or sitting at Nuno Bonito's side in the shack, he was not. Paulo answered that Abalo had been there up until two days ago, but he didn't want to wait any longer, and so he'd gone back to Manáos on another launch that had been tied up at the Teacup for a while. Abalo's men, the men on the steamer there now, had been directed to pay everyone. When he saw my face light up, Paulo added, "I hope you don't think you'll get much money. We barely made any ourselves, and Abalo didn't have to pay our expenses coming here from the other side of the world. One more season and you'll see a profit, if the work doesn't kill you first."

"You didn't see the rubber we brought in," Baxter boasted. "We brought in a grand rake of it."

Paulo turned his palms outward and shrugged.

"Let's see about this," Baxter said, and we turned and went back down to where C and the others were finishing the job of loading the rubber. There were two wooden crates on the beach, and we leaned against them and watched in silence until the man who seemed to be the leader, a large, muscular black man shouting orders with a Caribbean accent, finished weighing the last *pela* on a rigged-up weighing machine with a copper cylinder at one end and made his calculations. Then the Caribbean man said something to C, and C pointed to the crates and shouted down from the deck, "Those your things, for next season. Your food and supplies. Senhor Abalo say give you."

"We want our fuckin money. We don't want to stay another season," I shouted back.

C jumped off the boat, landing almost right in front of me with a thud. He stood so close I could smell his breath, and it was not pretty. "You have no choice. You owe Senhor Abalo."

"We owe him nothing. We did the work. We want to be paid," Bax said.

The Caribbean man jumped down too. He had been speaking in Portuguese to his fellow *muchachos* up on the deck, but now he switched to broken English. "No money this time," he said. "Just supplies and this." He took a piece of paper out of his pocket; he actually smiled as he held it out to us.

Bax snatched it from his hand and I read it over his shoulder. It was written in English and it confirmed that as long as we had brought in at least twelve *pelas* of rubber weighing an average of seventy-five pounds, we could consider our debt for our passage paid in full. We had brought in sixteen *pelas*. Baxter flapped the piece of paper in the big man's face. "What kind of horseshite is this? It says here if we brought in excess we should be paid. And here you're saying we ain't getting paid?"

The big man folded his arms. His face was stone now. "Supplies expensive. Your passage paid, but you need to pay what supplies you already got, and now you got more. Good stuff. Canned meats and whiskey. New boots. Next year you get money. You see."

"Are you fuckin coddin me?" Bax screamed in his face. "We worked the whole fuckin season. Abalo promised we'd get paid if we did the work! And we did the fuckin work. And now we want our fuckin dosh!"

Having heard the raised voices, the other *muchachos* jumped down from the steamer too now. They were gathering around, encircling us. I could feel the fury building in my body. It took the form of a fire that caught hold in my balls and shot up through my throat and flew out into my arms, turning my hands into rocks whose sole objective was to smash in their faces, C's and the other one, the big *muchacho* who was spouting the shite.

Without any warning my dukes flew up from my sides, ready to do what damage they could, but the big man ducked and in the same second, two of his fellow *muchachos* grabbed my wrists and twisted my arms, and next thing I knew, three of the *muchachos* were behind me, holding my arms back, trying to break them, and my back as well, by the feel of it. I kicked and spat but bag of bones that I was, I couldn't break their hold. When I took a breath I saw that three others were holding Bax the same way. C stood between us, looking from me to Bax and back again, pleased as Punch with the way things were unfolding.

"Ay, I see how it is now," Bax shouted. "All you bastards against two of us. Even things up and me and Jack will give you fucks a go." He jutted his chin towards C. "Go on. Even it up and let us show you what we still got left, or die trying."

C and the big man laughed. Without taking his eyes off Bax, C said something to the big man in a version of Portuguese I did not understand and they both laughed harder. I tried once more to break away from my assailants; I was ready to take them on for certain, one at a time or all at once. The fact that I couldn't win even a fair fight was not my concern at the moment.

Then I had a thought, which I played with for a half a minute before I dared execute it.

"You unloading and coming back again?" I asked the big man.

He nodded.

"I'm going back with you, then. Let me speak to Abalo myself, man to man."

"Ain't you the reasonable one," Bax spat. He was still struggling to break free from the men holding him.

"Abalo kill you, you show up at his door," the big man said.

"What's it to you? All I'm asking is for a ride back. What happens after is my affair."

He shrugged. "Ain't nothing to me." He turned to C, who also shrugged.

He gave his men a nod and they let go of me at once, though they stayed ready to grab me again. "Get on board. We leaving now."

"I'm going to kill the fucker. I'm going to lick him till he shites himself and then I'm going to rip his fuckin throat out!" Bax cried.

"That's why I'm going by myself, arsehole," I announced.

"Get on board," the big man shouted.

"Let me go up and get my stuff."

"What stuff? Your gun? You leave that here, with this other one."

"What do you mean, with this other one?" Bax cried, still struggling to free himself. "I'm going too. He ain't the boss of me. You've got it arseways if you're thinking that."

He jerked his body in every direction, his teeth clenched, a sort of squeaky growl escaping his throat, but the men holding him did not let go and he couldn't break free. They were watching C for an order, but the order didn't come.

"I'll explain we've had a change of heart and need our pay," I said to Bax, calmly, enjoying his fury. "I'll figure it out and then I'll come back on the next steamer and let you know our next move."

"Are you fuckin out of your mind? Who do you fuckin think you are, some kind of litigator going to settle our wee dispute?" He turned to C. "Tell these arsewipe loogins to let me go so I can break my brother's fuckin neck and save Abalo having to soil his fuckin hands doing so."

The men holding Bax seemed to like that idea. They smirked and looked at their boss again for a signal. C seemed to be considering. "Don't let him come with me," I cried. To Bax I said, "Two of us showing up is a threat. He'll kill us both. One of us shows up, there's a chance he'll listen. Besides, I need a break from seeing your fuckin ugly bullocks of a face day after day."

"Right. I get that, because every time I got to look on your ugly face it's all I can do to keep from puking up my fuckin *farinha*. But tell me this, Mr. fuckin milksop litigator: What if you *do* get him to give you what he owes us? Not that I think for a minute that will happen. What I think is he'll probably shoot you dead on the spot long before you open your gob and start pouring out your milksop excuses. But just say; just say he gives you our money. What's to keep you from hopping on the next steamer and going home without me?"

The fire in my balls blazed anew, and when it shot up to my mouth it tasted like metal. I grabbed hold of Baxter's neck. I would have put my fist in his face, but for the three minions holding him tight, and much as I wanted to, I could not hit a man who couldn't hit me back. "Who *are* you?" I shouted. My gaze drifted from Bax's piss-pot eyes to C, who was watching me intently, amused. "If you think I would take the dough and run, then I don't know who you are anymore. And you don't know who I am either. So much for fuckin brotherhood."

I let go of Baxter roughly, but as I turned away, he somehow got one hand free long enough to punch me, hard, in the shoulder. I stopped in my tracks. I could tell by the sound he emitted that the thugs had grabbed hold of him at once and bent his arm flat back to breaking point. I forced myself to swallow down the urge to turn and knock his teeth down into his bullocks while I had the chance.

C said something to his men and one of them cut down a vine and tied Baxter's hands behind him. Meanwhile I boarded the boat with the rest of them. "You hateful piece of shite," Bax shouted as the big man started up the motor. "Rot in hell, you fuckin burse. May the cat eat you and the devil himself eat the cat. May you fall overboard and may the piranhas nibble you slowly, bullocks first and then your useless fuckin pud and then your eyes and…"

I stood at the aft rail watching him as the launch began to pull away from the bank. In no time he'd worked himself free of his restraints and threw himself into the river like he thought he could catch up to us, but he never stopped cussing me. Even as he was choking up all the river water he swallowed trying, he was cussing. Even as he came to his senses and got out of the piranha-infested, branch-carrying, wasp-nest-embracing shite brown tide, I could still see his ugly gob working hard even then, even though I couldn't hear him anymore. And though I knew meeting up with Abalo would likely result in Jack Hopper with a hole in his heart—bleeding out at the end of the great floating docks where the rubber got delivered, with fish jumping in the air to get their fair share and birds descending from above for a shot at his gangy eyes and pick-axe snoot—I was glad in that one moment to have got one over on my brother, to be the one in charge for once.

11

THE STEAMER WAS FILLED to capacity with its precious cargo, and there was little room for walking about. Sleep each night was a nightmare of heat and humidity and other discomforts in a stinking hammock strung in the tightest space possible at the stern of the boat. But all that I was used to. What troubled me more was the two children on board, young Indians who looked just like the Gha-ru—though they were not Gha-ru, or I would have recognized them. They must have separated now and then, to stretch their legs or use the dung bucket, but whenever I looked I found them pressed tight together along the outer wall of the cabin, watching the activity with round eyes full of fear.

They had to have been stolen. I wanted to ask the Caribbean man, Magnânimo was his name, about it, but I knew my displeasure would be evident the minute I opened my gob, and so I restrained me miserable self. There was nothing I could do anyway. I needed to get to Abalo's. I needed to get the dough and get back to the camp and get me fuckin brother and get out. Much as Bax might will it, I didn't want to swim with the piranhas.

But the sight of the two boys, who couldn't have been more than seven or eight, set something off in me during the long days standing at the rail of the launch. I was a fallen man; I had lost my humanity. I was never much of a do-gooder, it's true, but I believed in the work do-gooders did, and I always thought age would reveal me to be, at the very least, a decent person, a good son, a good neighbor, a man who could be called upon when others needed help. Instead I'd sold my soul to make my fortune, and the fortune had turned out to be no more than a pipe dream.

At night I watched the men play cards. Since I didn't have any dosh, I couldn't play along, but Magnânimo took pity on me and let me share in the whiskey. And so I drank myself cock-eyed when I could. And what reason was there not to? The days on the boat were shorter when I was rat-arsed. My perplexity concerning the boys—and my own miserable mistakes as well—had a softer edge. My frustration, which was so deeply lodged in me that I could sometimes feel it screaming in my gut, merely hummed when I was rat-arsed, in tune to the hum of the engine.

The trip to Manáos took much less time than it had when I'd come the opposite way during the dry season. The Rio Purus curled like a snake, and now with the rains there were so many *furos* it was almost as if we traveled in a straight line. In no time we were on the Amazonas and approaching our destination. Before we docked, Magnânimo told me I had only a short time to deal with Abalo if I wanted to ride back when the steamer returned to the Teacup for its next load; the boat would unload and leave again at dawn two days out. I agreed to be at the dock in plenty of time, though I couldn't help fantasizing how nice it would be not to return at all. I shot a last look at the young buckos. They were still huddled together, one of them sleeping and the other staring ahead vacantly. One of the men had been charged with feeding them, but only the scraps the others left behind. They already looked thinner than they had the first days out.

Working against the setting sun, the men began unloading the rubber right away, and I went off to look for a place to spend the night. I found a spot down at the docks in a narrow alley between two warehouses, where there was nothing more than a few water rats to take note of me. C and Magnânimo were due to meet with Abalo the following morning. I thought I'd wait until the afternoon to go up to the mansion myself. That way Abalo would know I was coming and what I was coming for. Asking him for our pay for the season was a fair enough request. Maybe he would have a fair response if he had a moment to consider it. Anyway, I was giving him that chance, and if he didn't take it—well, I didn't know. I fell asleep with the possible outcomes spinning in my noggin, like the peg tops me and Bax used to spin when we were boys.

I kept myself hidden all morning and in the early afternoon I stole two *carambolas* from an outdoor market and made my way up the crowded streets to the mansion. It was quare enough to be walking among so many people, all of them clean and wearing what Mum would have called "their Sunday best," men in suits and women in bright-colored dresses carrying parasols to match. The streets seemed wider and cleaner than before, the buildings grander, the sunlight fiercer. It was a different world to me. I was like one of the rats I'd seen the night before, dirty, scuttling quickly to avoid observation.

I took a deep breath and rang the bell and a moment later Louisa appeared at the door. As soon as she saw me, her smile dropped from her pretty face and she tried to force the door closed. I pushed back on it. *"Vai! Ele quer te matar!"* she whispered. *Go, he wants to kill you!* She glanced behind her.

"He owes me money. I'm not going anywhere."

"*Não importa.* He'll kill you."

She looked over her shoulder again. Then she backed away from the door and bowed quickly and said, "The young man is here to see you, Senhor Abalo."

Abalo appeared in the door frame, nearly filling it with his bulk. He was dressed in a finely cut three-piece suit that the day was far too hot for and holding a lit cigar. I could see Louisa, though barely, lingering in the hallway behind him, wringing her hands and trying to mouth some message to me.

Abalo looked me up and down slowly, with immeasurable disdain, and I knew at once I'd been a fool to imagine I might be invited in for conversation. He took a step forward, forcing me to step back, so that I found myself down one step from the big man, looking up at him rather than eye to eye. "When my brother first went to meet you," I began, "you indicated there was a great deal of money to be made. Now your men are saying—"

"You young people have no patience," Abalo interrupted. He took a puff on his cigar and exhaled slowly, directing the smoke flow into my face. "Do you think it was cheap to bring you here from New York? You're an ungrateful son of a bitch."

"Our companions are dead. Did C tell you that? Me and my brother are half dead. We want our money. We worked for it. We near died for it. And now we fuckin want it. That's the beginning and the end of what I have to say."

Abalo leaned forward, so that now I had to tilt my head back and look up into his manky nostrils. His cigar burned so close that my eyes began to water. "I don't want trouble," he said softly, "but this is an argument you can't win. Some people die in the jungle, some don't. You're one of the lucky ones, you and your brother. You're still here. You do as well next season and this time next year there'll be plenty of money for you. Now please, get out of my sight."

He stepped back. Our conversation was over and he was turning toward the open doorway. But I struck out at him before he could enter through it, grabbing his arm and spinning him toward me fast. When I saw his cigar land near my feet, I thought I had a chance and was just about to smash his face in when a pistol appeared between my brows, cold and hard, sucking the flesh off my forehead. "You fuckin thieving piece of shite scruf," I said.

He cocked the gun and kept the muzzle where it was. The moment seemed to go on forever. "Get out of here," he growled at last. "Next time I see your face I'll kill you. You got any argument, you take it to C."

The weapon disappeared. The door slammed.

I stood there soaked, half in sweat and more in shame. I had come all this way for an audience of less than a minute, and with a gun pressed to my head for half of it. I was about to bang on the door again when it opened a crack and Louisa's small nose appeared. "Bruna stays at the green house on Rua Estreita," she said in her language. "Go. I'll find you there shortly."

"I'm not going anywhere," I replied.

She looked behind her and then back at me and lowered her voice to a whisper. "If he finds me talking to you, he'll kill me too. I don't want to die yet, thank you very much. Go, please, go. Rua Estreita."

Rua Estreita was a small street on the hillside near the docks at the east end of the city. It smelled of fish, and there were wooden cleaning tables all along it, with buckets and pails piled beneath them. I thought of the marble slab tables at the other end of the docks, where the big ships came in. This was where the fishermen lived, the men who provided for the elite of Manáos.

The green house was no more than a shack, up on stilts like the other structures on the road. It was above the waterline for now, but then the season was not yet at its apex. I walked right past it, down to the end of the dock, and then back up and then down again. I was waiting for my anger to level itself out. I walked for more than an hour, and finally I returned to the green house and knocked. I hadn't had the presence of mind to think of Bruna in a long time, but now that I was there, standing at her door, I saw myself as she'd see me, peeled down to me very core, looking (I hadn't seen me own puss in some time but I would wager) like a bucket of snots.

The door opened and a large woman smoking a pipe stuck her head out. She looked me up and down. "*O que você quer?*" she asked harshly. *What do you want?*

"*Eu sou um amigo de Bruna,*" I said.

The woman drew on her pipe and exhaled slowly, blowing smoke and taking me measure. Then her expression shifted. "You the boy who wrote the letter?" she asked in her language.

"That's me. Jack Hopper," I said, though I was ashamed to give my presence a name.

She drew on her pipe again and studied me some more, a manky bag of bones with stinking hair and a straggly beard and clothes near ripped to shreds. Eventually a half smile appeared around the stem of her pipe and she said, "Come in, young man. Come in. You are welcome here."

There were three other women within, one of them nursing a wee babe. She gave me the once-over and then covered her diddy and ran off into a back room separated from the kitchen by a heavy curtain. The other two were older women, the age of the woman who'd let me in. One was wearing a black scarf on her head, tied at the nape of her neck pirate-style. The other had a pair of rosary beads twisted around her wrist like a bracelet, as if to have them at the ready should she suddenly be called upon to pray.

They had been drinking strong-smelling coffee around an ipè wood table. Now they put down their cups and looked with curiosity to the woman with the pipe, waiting for an explanation. There was a plate of cakes at the center of the table, and I couldn't force me piss-pot eyes to abandon it. I told myself I'd give them a minute, and if they didn't offer, I'd snatch all I could and run for it.

The woman with the pipe was saying, "This here is Bruna's friend, the one who wrote the nice letter." The other two began to giggle. I glanced up to see one of them, the one with the scarf, cover her mouth and blush, shy as a school girl. I nodded, but my eyes were all for the cakes, and I could not concentrate on anything else in their presence. It was only when the door flew open that I shifted my gaze. In came Louisa, carrying a burlap sack, and Bruna was just behind her.

Louisa came forward and hugged me, as if we were the best of friends. She pulled an envelope half out of the sack, to show me it was full of mail. Then she backed away from me, grabbing her nose and mugging a face so as to assure the others I smelled as bad as I looked. Everyone laughed, except Bruna, who was still standing near the door. She smiled shyly when our eyes met. "*Estou faminto*," I whispered. *I'm starving.*

The three older women looked at one another and then exclaimed all at once and jumped up from the table. The one with the pipe, whose name, I soon learned, was Nilza, pulled her chair out and patted it with the flat of her hand while yelling, "*Sente-se, sente-se!*" *Sit, sit.* I was smiling uncontrollably by then, though I can't think why, other than that something seemed to have snapped in my mind once I knew I was to be fed. I sat, and someone shoved the plate of cakes before me, and soon enough a mug of hot coffee appeared beside it.

Now the older women got busy at the wood stove, putting together some concoction that involved the cutting of vegetables, and the younger women took their places at the table. While I shoveled food into my gob, one cake after another with no regard for whether anyone else might care for some, Louisa peppered me with questions. What was I going to do about getting my money from Abalo? Had I made another plan? Where was my brother? Weren't we working with two others? Where were they?

I couldn't stop eating. Louisa placed her lovely golden hand on me manky arm. I looked at it there, such a dainty thing in its gray sleeve with its starched white ruffle at the cuff. Perhaps she meant to slow me down, but there were only two cakes left by then and I was having them if it killed me. Meanwhile Bruna sat with her pretty chin on her palm, leaning in towards me, her eyes wide and a bit moist, waiting for what I could not wager. Adriana, Nilza's daughter, had finished breast-feeding her dote by then and joined us at the table with the wee cub, who bounced on her lap and laughed and dribbled, doing his best to garner all the attention away from me.

I began to answer Louisa's questions with my gob still full, the crumbs a-flying. But seeing as that wouldn't work, I went on chomping and let the women wait until the last cake was gone and I'd wet my disgusting pillock of a manky finger and used it to wipe the remaining crumbs from the plate. Then I had me a good burp, for which me mum would have slapped me upside the head, but it was beyond my control, and the young women must have agreed because they only laughed, and when the dote joined in, laughing like he even knew what was funny, the older women started laughing too, and soon we were all cackling like a barrel of ninnies.

It was a long moment before everyone had their fill. Then, once it was quiet again, Louisa lifted a brow to remind me she was still awaiting answers to her questions. And so I took a deep breath and began, and once I was going there was no stopping me.

I told them what happened to Leon and Teddy, and how me and Bax had almost died ourselves a time or two or three, and how we hadn't been paid what we'd been promised, and how my only choices were down to two—go back and work another season and hope for a fair deal thereafter, or kill Abalo, who would surely kill me first. I wanted to mention the Gha-ru there in the middle—who would they tell?—but a vision of my brother's scowl inspired me to close me manky gob in the nick of time.

By then the older women had two pots on the stove, one for the fish stew they were making on my account and another a kettle just for heating water. Nilza went out the back door of the shack and returned with a big tin tub, the sort clothes got washed in, and set it down noisily beside the table and poured water from the kettle into it and then went out again to refill the kettle with water from one of the rain barrels. I kept clacking away as the water in the tub swelled. It was as if I hadn't talked in years, and now someone had greased the wheels and I couldn't make them stop. For all my audience even cared, I told them about the books I'd brought to the jungle, not knowing everything would deteriorate into musty-smelling mold, about the spider Leon shot at in our hut and the jaguar that came to the door that same night, about poor Nuno Bonito trying to hang himself with an epiphyte. Whatever came to mind I puked it up the instant following.

The older women laughed heartily and with great delight whenever I mispronounced a word, which was frequent. The younger women insisted on halting my prattle every few sentences to give me lessons, making me repeat words until I could say them properly, and to be honest, I didn't give a dickens. Nilza cleared away the cake plate and replaced it with a bowl of steaming stew. The pirate woman went to hand me a spoon, but the other one, the one with the rosary, decided it wasn't entirely clean and snatched it from her and cleaned it on her skirt until it gleamed. That made me laugh. Here I was, the filthiest, mankiest, most disgusting grimy, slimy gobshite in all the world, and here was someone cleaning me spoon to make it all nice for me. She handed it over with a curtsey that sent everyone into peals of laugher.

I was full already, but ever aware of me good manners, I continued to eat so as not to appear ungrateful. I was jazzed, and I didn't want to ruin the moment. By the time I put my spoon down for good, the tub was half full, and Nilza handed me a rough bar of oily soap and ordered me to bathe. All the women, young and old, stayed in place for a moment, as if expecting me to strip down in their presence. Then Nilza yelled, "*Vá, vá,*" and they all laughed loudly, delighted with themselves, and ran off into the other room, each with her hand on the back of the one before her.

I stripped down at once and lowered me manky arse into the wee tub. If I had been my full size, it wouldn't have accepted me. But now I was thin as any corner boy, and able to fold myself in half. I could hear the women whispering and giggling in the other room, and Nilza occasionally shushing them, so that I thought they must be discussing me. Once Nilza yelled out, "Take your time, young man," which set everyone to laughing all over again. I laughed. I couldn't remember when I'd ever been so tickled.

And I did take my time, because nothing had ever felt so pleasant as sitting in five or so inches of steaming hot water—with six cheeky women giggling just on the other side of the curtain—and all without having to worry about being bitten in two by caiman or having a candiru swim up me flute.

I went through the mail Louisa had brought while I was sitting there. There were four letters from me mum, addressed to me and Baxter together—as if we were two sides of the same bad coin, and that was about right. I opened and read them one at a time and then carefully reached over the edge of the tub to place each on the table where it wouldn't get wet. Mum wasn't much of a writer. She talked about the comings and goings of neighbors, some of whom I didn't even know, or maybe I didn't remember them. But the fact that she was writing about the neighbors bespoke volumes in itself. It told me she was back to her old ways, curious about things going on around her, and it brought tears to my eyes to think how far away I'd gone from her—in my thoughts as well as in my fuckin life. And of course she wrote about Nora, who, she said, made time for her daily, even though her Aunt Becky would soon be leaving her, and about how much she missed her boys and how she hoped to see us soon. Her every word was a precious jewel to me and I found myself choked up tight, and I would have read all four letters a second time if not for the women waiting on the other side of the curtain for me to finish up and let them back into the room.

There were seven letters from Nora, but they were all addressed to Bax. Actually, they were addressed to *a ghrá* Baxter Hopper. The *a ghrá* was an endearment, like "my love." She'd probably thought she'd pulled one off on all the people who'd handled the letter since she'd posted it in Hoboken. If anyone had caught on it was a love letter, they might well have snagged it for themselves, just to have a gander. As for me, Nora had sent me one big envelope, and I saved it to open last. I could feel it was a magazine but I hoped there might be a letter or two as well. I tore open the package. It was just the magazine, *Mother Earth*. No note at all.

Still, it made me laugh out loud, which in turn made the women waiting behind the curtain laugh. Nora had told me about the editor of *Mother Earth*, Emma something or other, an anarchist she'd met on one of her outings with her auntie one day. Why, I wondered, would she send me such a dickens of a thing? I was pleased as Punch she'd thought of me at all, for fair, but I couldn't deny I would rather have a letter, something in her own words. And suddenly all my old resentments came rushing back at me, and I found myself feeling a wee bit muzzy because *I* should have been the one Nora had fallen in love with. *I* was the one she had everything in common with; *I* was the one closest to being her intellectual equal—if anyone could be said to come close to her fine mind. Why couldn't she see that? What would Bax do with a copy of *Mother Earth*, except maybe use its pages to wipe his arse. But even as I was thinking such thoughts, I was seeing in my mind's eye how Bax could make her laugh so easily. If he grabbed her round the waist and lifted her off her feet when she didn't expect it, she laughed. If he came up behind her when she was with her cronies and clapped his manky bullocks-squeezing hands over her eyes, she squealed with delight. The very sight of him set something astir in her heart. Did it have to have a name? Or maybe it did. *A ghrá.*

Once I called out that I was dressed again, the woman filed back in, all with big smiles on their faces, and found more food for me to eat, now fruits and cashews. I finally felt clacked out, so I asked no one in particular how they all knew one another.

They interrupted one another to answer, the older women all clacking at once, but I gleaned that the three were fishermen's wives and longtime friends. Adriana, Nilza's daughter, announced that she was Bruna's dearest friend after Louisa. Bruna blushed and Adriana went on, her little one up on her shoulder now so she could pat his arse while she talked, which made her own voice come out staccato. "I found Bruna out on the docks one fine night less than half a year ago," she said. The older women sat back in their chairs to give her the floor for her story. "One of the men who paid for her services back in those days licked her badly."

I looked at Bruna, but she lowered her head and pretended to be preoccupied with her fingernail.

"So I brought her home," Adriana continued, "and Mamãe nursed her back to health, and now she's part of our family."

"Good to hear this, Bruna," I said, "not that you were beaten but that you got away from that life."

She nodded but didn't lift her head.

"She makes her money like the rest of us now," said the old woman with the rosary, "repairing nets and cleaning fish. But we don't let her take the fishes up to the public houses, for the very reason we don't know what old Senhor Fabiano will do if he ever catches sight of her again."

I glanced back at Bruna once more, but she was still staring into her lap, no doubt embarrassed to have those hard times brought back to life in front of everyone. "He's never come looking for her," Louisa interrupted. "But no cause to take a chance. The man who beat her was all the way from Italy, one of Senhor Fabiano's best customers, so we don't let her go where she might be seen and recognized. We keep her close."

"What about Abalo? They're friends, aren't they?" I asked.

"Not exactly friends, though both are in rubber," Louisa said. "But then who isn't? I used to be afraid Senhor Abalo would ask me what I knew about Bruna's disappearance, but he never did. He probably figured she was dead and he was better off without the details."

Bruna lifted her head just then and looked me in the eye. "My father worked for Senhor Fabiano, a *seringueiro*, like you," she said in her wee voice. I leaned closer to hear her. "He got fever, in his first year, when he was still owing. I was the oldest child, so when he died, Senhor Fabiano took me into service to pay my papa's debt. I was twelve." She searched my face, but I didn't have a response at the ready. "I was housekeeper then; it wasn't so bad. And there was plenty of food and a good bed, which my mother could not have provided with four children younger than me. But as his business became more successful, he began to get visitors from faraway places, and..." She closed her mouth and bowed her head again, this time nearly to her lap.

There was silence for a moment. When it was clear she was done talking, Louisa announced that she didn't mind working for Senhor Abalo because he had never forced her to entertain any of his visitors. "Mostly," she said, "he leaves me alone to clean the house and prepare his meals."

Nilza nudged Louisa. "Tell him about his ways," she said, jerking her head in my direction.

Louisa laughed. Knowing what was coming, everyone else did too. Bruna looked up and smiled faintly. Everyone was counting on Louisa to dispel the sadness that had fallen over our gathering.

"*O homem é um porco!*" she cried loudly. *The man is a pig!* The others cackled gleefully to hear her go so far so fast. "The things he does no one would believe. The things they *all* do!"

In her excitement she got to her feet and crossed one leg over the seat of her chair and sat down on it. "I'll tell you this one. Once he had me clean his porcelain bathtub. I did so once a fortnight, but this time he wanted it sparkling, not a mark on it. When he was satisfied, he said I was to work with the cellar boy to fill it with champagne. Imagine that! I thought he'd lost his wits. I was about to ask him outright too, but he gave me the eye, which he does when I'm not to ask so many questions."

"*We* must learn how to do that here," Adriana joked.

"We spent all day," Louisa exclaimed. "Me and the cellar boy. He'd come up with four bottles and I would uncork them and pour them into the tub while he ran down for four more. When the tub was near full Senhor Abalo told us we were done for the day and could take some time for ourselves. The cellar boy left at once, as he lives with his pa in a separate residence, and I went up to my room. And sure enough, not an hour later, here comes a lovely white carriage pulled by two lovely horses and out steps these lovely ladies, all dressed in lovely gowns and their hair pinned up just so..." Her hands fluttered near the back of her head. "And then comes a second carriage, with two of the nasty old men Senhor Abalo plays cards with. And I can hear them all down in the parlor engaging in chitchat. And then—"

"I don't believe this part myself," the woman with the rosary confessed to me. "Louisa has been known to tell a tall tale now and again."

"It's true! It's all true. My room is right above, and I heard everything!" Louisa turned her attention back to me. "So I can hear them, and they're all of them in by the tub,

all in that one tiny room, and one of the women is saying..."
(She put her hand on her throat and spoke in a pseudo sexy
voice an octave higher than her own.) "*Oh, it feels so good,* and
the other cooing, *It's just lovely, and clean enough, you say, so I
can take myself a sip?*"

Now everyone was laughing, even the one with the
rosary who claimed she didn't believe the story. Only I was
confused. "You mean to say they got down on their knees and
drank from the tub like cows at a trough?"

The laughter got louder. "No, silly boy!" Nilza cried.
"They stripped themselves down to nothing and climbed
in full naked, the women did! The two of them, like *bouto* in
the river. It was the *men* there to do the drinking, and the
watching as well, of course."

"I still don't believe it," the one with the rosary said, but
you could tell by the look on her face she was jazzed enough
anyway, and she hoped it was true.

"The mess the next morning!" Louisa cried over the
chortling. "Champagne all over the floor. And plenty of it
still in the tub. I asked Senhor Abalo what should I do with
it, and he said, *Go out and give it to the horses.* So I told the
cellar boy, but he was disgusted when he heard what went
on the night before, and he said, *I won't be giving none of
that poison to those fine animals. Senhor Abalo will have to hang
me first.*" Louisa had changed her voice again, this time to
convey both the cellar boy's repugnance and his lack of class.

Louisa went on, telling about how some of Abalo's friends
would light their cigars with paper money, just to show off
how rich they were, and how they played horrible jokes on
one another, to offset the terrible boredom that comes, she
said, from having no notion what it's like to do a good day's
work. "Once Senhor Abalo pushed a friend of his into the
pond behind his house, fully dressed," she cried.

Nilza and the other older women burst out laughing. "That wasn't the worst of it," said the one with the scarf.

"Let me tell, let me tell," cried the other, banging her palm on the table so that her rosary beads jangled.

"Tell it, then," Louisa cried.

But Adriana beat her to it. "There were two caiman in the pond!"

They all hooted with glee.

"They were dead as bricks, mind you. But the man was drunk and he didn't know that. And he must not have known the pond was shallow either, for he began to flail about as if he was drowning—"

"He screamed like a madman," Louisa interrupted. "I saw the whole thing from the kitchen, where I was supposed to be preparing beverages for Senhor Abalo's other guests. It took everything I had not to fall down laughing. All the stupid man had to do was get to his feet and step out!"

They laughed harder yet, until their faces were red as beets and there were tears in their eyes. It took a long time for the last flare-ups of laughter to fade off, and then a period of cheerful silence followed. Louisa had run out of stories for the moment, and the others looked satisfied to reflect on all she had said already. But I suddenly remembered the two little boys, the Indians who had been on the launch, in the care of Magnânimo. As soon as I mentioned them, the smiles fell from the others' faces and Louisa bit her lip as if she were loath to answer. But as no one else did, she said, "As Senhor Abalo's launches move up and down the Rio Purus, from time to time they see children fishing at the edge of the water. When they're certain there are no adults nearby, they take them, for Abalo." She shrugged. "He gives them to his friends from Italy and Poland when they visit, to be raised as houseboys. He says he's doing them a service, that otherwise they'd live their lives in the dark as savages and never know a whit about the real world."

Everyone was watching me expectantly. I didn't know what to say. But then Louisa slapped her hand down on the table and announced she had to be going soon, much as she regretted it. Abalo had gone out just after I'd been there, to play cards, and she had to be back before he returned, to make his supper, after which time he would go out again. Then her smile got bigger and she sat forward conspiratorially. "But I can't leave until we've worked out how you're going to get your money, Jack," she said.

The older women hooted with delight and Adriana cried, "Wait! Wait. Don't start without me," and she ran into the back room to put down the baby, who had long since fallen asleep in her arms.

"Ah, we made our bed and now it seems we have to lie in it," I protested, though without much clout to back it up.

But Louisa was relentless. "Jack, you can't mean that. If you don't get your money now while you have the chance, you'll never get back to America. Can't you see that's how Abalo works? He fixes it so there's always the need to stay for one more season, and one more season after that."

"Is that so?"

"It is, and I wouldn't say so if it wasn't true."

We stared at each other then, me and Louisa, while the others looked on. Finally I sighed, to let her know I was ready to listen to what she had to say.

And so it came to pass that we devised a grand scheme, with Louisa leading the way and each of the women contributing, and there was more laughter as we imagined how it would unfold. The plan was that I would go to the mansion early in the morning, before dawn, and slip in through the back door. Abalo always used the back door when he returned from his outings, and he was often so drunk he failed to think to bolt it. But just to be sure, Louisa would get up after she heard him retire and check it was unlocked. She knew where Abalo kept his gun, the one he'd used hours earlier to brand the space between me eyes, and she would remove the bullets, so no danger would result should anything go arseways.

But more than likely, Abalo would be sleeping soundly when I arrived, and I could easily sneak in and find my way to the room off the foyer where Abalo had hosted me and Bax that first day. There was cash on the table in there. A pile of it, Louisa said. Abalo had a lot of people to pay now that the *pelas* were coming in; he'd been keeping it handy. I could take what I thought we'd earned, or more for all she cared, and leave the way I'd gone in, through the back door. When Louisa saw that I was safely gone, she'd return the bullets to the gun and go back to bed. Abalo generally slept late into the morning. By the time he awoke and realized some of his money was missing, I'd be long gone.

With my stomach full and my body as clean as it was likely to get, it all sounded doable, and everyone insisted it was only fair play after what the man had done to me and Bax. Louisa said Abalo had so many enemies he would never suspect me, and even if he did, he would never get to the dock before the steamer left. Nilza said Louisa was right; Senhor Abalo was an arrogant man who looked down on the poor and took liberties that hurt other people, and I would be a fool not to take advantage of this opportunity to put him in his place.

On and on they went, interrupting each other to list the reasons why I must do this—as if I hadn't already made up my mind—how in its way it would be as much a redressing on behalf of all the people who'd been cheated by Senhor Abalo—and God knew there were enough of them—as it would be justice for me and my brother.

I stopped listening after a time, because my own thoughts were piling up on one another. There would still be complications; me and Bax would have to put on a show and return to our camp as if to be ready for another season tapping. And how we would find our way back to Manáos to board a ship for home I couldn't even begin to hazard. I would have to leave the mail behind, so no one on the launch would know I'd seen Louisa. And I would be a true heap o' shite if I didn't admit the darker side of me would be pleased as Punch to deny my bullocks of a brother those seven letters Nora had written to him anyway. *A ghrá*, indeed. But the thought of getting out, of getting back to Hoboken, carried me along more swiftly than any river current, and I couldn't stop smiling.

The other women left not long after Louisa, and then there was only Nilza, Adriana, the baby, who was still asleep on Nilza's bed, and Bruna. Nilza heated water again and cut my beard and then shaved me while Adriana and Bruna looked on. I couldn't believe how good it felt to be free of the beard once it was gone. Nilza's husband, who drank and played cards with the other fishermen at the end of each day, was due home soon, and Nilza thought it would be safer if I spent the night elsewhere. Her husband was a good man, she said, but he loved a good story as much as anyone, and she feared if he knew they were hiding me, he might mention it one day when he'd had himself too much booze. There were a few launches sitting empty in the dock slips. Bruna could bring me to one of them and I would be safe enough through the night. Before I left, Nilza gave me a kiss on the cheek— and a small leather pouch to keep the dosh in, once I had it.

And then I found myself outdoors, alone with Bruna. There was lightning in the sky to the south, great jagged bolts that came out of the heavens vertically, like the legs of a spider. Bruna took my arm and said she would get me settled before the rain began.

She had been so quiet in the house, but now she was as chatty as a tree full of monkeys, jabbering on about how we should find a launch that was close enough to Rua Estreita that I could find my way back if there was trouble of any sort, but far enough that I would not be seen by any of the fishermen Nilza and the others knew when I got up in the morning. We walked quickly, in the shadows, and when we reached the launch she'd set her mind on, she had me wait until she was certain there was no one around. Then she gave me the signal and I climbed on board not knowing whether or not she would follow until I reached the cabin door and pulled it open and felt her come up against my back and squeeze in right behind me.

She had not brought a candle. We stood in the middle of the small cabin looking at each other in whatever light the storm across the river afforded, saying nothing. I had been rubbing my jaw continuously since Nilza had shaved me. It was as if a new appendage had appeared on my body and I couldn't get over how quare it felt. I rubbed it now; even with all the bites and scars, there were patches that felt as soft as Adriana's cub's cheek, which I'd touched with one knuckle earlier. I laughed. "It feels good," I said.

We stood a while longer in silence. Then Bruna whispered, "I can make you feel good, Jack."

"What do you mean?" I asked, though indeed I thought I knew.

"I know how to do it."

"Ah, you're free of all that now, Bruna. When you do it again, you must do it for love and not out of pity for a miserable stranger."

"You're no stranger," she said.

It was what I'd wanted to hear.

"And there's love there too," she added.

I almost didn't catch her words, because she'd tipped her head to her chest and mumbled them. I took a step toward her. "I thought about you all the time, Bruna, until our companions died, and then I stopped thinking altogether. I can't make no promises to you. I have nothing to offer you, nothing at all."

She lifted her head. "In my short life I learned this much, Jack Hopper. There's some things that happen don't need promises. This is for now. This is for love."

"For love," I whispered, and I put my arms around her and gently pulled her small body close to mine.

12

I AWOKE BEFORE SUNRISE, alone but happy, until I remembered what lay ahead. It had all seemed a grand scheme the night before, surrounded by women laughing and interrupting one another to add potatoes to the pot, but now it was another story.

It was not that I minded fleecing the man; for fair he had fleeced us first. But who knew what consequences would follow? When I'd left on the boat with the aim of confronting him, whether or not I ended up battered didn't matter a cow's tit to me, for I was barely human to begin with. But now that I was clean and full, and had spent the better part of the night basking in Bruna's mysterious displays of affection—and sweet Jaysus if they wasn't all bounteous beyond what I would have ever imagined from a girl so shy—the chance of getting mucked at my early age appealed to me not at all. What finally got me on my feet was nothing more or less than the picture in my head of what me piker brother's face would look like if I did have me a success—Bax, who expected me to come back empty-handed, or not at all.

It was still dark when I left the launch, but it wouldn't be for long. There were already men about, heading down towards the docks. I kept my head bent and hurried along the streets toward the mansion. As I got closer, the streets became empty, all the elite still fast asleep. My heart was slapping like the tailfin of a *pirarucu* gasping for his final breath.

I entered the back courtyard, which was so lush with trees and shrubs I didn't need to worry about being seen from the street. But there were windows, many of them, on the mansion itself, behind any one of which Abalo could be watching. I hurried around the pond where Abalo's mac had almost drowned in less than a foot of water and ran up the steps and turned the brass knob on the door, inertia alone carrying me along. It opened right away. I meant to close it quietly, but it was heavy and there was a thud and a click as it fell into place. I stood for a moment with my back to the door, wondering if anyone had heard. But as I didn't hear a sound, save the ticking of me own gammy heart, I moved on.

I hadn't thought to ask Louisa where Abalo's bedroom was, and now I wished I had. One long hall led from the back of the house to the front, and I hurried along as quietly as I could manage, past several doors leading left and right, until I reached the room off the foyer. I opened the door gingerly and had a peek in. There was the grand mahogany table where me and Bax had sat with Abalo our first day in Manáos, back when we was merry spalpeens, but there was no cash upon it. Something was wrong. Louisa had said there would be a pile of cash.

I entered the room and closed the door behind me and turned in a circle. There was no money anywhere. I could hear my breath coming harder, all my frustrations returning to me. Then there was another sound. Footsteps. *Now I am going to die,* I told myself, and I thought again of the night before, the sound of Bruna's breathing in my ear.

I braced for a fight, but when the door opened, it was none other than Louisa in her nightdress, her eyes hard with fear and a finger pressed to her lips. While I looked on, she shuffled past me and went to the China cabinet against the wall and opened the bottom drawer. When she turned she had a great wad of bills in her hand.

I looked at her and she at me. With a jerk of her hand she urged me to take it and be gone, and quickly. I did not want to take the time to count it, and lathered as I was, I could not have calculated its value otherwise. The bills were not dollars but mil-réis; I had not the foggiest notion how much was rightly mine. But every second of hesitation was dooming her as well as me, so I took half, or thereabouts, and then, since her hand was still extended, I took a wee bit more, for my troubles collecting it. "Will you be all right?" I whispered. Her lips drawn back by the force of dread, she nodded. I kissed her cheek and fled.

It took a great effort to walk rather than run to the steamer. But as it was all important that I not draw attention to myself, I forced myself to move at the pace of any other man heading off to a long day of work at the docks.

C and the others were already on board, moving crates of supplies from the bow to port and starboard equally for balance. When he saw me approaching, C jutted his chin in the air and then swiped his hand across it, as if to ask what had happened to me manky beard. With so much on my mind I had forgotten about it. My hand flew to my chin and a couple of C's men laughed and one called out, "He's been with the whores."

C turned sharply to the fellow who'd spoken. "How he been with whores? He got no money!"

The other man chuckled. "*Jovem bonito* like that don't need money. They give it free for them."

I shifted my expression quickly, from whatever it had been to a rat-arsed wild grin. If only I'd had me brother's gift of gab just then, I would have thought of the right words to accompany my aspect.

"Senhor Abalo?" C asked. "He give you money?" He was smirking. He knew the answer.

I shook my head. "Nothing, the manky bugger."

C and the others went back to work.

Now that I had the dough I wanted to be out of the harbor as quickly as possible, so I helped the fellows to carry the crates. I tried not to look in the direction of the mansion, but a few times I became aware of some activity in the distance and I momentarily lost control of me very own piss-pot eyes. Each time I found myself looking at the others afterward, wondering if they were on to me, never knowing for certain.

It seemed to take hours for the work to get done. I was sweating like the *porcão* I was, even though it was too early to be as hot as it would soon get. I'd told Louisa the boat would depart at dawn, and she'd promised me Abalo had never seen dawn in his life. But there was a first time for everything, as I well knew. The sun was rising fast now, dead center over the middle of the river to the east. The river and sky were golden, as brazen as I'd ever seen them. I tried to feel the wad of bills in the leather pouch that Nilza had given me. I'd stuffed it beneath my shirt, under the waistband of my cacks. But as I pushed and pulled and squatted and lifted with the other men, I felt nothing, and I imagined it had come loose and was lying about on the deck floor, that C would see it and know what had transpired and drag me up to the mansion so Abalo could blow a fine round hole dead center in the middle of my noggin.

Finally we were ready to leave. I could barely wait to find a place to stand alone for a moment between the crates and make sure the pouch was still on me. But just as we were casting off, I was distracted by the sight of C jumping off the boat. I ran to the rail. "You're not coming?" I hollered.

"I got other business," he shouted back.

Magnânimo appeared at my side. "He Abalo's man," he said in English. "Abalo have the itch, he scratch it."

I nodded to show I understood. But it vexed me deeply that C was not on board, that he would likely be the first one to hear that some of Abalo's dosh was gone missing.

I did the same as I'd done on the way to Manáos, keeping to my own self during the day and drinking whiskey and watching the others at cards each evening. But I was cautious now, drinking only enough to appear to be the doodle I'd been on the earlier trip, playing it the way I thought Bax would. The truth was everyone else got so rat-arsed jarred no one noticed me anyway. All the time I kept a good watch on the river behind us, half expecting to see C following on a smaller, faster launch. But the further along we got, the less likely it seemed that there would be any consequence to my thievery. For all I know, Abalo had a drawer full of cash and would never know some was gone.

When we reached the Teacup, there was already another load of rubber there, tied up to the bank, and another group of men, four of them, up at the house waiting for their *pelas* to be weighed. While these fellows were all ragged and sickly looking, the *caboclos* who stayed at the Teacup—Paulo and Gomez and Cabeça de Galinha (Nuno Bonito, who was still sick and in his hammock, being the exception)—looked somewhat better. They'd been eating well since the first boat had come in, and they'd received their new supplies. Baxter looked well too, though I tried not to look at him directly.

I had been worrying about coming into contact with Bax. We'd left things off badly, and I was afraid he'd want to clean my clock the moment he saw me, which could easily result in him finding my pouch and pulling it off me in front of everyone. But it seemed he'd made up his mind to ignore me. He only approached me once upon my arrival. He was moving toward the fire, where Gomez was roasting a nice fat curassow, and as he brushed by, he said, "Bootlicker, I can't even be bothered at this time to dirty my dukes giving you what you deserve. But it'll be coming, you can be certain. You're not safe anymore anywhere. Your life is good as over."

"I'll be waiting then," I replied with a grin I could not squash down, giddy as I was with my secret.

Everyone, including the strangers, had heard the story about the young bucko who'd gone off to argue with Abalo, and now they were all chubbed up to hear the result. The men who had known me before also wanted to know how I'd gotten my hair and beard cut. As we sat down around the fire to share the curassow, I fussed on about Abalo threatening me, describing in detail the barrel of his gun pressed between my eyes. But then I winked and said I'd run into a young woman I'd met the first time through, and thus the trip hadn't been a complete waste of my time.

The men laughed raucously and teased me about being a man for the ladies while Baxter scowled and called me names under his breath. I was astonished and delighted to realize my deception had convinced even my brother. I couldn't wait to tell Bax the truth. I couldn't wait to get going. I forced myself to turn my mug in his direction and say, "We should ready the canoe in the morning, beggar, and leave for our camp. There's sure to be cleanup on the *estradas*."

"Relax," Baxter replied. "I'm enjoying the companionship here." His response was punctuated with shouts from the others, telling me to take it easy, have some fun, not be such a *desmancha-prazeres*, a killjoy. What choice had I but to let it go? It would not do for anyone to realize how anxious I was. But anxious I remained beneath it all.

The following morning the four new men made their way down to the river so that Magnânimo could pay them. Me and Paulo and Gomez went down too, to observe the transactions. These were men who had been tapping for some years now. As each went before Magnânimo they beefed aloud about their pay, all of them believing they had earned more, but no one threatened it would be his last season if he was not better compensated. I guessed they were being paid just enough above the cost of supplies to ensure they'd risk their lives for one more season. Rubber was gold, after all. White gold.

Magnânimo had started the engine and was ready to untie the lines and cast off when we heard the sound of another engine. Another launch, a small one not capable of hauling rubber, appeared at the bend. There was a man standing at the bow, and as it got closer, I saw that it was none other than C, and something was off with his face. He was carrying both his *facão* and his rifle, and here I'd come down empty-handed. "I'm done for," I whispered, but no one heard me.

The launch pulled up near the bank and two of the three men on board with C extended their bodies over the bow to tie up to some trees. Then they jumped down from the bow to land. It had just begun to rain, but the others—Gomez and Paulo and the four *seringueiros*—stayed put, mesmerized by this unexpected event.

C's face had a hard look naturally, but it was enhanced on this grim day by a raw red welt running from the middle of his forehead toward the back of his head. Someone had walloped him recently, and good. He was looking down at me, the eye beneath his bruise black as coal and halfway shut. When the others saw how his good eye had hooked itself on me, they stepped back to make way for him. It took all the control I could muster to maintain an aspect of dumb curiosity. "What happened to your face, C?" I yelled up to him.

He jumped off the launch, his *facão* in hand—he'd passed his rifle on to the man who stayed behind on the boat—and strode quickly in my direction. He got right up close to me, so that we were mug to mug and I could smell his manky breath. At this range I could see someone had sewn a couple of stitches into his brow to keep it together. "You take Senhor Abalo's money?" he demanded.

"Of course not," I claimed. It's what I had to say to save my skin, but I wanted to shout in his face that it was *my* money, mine and Bax's, and he'd have to kill me if he wanted to take it away from me.

C pushed both my arms up away from my body and began to pat me down. Gomez stepped up, laughing nervously. "If it'd been me, you might have a worry," he said. "But this kid would sooner slit his own throat than steal another man's valuables."

Paulo piped up too, saying, "Kid's no thief. Anyone can see that."

C paid no attention. "Take them clothes off," he said. "Everything."

"Everything" was a pair of short pants, frayed at the bottom because they had once been trousers, and my boots. I removed them. The rain was coming harder now, and there was thunder and flashes of lightning. The wind picked up. Waves appeared in the river, and both launches (Magnânimo was lingering on his to watch the show too) began to buck like wild horses.

My blood was a river too now, and roiling as well. Only mine was a river of fire, and I knew if I spit, flames would shoot out of me ugly gob and I'd become the devil himself. I was stuck on the fact that C had come all this way to take back what was rightly mine. It was flying around my noggin like a rat in a box.

I didn't care a sack of beans what happened to me just then, but I didn't want to deny my brother—much as he was a great grievance to me—his chance to return to Hoboken and marry the love of his life. I weighed my options, and having decided nothing, I slammed my fist into C's face, and I'd be lying if I didn't say it felt fuckin good to hear the sound my knuckles made upon impact. I'd aimed for the bruise, because it wouldn't have taken much at all to split it wide open. But he turned just then, and I got the side of his mouth instead. You take what you can in this world.

In the same instant, a shot rang out from the boat and the bullet whizzed by my right ear. I paid the event no heed at all because C's head had snapped back with my assault, and I knew he was off balance and I'd get a second go at him if I played my cards right. But then his men grabbed me from behind, and as he regained his footing, I saw his face was throbbing with pain and anger.

He looked me over, his expression as mean as any creature I'd encountered since I'd come to the jungle, and then he lifted his arm and used the edge of his *facão* to slowly cut a fine line below my jaw, and when he was done he pressed the point of the weapon hard against the notch of my throat while his men laughed edgily behind us. Beyond the clamor I could hear someone yelling, "Stop there or else," and while I didn't dare to move my head for fear of finding it rolling at my feet, I knew it was Bax, come to my rescue in spite of all else.

"What the fuck are you doing?" Bax cried.

"He steal Abalo's money," C said without turning to look at him. I was pleased to see there was blood bubbling out of one side of C's mouth. He'd already been short on teeth. Another one or two wouldn't make a difference.

Baxter laughed. "No, he didn't, you arsewipe!" He had to shout over the downpour. "I'd have known if he did, 'cause he would have said so. Loogin like him couldn't keep a tight lip for all the water in Galway Bay. He didn't steal nothing. He come back here with his tail between his legs, like the shite-faced beggar he is."

It pleased me to think if C killed me now, it would be at a time when Bax and I were back on good terms. I dared to move my eyes just enough to take him in. He was standing about ten feet off, his rifle on the ground a few yards behind him, where someone must have kicked it soon as he came down.

I swung my gaze the other way and found two guns trained on my brother, one from Magnânimo, up on his boat, and the other from the fellow on the boat that had brought C our way.

"Where is it?" C demanded, looking from me to Bax and back again.

"How would I take Abalo's money? He didn't even let me in the fuckin house," I shouted.

C turned to Baxter now. My brother whistled when he saw his face full on. Knowing what was wanted, Baxter dropped his cacks and kicked off his boots, which had not been tied. One of C's men left my side to pick up the boots and shake them before throwing them back on the ground. "Go up to the house and find it," C said to his men.

The men turned for the shack. Meanwhile, the downpour continued. The tip of the machete was still at my throat. "You move and I kill you," C growled. I didn't move, so C added, "Maybe I kill you anyway."

The rain fell in torrents. It cascaded down me and Baxter's naked bodies and streamed down the bodies of C and the onlookers. The two guns from the boats were still pointed at Bax, and when I caught him turning to look at them, I knew he was calculating what would happen if he jumped C and tried to dodge bullets at the same time. I hoped he'd take the chance; the river was roiling and the boats were still bucking. The buckos with the guns would not have an easy shot. But in the end Bax stood there, doing nothing, meater that he was.

Eventually C's men returned, their hands over their brows to keep their piss-pot eyes from washing off their ugly mugs. They shook their heads. No snaked decks to be found. They'd checked everyone, they said, even Nuno Bonito, lying stinking and half rotted in his hammock. C turned back to me, and before I knew what was happening, he transferred his *facão* to his left hand and punched me in the face with his right. I heard two shots go off, one after the other, and I guessed my brother had seized the moment after all, but I was not at liberty to assess the scene.

In my fury I went for the hand that held the knife, when I should have gone for the man. As I grabbed at the handle, the other two jumped in and began to pummel me. Next I knew I was on the ground and all three were on me and there was nothing to do but cover my face and let them have at it. C kicked me hard in the ribs while his men licked me about the head with their feet—luckily only one fellow was wearing boots—and then with their hands when they began to slip and slide around in the mud. I could feel that I was bleeding from my nose and my forehead and from one ear, not to mention the cut C had made along my jaw.

My brother was not dead, for I could hear him exclaiming in the background, yelling that it looked to him like Abalo was ready to accuse just about anyone. It was only then I understood that Abalo's first suspect had been C himself; that's where his wound had come from. I lifted a hand from my face and opened an eye and took a quick look in Bax's direction. There were several feet surrounding him, all of them in motion, as if they were all participating in some kind of frenzied dance. I put it together that some of the men from Magnânimo's boat had jumped down to join in the fray. I couldn't be certain because blood and rain water were pouring over half my face and the other half was buried in the mud, some of which I'd swallowed. C kicked me one last time, hard, in the side. Then he said to his companions, "He didn't take nothing. Let's go."

Everyone stood in place until both launches had gone, one after the other. I had thought the one with the rubber would head back to Manáos now, but I could hear that it was heading south, the same direction as the one C was in. With the river swollen the way it was, it could be going anywhere. The rain had stopped, but big drops were still falling from the trees and mud was flowing all around me. "Get up," Bax said, but I continued to lie there. "You're okay," Bax said. I understood it to be a question even though it wasn't presented as one. I nodded.

The four new men grew disinterested now that the spectacle was over and drifted away. Gomez and Paulo stood a few minutes longer, taking turns apologizing for doing nothing while I'd had the shite beaten out of me and asking if I was all right. "Just need rest," I mumbled each time, and eventually they said something about checking

Nuno Bonito hadn't been roughed up too bad and turned for the shack too.

Only Bax remained behind. Eventually he picked up his cacks and wrung them out and put them on again. Then he poured the water out of his boots and set them back on the ground. He sighed loudly. "This shouldn't have happened," he said flatly. He stood awhile—pondering, looking out on the river, which was still heaving—his hands on what passed for his hips now that his body was narrow as a nail. When he allowed his gaze to travel back to me, he exclaimed, "You miserable shite, what in dickens are you smirking about?"

Although it hurt like blazes, I forced myself to roll to my side. The leather pouch, which I'd untied and let drop when I'd first seen C approaching, was no longer visible in the river of mud beneath me. But if you looked hard, you could see a few inches of the draw string, looking every bit like the piker earthworms we used to play with back when we were buckos without a care in the world.

13

BAX TIED THE POUCH onto a thick stalk of a low shrub and helped me up to the shack. The men cheered me good when I arrived, bent over and holding my ribs together, dripping water and gushing blood. Their cheering made me laugh, which only made me hurt more. They gave me rags to clean myself up; they praised the one good punch I'd thrown and told me it was *afortunado* the other men had grabbed me and kept me from doing more damage, because C could have killed me easily enough, with one blow from his *facão*.

Gomez and Paulo and Cabeça de Galinha catered to me well that night, bringing me water (they brought food too but I couldn't eat it) so that I could stay in the hammock they set up for me in the shack right next to the one where Nuno Bonito slept, mumbling to himself in a language even his fellow *caboclos* couldn't decipher. The other group of men left the next day in their dugout, and as soon as they had gone, I announced that I felt well enough to travel and wanted to return to my own camp. In truth I was licked inside and out; every bone in my body ached, and some were broken, and my face had swollen to twice its size and felt like a bag of spuds. It was hard just to talk and near impossible to see. But I wanted to get away as quick as I could now. I had a legitimate excuse too. I needed to rest before the season came around again. I would rest better back at our camp, where I wouldn't have to hear Nuno Bonito talking in his sleep. No one could argue with that. Nuno Bonito was mad as a box of frogs now, and when it gets that bad, it can be contagious. Also, the rivers were at their peak; now was the time to go.

The men helped Bax to get the supply crates into our canoe. Then they stood at the edge of the river and watched us as we moved away from the shore. I stared back, watching them get smaller and smaller, until we went around a bend and they disappeared completely.

All this time Bax had said not a word to me, about the dough or anything else. But after a time, he laid his paddle across the canoe and began to laugh. He couldn't stop. And though it caused me unimaginable pain to join in, I doubled over to hold my ribs together and laughed too.

"*Dia Uas*, we're getting out!" he hollered.

14

ONCE C QUESTIONED THE other suspects on his list and found them innocent, he would come back looking for us; we needed a place to hide. And I needed healing. In addition to my injuries, the first day out in the canoe I came down with a fever which made me hurt from the inside out, beginning in my bones; both Bax and me agreed it was not one of the malarial fevers we were used to; it was something more. I was so hot, Baxter said, he worried I'd set the canoe ablaze.

"You think I'm dying?" I asked him a time or two or three as he navigated through the *furos*. "Shite-faced beggars like you don't die easy," he said each time, and I would fall back to sleep content to think that Abalo's money, and maybe my fever too, had brought my brother around again.

What was freaky was that while everything was glazed over when I was awake—as if there was a gauze curtain between me and the rest of the world—as soon as I took myself a kip, there came the dreams, on parade, each one as clear as glass. I didn't tell Bax about the dreams, because my hunch was they were the sort people have just before they croak. First your life flashes in front of you, so they say, and once you've seen your share, next come visits from those already crossed over to the other side. Or maybe it can work arseways too. Meeting up with Da during the Gha-ru ceremony was only a preview of things to come, I thought now; and it explained why neither Mum nor Nora had been able to see me whereas I could see them. I was dying. There was no doubt in my mind.

I expected before long to be seeing my ancestors from out of the old country, the dead ones that is, which would be most of them—and all of them strangers to me—but in the meantime my dreams were all about me and Bax, mostly from when we were still wee chappies back in Hoboken. I dreamed about the rowboat we built with Da when we were six and seven. Bax hit his thumb with a hammer that day and I was impressed he didn't cry; I nearly cried myself it swelled so bad. I thought my brother must be the toughest boyo ever lived. Even Da said so. "Lad's as rough as a bear's arse," were his very words, and they made us laugh, which was what he intended. That night Mum made Bax sleep with his hand in a bucket of water so he wouldn't lose the nail, and sometime before dawn he awoke cussing because he'd peed the bed.

I remember thinking, I could tell the other boyos and gain me snagging self a laugh or two. Or, I could do myself a disservice and keep the incident under wraps. I believe it was my first moral dilemma. I kept waiting for Bax to threaten me, to say, *You tell the others and you're a dead man,* which might have helped me decide in favor of telling, but he didn't say a single word, and eventually I forgot the incident—until I remembered, there, dying in the canoe on a swollen river, dreaming my life over from beginning to end.

I dreamed us using the carving knife we stole from under Mum's nose to fashion swords out of poplar tree branches down on the banks of the Hudson so we could play at Eber and Eremon, two brothers who fought each other for control of all of Ireland, according to the stories our mammy told us when we couldn't calm down enough to sleep. I dreamed us out in the field with the other boyos, and here comes Da with a big fat grin on his face, carrying something in each hand. And when he gets close, me and Bax see it's baseball mitts, our first, and all the other boyos howling how lucky we are to have a father like him while we put on the gloves and hold them up to the sun.

I dreamed it all. And it was a gift for fair, and I was eager to stay with it, no matter it would eventually lead me on to Death's door…unless of course the Gha-ru could reverse the process, which seemed at least half possible. The chief might lay some ants on me, or some concoction made from vines and dead leaves, and I could be back to me miserable self the next morning.

In truth, I felt so weak I didn't care much how it went.

We found the cove. The water was so high we were able to tie up and step right out of the boat and onto land. Now it was *Baxter* who had to all but carry *me*, and as we hobbled along I couldn't help chuckling as I tried to imagine what this reversal in the fickle freaks of fortune would look like to the Gha-ru. I imagined they would laugh when they saw us. Baxter said I was almost uglier than Nuno Bonito now. My features had been rearranged, he said, so that my mouth was at the top of my head and my eyes were down by my chin and my nose was sticking straight out of my left ear. It hurt my head and everything else to laugh so hard but I did anyway. This was a version of Bax I hardly remembered. This was Bax the way he was sometimes with Nora, who laughed at everything he said. "Don't make me laugh," I begged him. It figured he would get me breaking up when every snicker came at such a cost.

"American," Baxter shouted as we made our way along the jungle path. We had passed the small clearing where we'd built our canoe, but now he wasn't sure we were heading in the direction of the *malocas*. This was the first time we were navigating the region without our Gha-ru companions. Everything looked different, Baxter complained as he dragged me along at his side. He was hoping someone would hear us and come for us, because he didn't want to waste time going in circles.

After a while he helped me slide my broken body onto a fallen trunk and he sat down beside me to catch his breath. It wasn't my weight so much he said, because there wasn't much of it anymore; it was how hot I was. I was burning him up. "I think we might be lost," he added flatly. "We found the cove easy enough. Why does everything look different up here?"

"We're going the right way."

Baxter studied me. "How would you know? You're nearly delirious and your eyes are swollen shut."

"Smoke," I said.

Baxter sniffed. "Rat-arsed kinker, I believe you're right!" he cried. He got up at once and pulled me to my feet and off we went again.

When he started walking faster, dragging me from under one arm like a wee cuttie's rag doll, I knew we were close. "American, American," Baxter shouted cheerfully. "I don't want to surprise them," he said to me. He chuckled. "Don't want to find my head shrunk and hanging like an ornament, if you take my meaning." But as he pushed aside some branches and dragged me into the cleaning, he came to a full stop and I heard him suck in his breath. I made myself look up. And something died inside me in that instant, gone forever—for all three buildings were gone, burned to cinders.

❖

I clung to the chance I was dreaming, but even fevered, I knew I was not. There were bodies...and body parts... protruding from behind blackened objects. They looked to be mostly children and older women. Some of them appeared to have been shot. Others had been mortally wounded with *facãos*. The gardens were charred black. The land was black. It had rained earlier that morning, and the mud was black with ash.

"They've taken the men and the younger women," Baxter whispered. His voice was horrible. I couldn't look at his face.

We didn't move for a long time. One little girl—I remembered her; she was the one who'd blown my gaff the night I'd stolen the food—had been decapitated. I recognized her head. It was behind a pile of rubble, a charred hammock and some painted gourds, and it looked like more of the debris, another ruined gourd. I hoped my brother wouldn't notice.

We stood there stiffly like two more things without any life. Then Bax turned his head sharply and I turned mine too and saw movement in the leaves on the other end of the clearing. Baxter had to drop me in order to ready his gun fast.

Survivors. They came out of the forest and stood at the edge of the clearing: three women, two young and one older one. One of the young women was wearing a basket against the front of her body. I knew what was in it: a baby.

These were women we had seen many times during our stay with the Gha-ru, women who sang to plants and shared their dreams and laughed and caressed their children. Women who had fussed over us, teased us, served us our meals. Now they came slinking in our direction, their faces contorted with grief. Bax hung his gun on his shoulder and dragged me to my feet and we made our way to them and met in the middle of the clearing. But the woman with the baby kept looking behind her, as if she expected the enemy who had done this to reappear. We followed them back into the forest.

The older woman slipped to her knees on the ground, and holding her arms across her chest, she began to rock and moan, all the while jabbering at us about, surely, what had happened. I looked at Bax for some sign he understood her, the way he'd understood the chief during the dream ceremony that time. But his face was a blur and I couldn't determine either way. The smaller of the two younger women petted the older woman's head and whispered to her. The other one, the one with the baby, reached out and touched my swollen mug. She left her hand on my face for a long time. Then she said something to the old woman, who stopped jabbering and got up slowly and touched my face and head too. The woman with the baby turned to Bax and began moving her hands, communicating something. She pointed in the direction of the river and tugged on his arm. She wanted him to follow her.

I sat on the ground with the two women who stayed behind. The older one helped me to lie down and then began to pray over me, singing with her eyes closed, her right hand moving up over my face and ribs, at least one of which I knew was broken. She gave some instructions to the younger woman and she ran off and returned with some leaves, but they were the wrong leaves, apparently, because when the older one saw them she tossed them aside and went back to her singing. The younger woman squatted at my feet.

I felt someone kick gently at my feet and realized Bax and the woman with the baby had returned. I was ashamed to have fallen asleep at a time like this, to have returned to the safety of Hoboken—where my brother and I had been rebuilding a kite we'd found caught in the branches of a tree near the river, one of its ribs broken. I opened my eyes and saw him looming over me, blocking the sun where it shone through the canopy. He looked like an old man. "What?" I said. My throat was blazing.

"Our canoe. She was concerned it would be seen from the river. We took the crates out and hid them. Then we pulled the canoe from the water and hid that too." He had brought up my rifle and both our *facãos*.

My fever was worse and I knew I was delirious because every time I tried to think how Bax might have communicated with the woman, I drifted into sleep. Such a small problem was impossible for me to solve—at first. Then I remembered that my brother was magical, that he had communicated with the chief. These were his people now. I would only be in the way. How long until they figured that out?

Bax dragged me to my feet, and we went with the three women deeper into the forest. They'd built a lean-to there. The area was rich with water vines, and they used the *facãos* to cut some of them. They made me drink, and when I shook my head that I was done after one sip, the woman with the baby pushed my lips apart roughly and made me swallow more. Then the three of them made me a bed of leaves.

I drifted. I could hear the women talking softly. Sometimes I could hear Baxter's voice. Sometimes the baby cried, and that seemed to cause a lot of anxiety, but I lacked the wits to understand why. I kept thinking of the baby back in Manáos, the one who could get all the women laughing just by lifting his brows.

In the morning Baxter told me the women wanted to take him somewhere, to see where the others had gone. I didn't feel any better, but I didn't feel worse either, and I wanted to come along. Baxter stayed firm. "You're staying here," he said. "You'll slow us down. If you die along the way, it will only add to our burden. She'll be looking after you." He jutted his head toward the woman with the baby. The basket was hanging from a tree now. The baby was sleeping and its mother was mashing palm hearts into some blackened manioc salvaged from the garden.

I did not want to be sick, especially now that the chief was gone and there was no one to save me from my destiny. I did not want to stay behind. But my brother was right. I could barely contemplate the idea of getting to my feet, let alone marching into the forest. I was on fire inside and out. I hurt so much I wanted to cry, but I didn't have the energy for it.

I slept all day. I awoke sometimes to hear the woman singing softly, whether to me or her child or a plant I didn't know. Once I awoke to find her leaning over me, her enlarged breasts brushing my chest. She fed me some of the mush she'd prepared with her fingers, a wee bit at a time. Then she cut another water vine and let the water drip down into my mouth before drinking herself. She put the basket back on her body and began singing again.

I shite me miserable self in my sleep. I groaned in contempt as my guardian rolled me to my side and removed what was left of my cacks and cleaned me with leaves and water from the vines overhead. Then she left the baby sleeping in its basket beside me and went down to the river to wash my duds.

Whatever was wrong got worse. I managed to lift my arm and see that my skin was beginning to turn blue. I'm dying, I reminded myself, that's all it is. Like Ted and Leon, I will never leave the jungle.

Sleep was peaceful, dark and dreamless now, as much as I could hope for. I awoke once to wailing and thought it must be the child. But when the woman clapped her hand over my mouth I realized it was me.

When I awoke next Baxter was there. He was leaning over me, shaking me. "Wake up, Jack. We're leaving. Right now. You need to get up."

I tried to sit up but couldn't. Baxter had to grab me around the chest and hoist me to my feet. I cried out in pain and Bax clapped his hand over me gob. "No noise, Jack," he said. "They're not so far from here. One of them ran away and they sent their thugs to capture him. If they come this way, they'll find us too."

I looked around. I didn't know what he was talking about, but I could see the women were in a lather too. The woman with the baby wasn't wearing her basket. She had her little one in her arms.

The older woman took hold of one of my arms and Baxter had the other and they began to drag me in the direction of the river. Every muscle in my body screamed for release. I thought I could see my pain spinning around me, red, like a flame engulfing me. I tried to keep my feet moving, but there were times they gave out and then the woman and Baxter had to pull me along, grunting under my dead weight, until I managed some control again. Once I stopped and pushed the woman away and vomited. Everyone looked at what had come up. Fire red it was, against the yellow-brown mat of leaves below—as if I'd been on a diet of beets and tomatoes.

The ground beneath us softened, and just before it turned all to mud, the woman with the baby said something to Bax and he replied, "Here? You sure?" She laid her baby down on some leaves and Bax lowered me as well and the four of them, my magical brother who could communicate with people who didn't speak his language, and the three women, got down in the wet dirt and began to dig with their hands.

I was thinking how proud I was of Bax, how much I loved him. Yeah, I had been all me miserable life jealous too; that was fair to say. But the fever had eaten through the jealousy now; it had even nibbled away at the hard times we'd had since coming to the jungle. What was left was my observation of Bax the doer, the chap who got things done, the fellow who could make friends with anyone. And what was the thing he was getting done now? Why, he was digging my grave of course.

I began to cry. I'd wanted to die to be rid of the pain and discomfort, but now that they were digging my grave, the four of them, the part of myself that didn't want to die asserted itself. I understood though. It had to be done. It was too much to expect them to drag me around half dead. I would only be a burden. Bax had said so and he was right. It was time to let go, to say so long to this good world.

The baby was crying too now, and when I looked up I saw that his mammy and the other two women were as well. We were all crying, and it was my fault. It was only a matter of time before Bax whaled me one for causing such a ruckus.

The little cub's mammy took him up in her muddy arms and began to feed him at her breast. He'd been hungry; that's all. I watched him suckle, and it seemed to me such a beautiful sight, the mammy bent over him like that, cooing, crying and cooing, and him at her nipple looking up into her wet eyes. I thought to myself, *This is the image I'll take along with me, down into that muddy hole. This is an image I can die with, and ain't it a sweet one.* I looked at the hole. It was coming along. The fickle freaks of fortune were coming for me. I would see Da soon. I wondered would he be sorry it was me dropping by for an extended visit and not Bax.

When the dote was full, his mammy put him on her shoulder and patted his back until he let out a wee belch. Then she hugged him tight to her chest and kissed his head and gave him to the older woman, who looked at her for a long time before placing him in the hole—my hole! I rubbed my face. I had to be seeing it all wrong. Was he coming along with me then? The three of them—the mammy had turned her back to the sight and was sobbing violently—began to cover the little fellow with dirt.

"Why?" I cried. Everyone looked at me but no one answered. What were they doing? Was I seeing what wasn't there?

I clenched my teeth and began to rock, until I had enough strength in my scrag of a body to propel myself forward, onto the earth where the wee thing had been only a moment ago. I clawed at the mud, trying to free the young fellow before he suffocated. "No," Bax said. "No, no, stop." But I didn't stop. I was crying and digging and crying and digging and I intended never to stop. But they took hold of me, even the young mammy. They took hold of me and they pushed me back.

Soon we were hurrying along again, my legs two dead weights attached to my lower body. "Where?" I asked, looking up, wiping my mouth with the back of my hand. I kept looking for the baby. I couldn't keep it in my head that he was back in the mud. "Where, Bax?"

He made a noise and I turned my head to glance at him. His face was wet. Snot was running from his nose and he was breathing fast through his mouth. I thought he'd realize and pull himself together, but a moment later he was squealing like a dote, dragging me along, keeping his focus on the path ahead, but crying full out.

He and the older woman, who had me on the other side again, leaned me against a tree and Baxter told me to hold on tight and not let myself slip to the ground. I wanted to please him, but I slipped away anyhow and watched from the mud as they got the canoe out of hiding and dragged it to the cove. Then they came back and hoisted me to standing and dragged me over to it, and Bax lifted me in his arms like I was a wee babe myself and placed me in the middle.

"Baby," I said. The sun on the water hurt my head. I leaned over the side of the boat to puke, but this time nothing came up. Nothing was inside me anymore. I'd shite out some and puked the rest and now I was only empty.

Baxter wiped his hands up and down his face harshly, as if he hoped to tear his skin away. Then he bent over the side of the boat and splashed water on his mug and wiped his hands over it once more. The women had the paddles, the older one and the young one, the short one. The one with the baby—the one who should have had the baby but didn't anymore—was curled up on the floor of the boat, between me and my brother. I sank to the floor beside her head and leaned against the board there to keep myself halfway upright.

"Jack, you may not live," Baxter said. It took me a minute to realize he was talking to me. He sucked in a deep breath and shuddered as he exhaled. Then he looked around, taking in the shoreline on either side and then the sun overhead. "But if you do, I'm going to tell you what you need to know. I know your mind ain't working right, but you got to try to remember the words, and you can put it together later, if you..."

I didn't know what he was talking about.

"The worthless muckers who burned the *maloca* and killed the women and children took the men and some of the younger women away, to tap. They're not far from here. There's a *furo* that cuts through where we are and where they are. That's where they went."

A lizard dropped into the water, making a plopping sound. Baxter turned his head to look at it. Then he continued. "They've got them cutting *estradas*. The Gha-ru men have machetes and the women are working with their hands, pulling brush. Behind every group of Gha-ru there's a *muchacho* with a whip, and behind every *muchacho* with a whip there's a Portuguese with a gun. If they so much as turn around, they get shot.

"We hid behind their base camp, where the bosses built a shack for themselves. There were chains on the ground there. The Gha-ru are sleeping outside, all chained one to the other. We saw them at work. When the one escaped, the leaders took up their guns and fired. You must have heard. Or maybe not, state you're in. One woman, she started yelling out, giving herself away that she was wife to the one escaped. When they realized, they made everyone stop working and come to the base and they tied her to a tree and gathered some twigs and dry leaves and lit a fire beneath her feet, and—"

He broke off crying. He rubbed his hand back and forth over his face. Then he dropped his head into his palms and it was a long time until he lifted it again. "It's not believable, what's happening." He worked his lips for a while. "They whipped her while she burned. They wanted to make her yell out again, so her husband would hear and come back. Setting the example for the others. But she knew what they were up to, and she didn't say a word."

Baxter kept talking. I focused on the irony; I had always been the one to tell Bax stories, and now it was arseways. My eyes were heavy and wanted to close. I had to force them to stay open, which made them burn something fierce.

I drifted. When I came back again, Baxter was saying that some of the men had had their fingers cut off, and one an ear. They all had open wounds, lashes from the *muchachos'* whips. Many of the women you could tell had been violated. Bodies of men and women who could no longer work were piled up to be burned. Some were dead and some were almost. He saw the chief among them, there in the burn pile, dead already, thankfully. He wanted to rescue the ones still alive, but they were guarded, mostly by *muchachos*, and the Gha-ru women he was with wouldn't let him try because there was no chance for success with only two guns and him the only one who knew how to shoot.

"Baby," I said.

Baxter looked at me, so I said it again, softly, so he wouldn't get angry. "Baby."

"He wouldn't stop crying, Jack. She had no choice. Stop saying it. You're making things worse."

I closed my eyes. I drifted again. I slept. Then I felt Baxter lifting my arm and placing something into my hand. Even when I looked at what I was holding I didn't know what it was. I stared at it, blinking my burning eyes. When I was able to focus I saw it was a leather money bag.

It lay on my open palm, tilting toward the bottom of the boat. I didn't know what Bax intended me to do with it. The woman who had been curled on the floor of the canoe got to her knees, then her feet. She said something to the other women, the two guiding the boat. We were close to shore, hugging the bank. They brought the boat closer yet and the woman who no longer had her baby pulled down an epiphyte and tore some ligaments from it and sat back down on the canoe floor and began braiding them together. She worked for a long time. Then she picked up the pouch—it had fallen out of my hand by then—and threaded the thin braided belt through the holes at the top along with the drawstring. Kneeling before me, she tied the narrow cord around my waist and pushed the pouch down into my cacks. Then she curled up into a ball again, like a flower closing against the dark.

I was eager to sleep, but Baxter wouldn't have it. "Magnânimo's launch was tied up near the camp where they're working the Gha-ru," he said. "You might remember it headed out in the wrong direction when we were still at the Teacup. I wondered about that myself. They would have already captured the Gha-ru by then, and Magnânimo must have had orders to deliver supplies to the camp there. That's why he headed out the wrong way. That means Magnânimo is working for whoever caused all this to happen, the filthy fuckin piker, and since Magnânimo is Abalo's man, this can only be Abalo's doing." His face twisted in disgust. I forced a nod so as to make like I understood.

"When I saw Magnânimo's launch there, it added up. C knew all along we'd had help. He knew from the way we looked, and he knew from the amount of rubber we had…" He drifted off and stretched his head back to look at the sky.

"The way I see it, C told Abalo, and Abalo saw an opportunity to turn the situation to a profit. Abalo was losing too many men. Sick like you, or stuff like what happened to Leon and… Anyway, I took the chance Magnânimo is nothing more than a runner, like the other *muchachos*, not under Abalo's thumb the way C is. The camp is large, about forty men supervising, mostly *muchachos*, like I said, but also Portuguese. The Portuguese are the bosses, and the *muchachos*, the Caribbeans, don't look too happy about what they're being made to do—about having to whip and beat the Gha-ru, even kill them. The *muchachos* are there to keep the Gha-ru working. They have the whips, yeah, but the Portuguese have the guns and they can shoot anyone who doesn't comply, whether Indian or *muchacho*. The *muchachos* tied the woman to the tree and built the fire beneath her, but they did it at gunpoint. Not that it matters. None of it matters a single fuck, does it now? But I saw some looks pass between them, the *muchachos*. So I took me chances that I could bargain with Magnânimo."

The story had become worse than tedious. I promised myself I would keep the words, all in sequence, in my noggin and make sense of them later. I took a deep breath to brace myself for more, because I could see Bax wasn't yet done.

"When I saw Magnânimo boarding the launch and preparing to leave, I had the lasses hide in the forest and I slid the canoe into the river and intercepted him at some small distance from their camp. Magnânimo recognized me and helped me tie up alongside his vessel and climb on board. He was pissed at first, probably thinking I'd spied on him, that I knew he'd sold his manky soul to the devil himself. He demanded to know why I was there and why I was away from the Teacup with you all beaten to shite and all. I didn't let on we'd been to the *maloca* or that we even knew anything about the Gha-ru. I was working on my hunch there was no reason for Abalo and C to tell any of the *muchachos*, Magnânimo included, how they come to know the Gha-ru's whereabouts.

"I told Magnânimo I'd left you up at the Teacup, sleeping in a hammock beside Nuno Bonito, and gone looking for him, hoping to secure his help. I asked him would he take you back to Manáos with him. When I saw he was about to deny me, I said I had money. I didn't tell him where the money was from, but he must have realized. Whether we can trust him I wouldn't want to wager. He took the dough I offered, which was about half of it. He only had one other man on board with him, and the piker watched from the bow and didn't say a word. Magnânimo said I should get back to the Teacup and have you ready. He's making a stop at the Teacup in three days' time, to pick up more rubber, and then he's heading directly to Manáos. But I said to him, as I had to, that it might arouse suspicion among the other men if he picked you up there, that I'd wait for him north of the Teacup, just past the bend. He thought it over and agreed. He said he'd drop you at the docks in Manáos, and after that you're on your own. It's the best I could do for you, Jack."

I lowered my head to my chest and tried hard to concentrate. "You?" I managed.

Baxter shook his head. "We got the two guns and she…" He pointed to the older woman. "…thinks she knows where we can find more. We're going to fight."

"Me? Me." I tried to touch my chest with my finger but I couldn't lift my hand that high.

"Jack, listen to me. You're dying. Your skin color's all wrong. You're too hot. You got to try to get home. It's your only chance."

"Because I'm a burden?" None of it was making sense.

"That too, my man. I won't lie to you." He looked out on the river. "What can I do? Put you over my shoulder and carry you when we march on them?" His gaze drifted to the woman on the floor between us. "Is that what you want?"

I got sicker that night. We got off the river and the women went into the forest and came back with leaves of all sorts and ministered to me, but nothing helped. We needed the chief clacking his hokum with his gods, and he was dead; that I remembered Bax saying. I lay for hours breathing rapidly, on my back, looking up at the stars, with nothing at all going on in my head. *I'm ready*, I said to the night sky, to the bats and the insects and the howler monkeys and the jaguars. *Come and get me.* But in the morning I was still there.

After a few more days of traveling through *furos* we made it to the Teacup. Magnânimo's launch was already there. We waited for dark to pass through that part of the river. Once we reached the point on the other side, we tied up and slept in the canoe and climbed the bank in the morning.

"Today's the day," Baxter said after he and the women had put together a lean-to up on a rise above the river. He looked out at the water. "Unless he motors by us, fuckin sop that he is. We can't know ahead though, can we?"

Something occurred to me, though it took a minute to fish out the word I needed to express it. "Nora," I finally managed.

Baxter shot me a quick look. Then he went back to staring out at the river. He chewed on his lips for a while. "I'm needed here, Jack. I'm the only chance they have. You see that, don't you?"

I had more to say but I had no strength left in me at all. I turned to the side and puked. The woman who'd had the baby was sitting nearby, squeezing breast milk into a cup she'd fashioned with leaves and vine. She stopped what she was doing to look at my vomit. There was blood in it but not as much as there had been earlier that day.

Baxter snapped his head to the side. It was the launch. He signaled for the woman to get up, to hide. Then he looked behind him to make sure the other two, who were searching for fruit trees, were out of sight.

"Come on," Bax said. "We need to get down where he can see us."

He pulled me up from the ground. "You can't," I said. I had to stop and catch my breath. I was agitated, and I didn't have the lungs for it. "Please, come home." My eyes were filling with tears. This was all happening, and it was happening too fast. There was more I needed to say. If I clacked on long enough, I could get him to change his mind; I knew I could.

He dragged me down to within ten feet of the water and I slid to the ground. For a while Baxter stood with his hands on his hips, looking at the point from which Magnânimo would appear once he'd rounded the bend. Then he sat down beside me. As the sound of the launch grew louder, he put his arm around me and pulled me to his side.

Even in my deranged state, I could remember Bax would put his arm around me when we were young boyos. When I got hurt or got yelled at or was bawling over something, Bax would come and sit by my side and pull me in tight, because he was the big brother.

Magnânimo's boat appeared. Shoo, I thought, go away. He was headed right for us.

I let my head rest on Baxter's shoulder. It bobbed there, up and down, because his chest was heaving. He was making a noise, a kind of squeal through his teeth. I could see Magnânimo looking for a limb to tie up to, his man out on the bow with the rope in hand. "Best thing you can do…," Bax said. He had to stop because he was choked up. He whacked the back of his hand against his mouth. Meanwhile Magnânimo's man tied up and jumped off the bow, landing in water up to his hips. "Best thing to do," Bax started again, "if you make it back…"

"You bring him," the *muchacho* yelled. He'd had a look at me. He didn't want to have to carry me himself.

Bax got up and pulled me to my feet. "Tell them I came to a bad end. That way they won't spend their lives, you know, wondering why and—"

"Come on, man," Magnânimo yelled from the boat.

"You see what I'm saying? It will just make it easier."

He picked me up like a sack of spuds and threw me over his shoulder. "I'm coming, you fuckin loogin," he said to Magnânimo, but he didn't say it loud.

15

THE DOOR OPENED, A crack, white knuckles appearing around its edge. A woman peeked out, her lips a tight gray line, as pale as her skin. Her one visible eye looked us up and down guardedly.

I was in the middle, my arms draped over the shoulders of the two burly macs delivering me, my hands kept from slipping away by their grip on my wrists. These were boys I'd known from the docks, Bill Thorn and Michael Weber. There'd been quite a carry-on over who was to bring me to the house. Nobody wanted to have to inform me mum it was only me back from the jungle, and just about dead at that. The boss on the job made the final decision, saying Thorn and Weber were the ones bragging all the time how strong they were, and as I was dead weight (what little there was of me) and it was a good half mile to the Hopper residence, they could take on the task. But they were less than jazzed about it, especially after Daniel Ahern, one of the Germans on the crew, piped up to say he wouldn't be surprised if I was contagious.

The eye stopped roving and settled on the note that was pinned to my coat, on which were printed three words in big letters: Hoboken in America. Then the eye traveled up to me ugly mug, and when a margin of white appeared over the top of its pupil, I knew I'd been recognized.

Quietly, the door shut, and the macs turned to each other in alarm. But I held my gaze steady, knowing full well it would open again. When it did, it was not me mum's eye I saw but a stranger's, her iris as black as coal. Then all at once the door was thrown wide open and an old woman I didn't recognize took a step back and began swinging her arm and screaming, "Get him in, get him in here at once. Lay him out on the sofa. That's right. Slowly, slowly now. Center him. Center him. Feet up, yes. That's right. That's right. Nora, go and fetch a tea towel. He's got dried blood all under his nose."

As I was being manipulated, I caught a glimpse of me mum flattened against the wall, muttering to herself. Her hands were crossed over her neck. I'd seen her like that before, but I couldn't say where or when.

The boys from the dock introduced themselves and said a few words by way of condolence and left quickly, and the old woman got busy getting me out of my wool coat. Everything I was wearing had been an offering from one of the kind souls who'd encountered me on the long trip home. Half the time I didn't get to meet these ward-heelers. I would simply awaken and find myself wearing something I hadn't been wearing before. I was grateful, because the further north we traveled, the colder it became. But the shoes hurt my dogs like the dickens. Even though I hadn't put any weight on my feet in as far back as I could remember, the feeling that my bones were being crushed was constant. And while people came by to bring me scraps of food, and now and then to drag me around the deck on the off-chance I might undergo a spontaneous recovery, no one thought to remove the shoes once they'd been placed on me. So I wore them day and night, and I was glad when the old woman—I recognized her now; it was the hag, the raven, my mother's fortuneteller, Clementine!—removed them. "*Dio mio*, the stench!" she exclaimed. My mouth twitched. I would have laughed if I'd had the brawn for it.

I slept, and when I awoke Nora was sitting beside me on the edge of the sofa. I wanted to study her face, but it hurt to turn my head, and I couldn't have focused anyway. My eyes were tired all the time now; it took a grand effort to open them at all.

I stared at the ceiling. She was talking, talking and crying. I didn't bother to follow the words. The matters of life, the minutiae, had been sloughing away from me for a long time now. Who would have ever thought it could take a dying man so long to get there? I could no longer concentrate for more than a second or two even on the things that had happened in the jungle. Or I could, but it was all vague now, as if I had dreamed it. The stiller I became, the quieter I got inside myself, the more it seemed that everything earthly was meaningless in the end anyway, a dream *meant* to be forgotten, and I looked forward to passing on to whatever would follow, even if it were nothing at all.

When Nora reached over me to better position my head on the pillow, her face came into view, surprising me. She looked older. Her eyes were red and her face was puffy. She was wearing a dress the color of an eggplant, buttoned up to her throat. It made her white skin look deathly pale. I heard a voice from behind her, the hag again. I didn't hear anyone else; I didn't think Mum was in the room.

The hag's face appeared where Nora's had been. "He's gone, ain't he?" she croaked.

At first I thought she meant me, that I had passed on and here I hadn't realized. But then it registered she was speaking to me, not Nora, and thus would be asking about my brother.

I nodded, one nod, the most I could manage. Nora emitted a harsh sound from her throat, a wheeze.

I was in no position to puzzle out whether my affirmation had been the right or wrong response. In the end, what did it matter? For all intents and purposes, we were both dead, me and Bax, whether it was deducible yet or not. And how could I explain the truth anyway? I remembered the way he'd held me there at the edge of the river, the way my head bounced against his heaving chest, our last moment together before we died. I would remember *that*, I knew, forever. Even if I took on a new form, that would come along with me.

"I told you to be prepared for this," the hag said to Nora. Then she spoke to me again. "I thought it would be the both of you. This I didn't foresee. I tried to prepare your mum and this one here for the losses. I seen them coming to the door a few weeks ago, those big boys, and I told your mum, Someone's coming to bring the news. There'll be a knock. Three times." She lifted her arm and made a fist. "Knock, knock, knock, just so. And there came the knock, today, just as I said so. And there was those boys, just like I seen. But I didn't foresee you there, hanging between them like a scarecrow on a fence. It's a shock, you know. Someone should have let us know, sent a telegraph or—"

"Clementine, no more!" Nora cried.

The old woman snapped her head in Nora's direction. "You must accept... Look at him, halfway there. When they're like this, half in half out, it don't upset them none to—"

"Please, leave now, Clementine," Nora spat.

The old woman gasped and Nora came into view as she stepped forward and placed her white palm alongside the hag's gaunt cheek. "The doctor will be here very soon," she said gently, but the hag's expression remained indignant.

"Tomorrow, though," Nora added. "Please, if you can spare the time, we'll need you to come by tomorrow."

❖

I awoke later to the sound of a man's voice—the doctor. The doctor had apparently just examined me because my shirt was open and I could feel the cool air on my chest. The doctor was standing, but when he saw my eyes open, he sat at my side, where Nora had been earlier, and took my chin in his hand and gently turned my head until it was facing in his direction. "Jack, do you remember me?"

"It's Dr. Burns, Jack," Nora said from somewhere behind him. And then to the doctor, "Mostly he's not been tracking. His eyes pop open now and then but they don't appear to see anything. But sometimes—like now—it almost seems he's looking right at you for a second. And before; he seemed to nod in response to…" She ended her explanation mid-sentence.

"I treated you when you were a boy. You and your…" Dr. Burns broke off and turned his stunned expression to Nora. Then he cleared his throat and quickly returned his gaze to me. "Can you say how long you've been this way?" he asked. "Can you show me about how many weeks with your fingers?"

I understood the question but had no energy or will to answer. I knew it began in the jungle, and that when I left the jungle I lay against the wall of the cabin in Magnânimo's launch for a long time, tended to not by Magnânimo or his man but by the three young Indian boys who were the only other passengers. Then I lay some hours in the hot bright sun where Magnânimo had dropped me, at the end of the dock in the section of Manáos where the fishermen live, and where, as the fates would have it, I was observed not by the fishermen, who would surely have thrown me into the river like the rotted fish I was, but by their wives and daughters, one of whom happened to be Adriana, the daughter of Nilza, the woman who had taken me in and fed me before everything went arseways. After that, I lay in a vacant launch, ministered to by Louisa and Bruna and Adriana, for how long I could not say. Then one night the three of them carried me down to the docks, covered over with a tablecloth. I remember Louisa saying to the others that if anyone stopped them, they should say they'd caught a *pirarucu* and had arranged to sell it at one of the steamers. I laughed then—the thought of little Louisa and her companions pulling a *pirarucu* out of the river—from under my covering, a single bark no one seemed to hear.

It was the last sound I remember making. Even then Death was at my heels, had been for a long time, and I was reluctant to inject anything as earthly as a word into the world. A word could break the spell—and I did not wish it to be broken.

Two men took me from the women at the entrance to the ship, one man lifting me in his arms like a baby, and the other, I saw as the cloth slipped away, holding a lantern, the only glim in the dark night other than the stars. Louisa said, "You be careful with him now. You've been paid, and if you should ever think to throw him overboard, you'll be haunted 'til your dying day, I can promise you that," to which the man holding me replied, "Don't give it a thought, little lady. I'll treat him like my very own tiny baby." The man with the lantern began to laugh, but someone must have given him the stink eye, for he stopped abruptly. "And make sure that note stays with him," Louisa snapped. "It's the name of the place he needs to get to. If he doesn't arrive, the blame falls on your shoulders."

I spent days and days and days on the steamer after that, in a dark storeroom on the upper deck, with the door ajar to let in the air and give the curious the chance to take a look, to donate if they chose to, or to feed me scraps from their pockets. I had only one specific memory the entire time: someone had shaved me, a woman, an Irish woman, as gentle as a saint. She sang while she worked—*Ma'am dear, did you ever hear/ Of pretty Molly Brannigan?/ The times are going hard with me,/ I'll never be a man again./ There's not a bit of all me hide/ The sun'll ever tan again/ Since Molly's gone and left me/ Here alone for to die.*

The doctor lifted his bag from the floor and got to his feet. When his voice came next, it was at a distance. "He's suffering from paralysis of the muscles, except the ocular muscles of the eyes, but those could be next. He's near comatose, fading in and out. He may be brain dead, hard to say. That bluish tint to his skin means he's not getting enough oxygen. I can't imagine it's contagious, what he's got, but this is a jungle disease that science don't know much about, so just to be safe, don't get yourself too close. And if you notice any changes in your own health, you let me know right way."

Ah, I thought, the doctor has spoken. It will be soon.

"Keep checking his ears in case they start bleeding again, not that there's anything you can do besides clean out the blood when it's over and done. Keep giving him the Aspirin too. It will dull any discomfort. He should be in the hospital, but you're as stubborn a lass as I've come across and I'm not about to argue with you any further. No point to try to feed him. He's beyond that. Once the organs begin to shut down, digestion doesn't happen as it should. It can be painful for him. So just let him go naturally. As for Maggie, keep her on the Veronal. It will make her sleep. I'll cut her dosage over time, and—"

"With all due respect, sir, in my opinion Mrs. Hopper's better off without the Veronal. She'll never get over losing Bax. Neither of us will. But she's got Jack here. And if she's sleeping all the time..."

"Whose well-being are you worried about? Maggie's or Jack's?"

"Why, both, sir, of course."

"Keep her on the Veronal. There's nothing she can do for this one here."

"But, sir—"

"I'm sorry to be so blunt, but... Was this the one you were to wed?"

She bleated sharply, as if he'd slapped her. "No, his brother."

"Well, I'm sorry for your losses. I wish I could offer you some hope, but there is none here."

The door opened, and then it shut, and the house fell silent. When Nora's voice came again, it was from nearby, and I realized she was sitting at my side again. "I don't like Dr. Burns," she said. Her voice was thick with mucus.

If I had been inclined to talk, I might have said, *I don't either*, out of habit, out of a lifelong practice of trying to be agreeable wherever possible, but for fair I had liked Dr. Burns, a good deal. I remembered in a flash how when me and Bax were chappies, Dr. Burns would let us play with the small wooden animals he kept in his scruffy brown leather bag in those days. There were six of them, hand-carved by the doctor himself, two cats, two dogs, a horse, and something we'd never been able to identify. When we asked Dr. Burns about it he said it was a mess-up, and for a long time we thought a mess-up was a real animal.

All six carvings were smooth and weighty and felt good in our hands. We divided them up and let them clout one another while Dr. Burns peeked into our ears and between our toes and squeezed our tummies, all as a prelude to announcing us the healthiest chaps in the land, at which time he would put his hands out and we would sadly return the wooden animals while our mum stood proud and smiling, nodding because we'd rehearsed the moment, the return of the toys, and were doing just as she'd told us we must.

Nora's voice startled me when it came again. "I do not intend to let you die," she said firmly.

It will happen whether you intend it or not, I thought to myself.

"You're all we've got now, Jack, and I will bring you back to life if it kills me."

A scamp and a cooch, I thought. *Everyone had always said so.*

"For your mom's sake if nothing else, because she'll die of a broken heart otherwise… I hope you're listening, Jack. I hate to be so severe…"

Yes, yes, I was listening. How could I not? She was just over me, screaming in my face. Brazen thing, she was. I couldn't wait for her to leave so I could sleep again. And I did sleep, on and off, but every time I awoke she was still there, making her argument.

Acknowleðgments

THANKS TO CARLOS DAMASCENO (aka Carlos the Jaguar) of Manaus, Brazil, who took me (and my traveling companions) out on the Amazon and Rio Negro in a small launch for an eight-day trip to introduce us to rubber trees, *bouto*, caiman, squirrel monkeys, howler monkeys, *pirarucu*, piranha, vampire bats, and much more. His incredible knowledge of the jungle, its many creatures and its many moods, was invaluable to me during the writing of this book.

Thanks to Julián Larrea, Ecuadorian guide from Quito, for a blissful experience on the Pastaza River and in the jungles of Ecuador.

Thanks to the Achuar people of the Pastaza River for sharing their world—their wisdom, customs, and even some of their ceremonies—with those of us who came to visit with the Pachamama Alliance Journey group in October 2010.

Thanks to my two Portuguese-speaking readers for taking the time to check that the Portuguese words and phrases in this book were used correctly. Leidiana Marques, of Manaus, Brazil, is a teacher and the author of *Nas Nuvens*, an unconventional love story, and Ana Claudia Domene, who grew up in Brazil, is the author of *The Path to Aaran: A Novel About Finding the Soul's True Desire*.

Thanks to Michael Dooley, my best friend and traveling companion, for ongoing support and for being a wonderful photographer whose photos not only helped me to revive my memory as I wrote this book but also provided continuous inspiration.

Thanks to Deborah Parrish Snyder at Synergetic Press, who unwittingly put me on the path that brought me to write *Before We Died.* My obsession with the jungle began when I was a kid, but my infatuation with the history of rubber tapping only came about after reading a short diary of a real rubber tapper: *White Gold: The Diary of a Rubber Cutter in the Amazon*, by John C. Yungjohann, edited by Ghillean T. Prance, published by Synergetic Press. Not only did I fall in love with the story, but several other books published by Synergetic Press provided me with invaluable information about tribal cultures, plants of the rainforest, and much more.

Very special thanks to Elizabeth Trupin-Pulli, for believing in my work against all odds. Thanks to Paula Coomer, Ellen Deck, Stephen Bogoff, Damian McNicholl, Julie Mars and Rocco LoBosco for boundless support.

Thanks to the brilliant Lacey Seidman for endless patience in working with me to develop social media skills. Thanks to Kellie Rendina, Emma Boyer and the team at Smith's for both in-the-box and out-of-the-box PR support.

Last but never least, thanks to everyone at Five Directions Press, especially the founders, C. P. Lesley, Courtney J. Hall and Ariadne Apostolou. All wonderful writers themselves, they spend hours each week using their many additional talents to ensure that all Five Directions authors are sent forward into the literary combat zone equipped with books that are well-edited, well-designed, and beautifully covered.

Many books informed and inspired *Before We Died*: I am deeply thankful to have come across the following:

Don Jose Campos and Geraldine Overton, *The Shaman and Ayahuasca: Journeys to Sacred Realms*

Roger Casement, *The Amazon Journal of Roger Casement*

Daniel Cassidy, *How the Irish Invented Slang*

Euclides de Cunha, *The Amazon: Land Without History*

Wade Davis, *One River: Explorations and Discoveries in the Amazon Rain Forest*

Warren Dean, *Brazil and the Struggle for Rubber*

Doug Gelbert, *A Walking Tour of Hoboken, New Jersey*

David Grann, *The Lost City of Z*

John Hemming, *Tree of Rivers: The Story of the Amazon*

Joe Jackson, *Thief at the End of the World: Rubber, Power, and the Seeds of Empire*

Algot Lange, *In the Amazon: Jungle Adventures in Remote Parts of the Upper Amazon River*

Luis Eduardo Luna and Steven F. White, *Ayahuasca Reader: Encounters with the Amazon's Sacred Vine*

Candice Millard, *The River of Doubt: Theodore Roosevelt's Darkest Journey*

Richard Evans Schultes, *Where the Gods Reign: Plants and Peoples of the Colombian Amazon*

Richard Evans Schultes and Robert Raffauf, *Vine of the Soul: Medicine Men, Their Plants & Rituals*

Scott Wallace, *The Unconquered: In Search of the Amazon's Last Unconquered Tribes*

About the Author

JOAN SCHWEIGHARDT IS THE author of six novels, a memoir written under a pseudonym, and various magazine articles, including several stories in travel magazines. She lives in Albuquerque, New Mexico.

Before We Died Discussion Questions

1. Were you surprised to learn about the atrocities that occurred in conjunction with the South American rubber boom?

2. Which brother—if either—did you like better, and why? Did you find them to be very different?

3. Do you agree with Jack that of the two, he would have made a more suitable match with Nora? What do you think Nora's choice of Baxter was based on?

4. Do you think any of the characters responded appropriately to Ted's inability to keep up? To the tensions arising between Leon and Baxter? To the physical discomforts of spending so much time in the deep jungle? To Abalo's refusal to pay what was expected of him? If not, what other responses might have had better outcomes?

5. Why do you think the Gha-ru showed kindness to Jack and Baxter? Do you think they were really responsible for Ted's disappearance?

6. What did you think of the decision that Baxter Hopper makes towards the end of the book?

7. Promises are made in this book, sometimes kept and sometimes broken. Did you feel Nora had a right to ask Jack to promise not to tell anyone, especially his mother, about "the German lady"? Do you feel people from that time period were more likely than people today to make and keep their promises? If yes, why?

8. What did you think of the "colorful" slang the brothers use? Were there any phrases you can imagine incorporating into your own discourse?

9. Has this novel broadened your perspective regarding man's inhumanity to man? Are there events going on in today's world that resemble events that occurred during the rubber boom?

10. Did the ending of the book leave you eager to read *Gifts for the Dead*, the second book in the series?